GO SET A
WATCHMAN

ALSO BY HARPER LEE

To Kill a Mockingbird

GO SET A WATCHMAN

Harper Lee

An Imprint of HarperCollins*Publishers*

HarperCollins books may be purchased for educational, business, or sales promotional use. For information, please e-mail the Special Markets Department at SPsales@harpercollins.com.

FIRST PAPERBACK HARPERLUXE EDITION

HarperLuxe™ is a trademark of HarperCollins Publishers

Library of Congress Cataloging-in-Publication Data has been applied for.

ISBN: 978-0-06-243365-7

15 16 17 18 19   ID/RRD   10 9 8 7 6 5 4 3 2

In memory of Mr. Lee and Alice

PART I

1

Since Atlanta, she had looked out the dining-car window with a delight almost physical. Over her breakfast coffee, she watched the last of Georgia's hills recede and the red earth appear, and with it tin-roofed houses set in the middle of swept yards, and in the yards the inevitable verbena grew, surrounded by whitewashed tires. She grinned when she saw her first TV antenna atop an unpainted Negro house; as they multiplied, her joy rose.

Jean Louise Finch always made this journey by air, but she decided to go by train from New York to May-comb Junction on her fifth annual trip home. For one thing, she had the life scared out of her the last time she was on a plane: the pilot elected to fly through a tornado. For another thing, flying home meant her father rising at three in the morning, driving a hundred miles to meet her in Mobile, and doing a full day's work afterwards: he was seventy-two now and this was no longer fair.

She was glad she had decided to go by train. Trains had changed since her childhood, and the novelty of the experience amused her: a fat genie of a porter materialized when she pressed a button on a wall; at her bidding a stainless steel washbasin popped out of another wall, and there was a john one could prop one's feet on. She resolved not to be intimidated by several messages stenciled around her compartment—a roomette, they called it—but when she went to bed the night before, she succeeded in folding herself up into the wall because she had ignored an injunction to PULL THIS LEVER DOWN OVER BRACKETS, a situation remedied by the porter to her embarrassment, as her habit was to sleep only in pajama tops.

Luckily, he happened to be patrolling the corridor when the trap snapped shut with her in it: "I'll get you out, Miss," he called in answer to her poundings from within. "No please," she said. "Just tell me how to get out." "I can do it with my back turned," he said, and did.

When she awoke that morning the train was switching and chugging in the Atlanta yards, but in obedience to another sign in her compartment she stayed in bed until College Park flashed by. When she dressed, she put on her Maycomb clothes: gray slacks, a black sleeveless blouse, white socks, and loafers. Although it was four hours away, she could hear her aunt's sniff of disapproval.

When she was starting on her fourth cup of coffee the Crescent Limited honked like a giant goose at its northbound mate and rumbled across the Chattahoochee into Alabama.

The Chattahoochee is wide, flat, and muddy. It was low today; a yellow sandbar had reduced its flow to a trickle. Perhaps it sings in the wintertime, she thought: I do not remember a line of that poem. Piping down the valleys wild? No. Did he write to a waterfowl, or was it a waterfall?

She sternly repressed a tendency to boisterousness when she reflected that Sidney Lanier must have been somewhat like her long-departed cousin, Joshua Singleton St. Clair, whose private literary preserves stretched from the Black Belt to Bayou La Batre. Jean Louise's aunt often held up Cousin Joshua to her as a family example not lightly to be discountenanced: he was a splendid figure of a man, he was a poet, he was cut off in his prime, and Jean Louise would do well to remember that he was a credit to the family. His pictures did the family well—Cousin Joshua looked like a ratty Algernon Swinburne.

Jean Louise smiled to herself when she remembered

her father telling her the rest of it. Cousin Joshua was cut off, all right, not by the hand of God but by Caesar's hosts:

When at the University, Cousin Joshua studied too hard and thought too much; in fact, he read himself straight out of the nineteenth century. He affected an Inverness cape and wore jackboots he had a black-smith make up from his own design. Cousin Joshua was frustrated by the authorities when he fired upon the president of the University, who in his opinion was little more than a sewage disposal expert. This was no doubt true, but an idle excuse for assault with a deadly weapon. After much passing around of money Cousin Joshua was moved across the tracks and placed in state accommodations for the irresponsible, where he remained for the rest of his days. They said he was reasonable in every respect until someone mentioned that president's name, then his face would become dis-torted, he would assume a whooping crane attitude and hold it for eight hours or more, and nothing or nobody could make him lower his leg until he forgot about that man. On clear days Cousin Joshua read Greek, and he left a thin volume of verse printed privately by a firm in Tuscaloosa. The poetry was so ahead of its time no one has deciphered it yet, but Jean Louise's aunt keeps it displayed casually and prominently on a table in the livingroom.

Jean Louise laughed aloud, then looked around to see if anyone had heard her. Her father had a way of undermining his sister's lectures on the innate superiority of any given Finch: he always told his daughter the rest of it, quietly and solemnly, but Jean Louise sometimes thought she detected an unmistakably profane glint in Atticus Finch's eyes, or was it merely the light hitting his glasses? She never knew.

The countryside and the train had subsided to a gentle roll, and she could see nothing but pastureland and black cows from window to horizon. She wondered why she had never thought her country beautiful.

The station at Montgomery nestled in an elbow of the Alabama, and when she got off the train to stretch her legs, the returning familiar with its drabness, lights, and curious odors rose to meet her. There is something missing, she thought. Hotboxes, that's it. A man goes along under the train with a crowbar. There is a clank and then *s-sss-sss*, white smoke comes up and you think you're inside a chafing dish. These things run on oil now.

For no reason an ancient fear gnawed her. She had not been in this station for twenty years, but when she was a child and went to the capital with Atticus, she was terrified lest the swaying train plunge down the riverbank and drown them all. But when she boarded again for home, she forgot.

The train clacketed through pine forests and honked derisively at a gaily painted bell-funneled museum piece sidetracked in a clearing. It bore the sign of a lumber concern, and the Crescent Limited could have swallowed it whole with room to spare. Greenville, Evergreen, Maycomb Junction.

She had told the conductor not to forget to let her off, and because the conductor was an elderly man, she anticipated his joke: he would rush at Maycomb Junction like a bat out of hell and stop the train a quarter of a mile past the little station, then when he bade her goodbye he would say he was sorry, he almost forgot. Trains changed; conductors never did. Being funny at flag stops with young ladies was a mark of the profession, and Atticus, who could predict the actions of every conductor from New Orleans to Cincinnati, would be waiting accordingly not six steps away from her point of debarkation.

Home was Maycomb County, a gerrymander some seventy miles long and spreading thirty miles at its widest point, a wilderness dotted with tiny settlements the largest of which was Maycomb, the county seat.

Until comparatively recently in its history, Maycomb County was so cut off from the rest of the nation that some of its citizens, unaware of the South's political predilections over the past ninety years, still voted Republican. No trains went there—Maycomb Junction, a courtesy title, was located in Abbott County, twenty miles away. Bus service was erratic and seemed to go nowhere, but the Federal Government had forced a highway or two through the swamps, thus giving the citizens an opportunity for free egress. But few people took advantage of the roads, and why should they? If you did not want much, there was plenty.

The county and the town were named for a Colonel Mason Maycomb, a man whose misplaced self-confidence and overweening willfulness brought confusion and confoundment to all who rode with him in the Creek Indian Wars. The territory in which he operated was vaguely hilly in the north and flat in the south, on the fringes of the coastal plain. Colonel Maycomb, convinced that Indians hated to fight on flat land, scoured the northern reaches of the territory looking for them. When his general discovered that Maycomb was meandering in the hills while the Creeks were lurking in every pine thicket in the south, he dispatched a friendly Indian runner to Maycomb with the message, *Move south, damn you.* Maycomb was convinced this was a Creek plot to trap him (was there not a blue-eyed, red-headed devil leading them?), he made the friendly Indian runner his prisoner, and he moved farther north until his forces became hopelessly lost in the forest primeval, where they sat out the wars in considerable bewilderment.

After enough years had passed to convince Colonel Maycomb that the message might have been genuine after all, he began a purposeful march to the south, and on the way his troops encountered settlers moving inland, who told them the Indian Wars were about over. The troops and the settlers were friendly enough to become Jean Louise Finch's ancestors, and Colonel Maycomb pressed on to what is now Mobile to make sure his exploits were given due credit. Recorded history's version does not coincide with the truth, but these are the facts, because they were passed down by word of mouth through the years, and every Maycombian knows them.

". . . get your bags, Miss," the porter said. Jean Louise followed him from the lounge car to her compartment. She took two dollars from her billfold: one for routine, one for releasing her last night. The train, of course, rushed like a bat out of hell past the station and came to a stop 440 yards beyond it. The conductor appeared, grinning, and said he was sorry, he almost forgot. Jean Louise grinned back and waited impatiently for the porter to put the yellow step in place. He handed her down and she gave him the two bills.

Her father was not waiting for her.

She looked up the track toward the station and saw a tall man standing on the tiny platform. He jumped down and ran to meet her.

He grabbed her in a bear hug, put her from him, kissed her hard on the mouth, then kissed her gently. "Not here, Hank," she murmured, much pleased.

"Hush, girl," he said, holding her face in place. "I'll kiss you on the courthouse steps if I want to."

The possessor of the right to kiss her on the courthouse steps was Henry Clinton, her lifelong friend, her brother's comrade, and if he kept on kissing her like that, her husband. Love whom you will but marry your own kind was a dictum amounting to instinct within her. Henry Clinton was Jean Louise's own kind, and now she did not consider the dictum particularly harsh.

They walked arm-in-arm down the track to collect her suitcase. "How's Atticus?" she said.

"His hands and shoulders are giving him fits today."

"He can't drive when they're like that, can he?"

Henry closed the fingers of his right hand halfway

and said, "He can't close them any more than this. Miss Alexandra has to tie his shoes and button his shirts when they're like that. He can't even hold a razor."

Jean Louise shook her head. She was too old to rail against the inequity of it, but too young to accept her father's crippling disease without putting up some kind of fight. "Isn't there anything they can do?"

"You know there isn't," Henry said. "He takes seventy grains of aspirin a day and that's all."

Henry picked up her heavy suitcase, and they walked back toward the car. She wondered how she would behave when her time came to hurt day in and day out. Hardly like Atticus: if you asked him how he was feeling he would tell you, but he never complained; his disposition remained the same, so in order to find out how he was feeling, you had to ask him.

The only way Henry found out about it was by accident. One day when they were in the records vault at the courthouse running a land title, Atticus hauled out a heavy mortgage book, turned stark white, and dropped it. "What's the matter?" Henry had said. "Rheumatoid arthritis. Can you pick it up for me?" said Atticus. Henry asked him how long he'd had it; Atticus said six months. Did Jean Louise know it? No. Then he'd better tell her. "If you tell her she'll be down here trying to nurse me. The only remedy for this is not to let it beat you." The subject was closed.

"Want to drive?" said Henry.

"Don't be silly," she said. Although she was a respectable driver, she hated to operate anything mechanical more complicated than a safety pin: folding lawn chairs were a source of profound irritation to her; she had never learned to ride a bicycle or use a typewriter; she fished with a pole. Her favorite game was golf because its essential principles consisted of a stick, a small ball, and a state of mind.

With green envy, she watched Henry's effortless mastery of the automobile. Cars are his servants, she thought. "Power steering? Automatic transmission?" she said.

"You bet," he said.

"Well, what if everything shuts off and you don't have any gears to shift. You'd be in trouble then, wouldn't you?"

"But everything won't shut off."

"How do you know?"

"That's what faith is. Come here."

Faith in General Motors. She put her head on his shoulder.

"Hank," she said presently. "What really happened?"

This was an old joke between them. A pink scar started under his right eye, hit the corner of his nose, and ran diagonally across his upper lip. Behind his lip were six false front teeth not even Jean Louise could induce him to take out and show her. He came home from the war with them. A German, more to express his displeasure at the end of the war than anything else, had bashed him in the face with a rifle butt. Jean Louise had chosen to think this a likely story: what with guns that shot over the horizon, B-17s, V-bombs, and the like, Henry had probably not been within spitting distance of the Germans.

"Okay, honey," he said. "We were down in a cellar in Berlin. Everybody had too much to drink and a fight started—you like to hear the believable, don't you? Now will you marry me?"

"Not yet."

"Why?"

"I want to be like Dr. Schweitzer and play until I'm thirty."

"He played all right," said Henry grimly.

Jean Louise moved under his arm. "You know what I mean," she said.

"Yes."

There was no finer young man, said the people of

Maycomb, than Henry Clinton. Jean Louise agreed. Henry was from the southern end of the county. His father had left his mother soon after Henry was born, and she worked night and day in her little crossroads store to send Henry through the Maycomb public schools. Henry, from the time he was twelve, boarded across the street from the Finch house, and this in itself put him on a higher plane: he was his own master, free from the authority of cooks, yardmen, and parents. He was also four years her senior, which made a difference then. He teased her; she adored him. When he was fourteen his mother died, leaving him next to nothing. Atticus Finch looked after what little money there was from the sale of the store—her funeral expenses took most of it—he secretly supplemented it with money of his own, and got Henry a job clerking in the Jitney Jungle after school. Henry graduated and went into the Army, and after the war he went to the University and studied law.

Just about that time, Jean Louise's brother dropped dead in his tracks one day, and after the nightmare of that was over, Atticus, who had always thought of leaving his practice to his son, looked around for another young man. It was natural for him to engage Henry, and in due course Henry became Atticus's legman, his eyes, and his hands. Henry had always respected

Atticus Finch; soon it melded to affection and Henry regarded him as a father.

He did not regard Jean Louise as a sister. In the years when he was away at the war and the University, she had turned from an overalled, fractious, gun-slinging creature into a reasonable facsimile of a human being. He began dating her on her annual two-week visits home, and although she still moved like a thirteen-year-old boy and abjured most feminine adornment, he found something so intensely feminine about her that he fell in love. She was easy to look at and easy to be with most of the time, but she was in no sense of the word an easy person. She was afflicted with a restlessness of spirit he could not guess at, but he knew she was the one for him. He would protect her; he would marry her.

"Tired of New York?" he said.

"No."

"Give me a free hand for these two weeks and I'll make you tired of it."

"Is that an improper suggestion?"

"Yes."

"Go to hell, then."

Henry stopped the car. He turned off the ignition switch, slewed around, and looked at her. She knew when he became serious about something: his crew cut bristled like an angry brush, his face colored, its scar reddened.

"Honey, do you want me to put it like a gentleman? Miss Jean Louise, I have now reached an economic status that can provide for the support of two. I, like Israel of Old, have labored seven years in the vineyards of the University and the pastures of your daddy's office for you—"

"I'll tell Atticus to make it seven more."

"Hateful."

"Besides," she said, "it was Jacob anyway. No, they were the same. They always changed their names every third verse. How's Aunty?"

"You know good and well she's been fine for thirty years. Don't change the subject."

Jean Louise's eyebrows flickered. "Henry," she said primly, "I'll have an affair with you but I won't marry you."

It was exactly right.

"Don't be such a damn child, Jean Louise!" Henry sputtered, and forgetting the latest dispensations from General Motors, grabbed for a gearshift and stomped at a clutch. These denied him, he wrenched the ignition key violently, pressed some buttons, and the big car glided slowly and smoothly down the high-way.

"Slow pickup, isn't it?" she said. "No good for city driving."

Henry glared at her. "What do you mean by that?"

In another minute this would become a quarrel. He was serious. She'd better make him furious, thus silent, so she could think about it.

"Where'd you get that appalling tie?" she said.

Now.

She was almost in love with him. No, that's impossible, she thought: either you are or you aren't. Love's the only thing in this world that is unequivocal. There are different kinds of love, certainly, but it's a you-do or you-don't proposition with them all.

She was a person who, when confronted with an easy way out, always took the hard way. The easy way out of this would be to marry Hank and let him labor for her. After a few years, when the children were waist-high, the man would come along whom she should have married in the first place. There would be searchings of hearts, fevers and frets, long looks at each other on the post office steps, and misery for everybody. The hollering and the high-mindedness over, all that would be left would be another shabby little affair à la the Birmingham country club set, and a self-constructed private Gehenna with the latest Westinghouse appliances. Hank didn't deserve that.

No. For the present she would pursue the stony path of spinsterhood. She set about restoring peace with honor:

"Honey, I'm sorry, truly sorry," she said, and she was.

"That's okay," said Henry, and slapped her knee. "It's just that I could kill you sometimes."

"I know I'm hateful."

Henry looked at her. "You're an odd one, sweet. You can't dissemble."

She looked at him. "What are you talking about?"

"Well, as a general rule, most women, before they've got 'em, present to their men smiling, agreeing faces. They hide their thoughts. You now, when you're feeling hateful, honey, you *are* hateful."

"Isn't it fairer for a man to be able to see what he's letting himself in for?"

"Yes, but don't you see you'll never catch a man that way?"

She bit her tongue on the obvious, and said, "How do I go about being an enchantress?"

Henry warmed to his subject. At thirty, he was an adviser. Maybe because he was a lawyer. "First," he said dispassionately, "hold your tongue. Don't argue with a man, especially when you know you can beat him. Smile a lot. Make him feel big. Tell him how wonderful he is, and wait on him."

She smiled brilliantly and said, "Hank, I agree with everything you've said. You are the most perspicacious individual I've met in years, you are six feet five, and may I light your cigarette? How's that?"

"Awful."

They were friends again.

2

Atticus Finch shot his left cuff, then cautiously pushed it back. One-forty. On some days he wore two watches: he wore two this day, an ancient watch and chain his children had cut their teeth on, and a wristwatch. The former was habit, the latter was used to tell time when he could not move his fingers enough to dig in his watchpocket. He had been a big man before age and arthritis reduced him to medium size. He was seventy-two last month, but Jean Louise always thought of him as hovering somewhere in his middle fifties—she could not remember him being any younger, and he seemed to grow no older.

In front of the chair in which he was sitting was a steel music stand, and on the stand was *The Strange Case of Alger Hiss*. Atticus leaned forward a little, the better to disapprove of what he was reading. A stranger would not have seen annoyance on Atticus's face, for he seldom expressed it; a friend, however, would expect a dry "H-rm" to come soon: Atticus's eyebrows were elevated, his mouth was a pleasant thin line.

"H-rm," he said.

"What, dear?" said his sister.

"I don't understand how a man like this can have the brass to give us his views on the Hiss case. It's like Fenimore Cooper writin' the Waverley Novels."

"Why, dear?"

"He has a childlike faith in the integrity of civil servants and he seems to think Congress corresponds to their aristocracy. No understanding of American politics a-tall."

His sister peered at the book's dust jacket. "I'm not familiar with the author," she said, thus condemning the book forever. "Well, don't worry, dear. Shouldn't they be here now?"

"I'm not worrying, Zandra." Atticus glanced at his sister, amused. She was an impossible woman, but a sight better than having Jean Louise permanently home and miserable. When his daughter was miserable she prowled, and Atticus liked his women to be relaxed, not constantly emptying ashtrays.

He heard a car turn into the driveway, he heard two of its doors slam, then the front door slam. He carefully nudged the music stand away from him with his feet, made one futile attempt to rise from the deep armchair without using his hands, succeeded the second time, and had just balanced himself when Jean Louise was upon him. He suffered her embrace and returned it as best he could.

"Atticus—" she said.

"Put her suitcase in the bedroom, please, Hank," said Atticus over her shoulder. "Thanks for meeting her."

Jean Louise pecked at her aunt and missed, took a package of cigarettes from her bag, and hurled it at the sofa. "How's the rheumatism, Aunty?"

"Some better, sweet."

"Atticus?"

"Some better, sweet. Did you have a good trip down?"

"Yes sir." She collapsed on the sofa. Hank returned from his chores, said, "Move over," and sat down beside her.

Jean Louise yawned and stretched. "What's the news?" she asked. "All I get these days is reading between the lines in the *Maycomb Tribune*. You all never write me anything."

Alexandra said, "You saw of the death of Cousin Edgar's boy. That was a mighty sad thing."

Jean Louise saw Henry and her father exchange

glances. Atticus said, "He came in late one afternoon hot from football practice and raided the Kappa Alpha icebox. He also ate a dozen bananas and washed 'em down with a pint of whiskey. An hour later he was dead. It wasn't sad at all."

Jean Louise said, "Whew."

Alexandra said, "*Att*icus! You know he was Edgar's baby boy."

Henry said, "It *was* awful, Miss Alexandra."

"Cousin Edgar still courtin' you, Aunty?" asked Jean Louise. "Looks like after eleven years he'd ask you to marry him."

Atticus raised his eyebrows in warning. He watched his daughter's daemon rise and dominate her: her eyebrows, like his, were lifted, the heavy-lidded eyes beneath them grew round, and one corner of her mouth was raised dangerously. When she looked thus, only God and Robert Browning knew what she was likely to say.

Her aunt protested. "Really, Jean Louise, Edgar is your father's and my first cousin."

"At this stage of the game, it shouldn't make much difference, Aunty."

Atticus asked quickly, "How did you leave the big city?"

"Right now I want to know about this big city. You

two never write me any dirt. Aunty, I'm depending on you to give me a year's news in fifteen minutes." She patted Henry on the arm, more to keep him from starting a business conversation with Atticus than anything else. Henry interpreted it as a warm gesture and returned it.

"Well—" said Alexandra. "Well, you must have heard about the Merriweathers. That was a mighty sad thing."

"What happened?"

"They've parted."

"What?" said Jean Louise in genuine amazement. "You mean separated?"

"Yes," her aunt nodded.

She turned to her father. "The Merriweathers? How long have they been married?"

Atticus looked at the ceiling, remembering. He was a precise man. "Forty-two years," he said. "I was at their wedding."

Alexandra said, "We first got wind of something wrong when they'd come to church and sit on opposite sides of the auditorium . . ."

Henry said, "They glared at each other for Sundays on end . . ."

Atticus said, "And the next thing you know they were in the office asking me to get 'em a divorce."

26

"Did you?" Jean Louise looked at her father.

"I did."

"On what grounds?"

"Adultery."

Jean Louise shook her head in wonder. Lord, she thought, there must be something in the water—

Alexandra's voice cut through her ruminations: "Jean Louise, did you come down on the train Like That?"

Caught offside, it took a moment for her to ascertain what her aunt meant by Like That.

"Oh—yessum," she said, "but wait a minute, Aunty. I left New York stockinged, gloved, and shod. I put on these right after we passed Atlanta."

Her aunt sniffed. "I do wish this time you'd try to dress better while you're home. Folks in town get the wrong impression of you. They think you are—ah— slumming."

Jean Louise had a sinking feeling. The Hundred Years' War had progressed to approximately its twenty-sixth year with no indications of anything more than periods of uneasy truce.

"Aunty," she said. "I've come home for two weeks of just sitting, pure and simple. I doubt if I'll ever move from the house the whole time. I beat my brains out all year round—"

She stood up and went to the fireplace, glared at the mantelpiece, and turned around. "If the folks in Maycomb don't get one impression, they'll get another. They're certainly not used to seeing me dressed up." Her voice became patient: "Look, if I suddenly sprang on 'em fully clothed they'd say I'd gone New York. Now you come along and say they think I don't care what they think when I go around in slacks. Good Lord, Aunty, Maycomb knows I didn't wear anything but overalls till I started having the Curse—"

Atticus forgot his hands. He bent over to tie perfectly tied shoelaces and came up with a flushed but straight face. "That'll do, Scout," he said. "Apologize to your aunt. Don't start a row the minute you get home."

Jean Louise smiled at her father. When registering disapprobation, he always reverted back to her childhood nickname. She sighed. "I'm sorry, Aunty. I'm sorry, Hank. I am oppressed, Atticus."

"Then go back to New York and be uninhibited."

Alexandra stood up and smoothed the various whalebone ridges running up and down her person. "Did you have any dinner on the train?"

"Yessum," she lied.

"Then how about coffee?"

"Please."

"Hank?"

28

"Yessum, please."

Alexandra left the room without consulting her brother. Jean Louise said, "Still haven't learned to drink it?"

"No," said her father.

"Whiskey either?"

"No."

"Cigarettes and women?"

"No."

"You have any fun these days?"

"I manage."

Jean Louise made a golf grip with her hands. "How is it?" she asked.

"None of your business."

"Can you still use a putter?"

"Yes."

"You used to do pretty well for a blind man."

Atticus said, "There's nothing wrong with my—"

"Nothing except you just can't see."

"Would you care to prove that statement?"

"Yes sir. Tomorrow at three okay?"

"Yes—no. I've got a meeting on. How about Monday? Hank, do we have anything on for Monday afternoon?"

Hank stirred. "Nothing but that mortgage coming up at one. Shouldn't take more than an hour."

Atticus said to his daughter, "I'm your man, then.

From the looks of you, Miss Priss, it'll be the blind leading the blind."

At the fireplace, Jean Louise had picked up a blackened old wooden-shaft putter which had done years of double-duty as a poker. She emptied a great antique spittoon of its contents—golf balls—turned it on its side, kicked the golf balls into the middle of the livingroom, and was putting them back into the spittoon when her aunt reappeared carrying a tray of coffee, cups and saucers, and cake.

"Between you and your father and your brother," Alexandra said, "that rug is a disgrace. Hank, when I came to keep house for him the first thing I did was have it dyed as dark as I could. You remember how it used to look? Why, there was a black path from here to the fireplace nothing could take out. . . ."

Hank said, "I remember it, ma'am. I'm afraid I was a contributor to it."

Jean Louise drove the putter home beside the fire tongs, gathered up the golf balls, and threw them at the spittoon. She sat on the sofa and watched Hank retrieve the strays. I never tire of watching him move, she thought.

He returned, drank a cup of scalding black coffee at an alarming rate of speed, and said, "Mr. Finch, I'd better be going."

"Wait a bit and I'll come with you," said Atticus.

"Feel like it, sir?"

"Certainly. Jean Louise," he said suddenly, "how much of what's going on down here gets into the newspapers?"

"You mean politics? Well, every time the Governor's indiscreet it hits the tabloids, but beyond that, nothing."

"I mean about the Supreme Court's bid for immortality."

"Oh, that. Well, to hear the *Post* tell it, we lynch 'em for breakfast; the *Journal* doesn't care; and the *Times* is so wrapped up in its duty to posterity it bores you to death. I haven't paid any attention to it except for the bus strikes and that Mississippi business. Atticus, the state's not getting a conviction in that case was our worst blunder since Pickett's Charge."

"Yes, it was. I suppose the papers made hay with it?"

"They went insane."

"And the NAACP?"

"I don't know anything about that bunch except that some misguided clerk sent me some NAACP Christmas seals last year, so I stuck 'em on all the cards I sent home. Did Cousin Edgar get his?"

"He did, and he made a few suggestions as to what I should do with you." Her father was smiling broadly.

"Like what?"

"That I should go to New York, grab you by the hair of the head, and take a switch to you. Edgar's always disapproved of you, says you're much too independent. . . ."

"Never did have a sense of humor, pompous old catfish. That's just what he is: whiskers here and here and a catfish mouth. I reckon he thinks my living alone in New York is ipso facto living in sin."

"It amounts to that," said Atticus. He hauled himself out of the armchair and motioned for Henry to get going.

Henry turned to Jean Louise. "Seven-thirty, honey?"

She nodded, then looked at her aunt out of the corner of her eye. "All right if I wear my slacks?"

"No ma'am."

"Good for you, Hank," said Alexandra.

3

There was no doubt about it: Alexandra Finch Hancock was imposing from any angle; her behind was no less uncompromising than her front. Jean Louise had often wondered, but never asked, where she got her corsets. They drew up her bosom to giddy heights, pinched in her waist, flared out her rear, and managed to suggest that Alexandra's had once been an hourglass figure.

Of all her relatives, her father's sister came closest to setting Jean Louise's teeth permanently on edge. Alexandra had never been actively unkind to her—she had never been unkind to any living creature, except to the rabbits that ate her azaleas, which she poisoned—but she had made Jean Louise's life hell on wheels in her day, in her own time, and in her own way. Now that Jean Louise was grown, they had never been able to sustain fifteen minutes' conversation with one another without advancing irreconcilable points of view, invigorating in friendships, but in close blood relations producing only uneasy cordiality. There were so many things about her aunt Jean Louise secretly delighted in when half a continent separated them, which on contact were abrasive, and were canceled out when Jean Louise undertook to examine her aunt's motives. Alexandra was one of those people who had gone through life at no cost to themselves; had she been obliged to pay any emotional bills during her earthly life, Jean Louise could imagine her stopping at the check-in desk in heaven and demanding a refund.

Alexandra had been married for thirty-three years; if it had made any impression on her one way or another, she never showed it. She had spawned one son, Francis, who in Jean Louise's opinion looked and behaved like a horse, and who long ago left Maycomb for the glories of selling insurance in Birmingham. It was just as well.

Alexandra had been and was still technically married to a large placid man named James Hancock, who ran a cotton warehouse with great exactitude for six days a week and fished on the seventh. One Sunday fifteen years ago he sent word to his wife by way of a Negro boy from his fishing camp on the Tensas River that he was staying down there and not coming back. After

Alexandra made sure no other female was involved, she could not have cared less. Francis chose to make it his cross to bear in life; he never understood why his Uncle Atticus remained on excellent but remote terms with his father—Francis thought Atticus should Do Something—or why his mother was not prostrate from his father's eccentric, therefore unforgivable, behavior. Uncle Jimmy got wind of Francis's attitude and sent up another message from the woods that he was ready and willing to meet him if Francis wanted to come shoot him, but Francis never did, and eventually a third communication reached Francis, to wit: *if you won't come down here like a man, hush.*

Uncle Jimmy's defection caused not a ripple on Alexandra's bland horizon: her Missionary Society refreshments were still the best in town; her activities in Maycomb's three cultural clubs increased; she improved her collection of milk glass when Atticus pried Uncle Jimmy's money loose from him; in short, she despised men and thrived out of their presence. That her son had developed all the latent characteristics of a three-dollar bill escaped her notice—all she knew was that she was glad he lived in Birmingham because he was oppressively devoted to her, which meant that she felt obliged to make an effort to reciprocate, which she could not with any spontaneity do.

To all parties present and participating in the life of the county, however, Alexandra was the last of her kind: she had river-boat, boarding-school manners; let any moral come along and she would uphold it; she was a disapprover; she was an incurable gossip.

When Alexandra went to finishing school, self-doubt could not be found in any textbook, so she knew not its meaning; she was never bored, and given the slightest chance she would exercise her royal prerogative: she would arrange, advise, caution, and warn.

She was completely unaware that with one twist of the tongue she could plunge Jean Louise into a moral turmoil by making her niece doubt her own motives and best intentions, by tweaking the protestant, philistine strings of Jean Louise's conscience until they vibrated like a spectral zither. Had Alexandra ever pressed Jean Louise's vulnerable points with awareness, she could have added another scalp to her belt, but after years of tactical study Jean Louise knew her enemy. Although she could rout her, Jean Louise had not yet learned how to repair the enemy's damage.

The last time she skirmished with Alexandra was when her brother died. After Jem's funeral, they were in the kitchen cleaning up the remains of the tribal banquets that are a part of dying in Maycomb. Calpurnia, the Finches' old cook, had run off the place and not come back when she learned of Jem's death. Alexandra attacked like Hannibal: "I do think, Jean Louise, that now is the time for you to come home for good. Your father needs you so."

From long experience, Jean Louise bristled immediately. You lie, she thought. If Atticus needed me I would know it. I can't make you understand how I'd know it because I can't get through to you. "Need me?" she said.

"Yes, dear. Surely you understand that. I shouldn't have to tell you."

Tell me. Settle me. There you go, wading in your clodhoppers through our private territory. Why, he and I don't even talk about it.

"Aunty, if Atticus needs me, you know I'll stay. Right now he needs me like a hole in the head. We'd be miserable here in the house together. He knows it, I know it. Don't you see that unless we go back to what we were doing before this happened, our recovery'll be far slower? Aunty, I can't make you understand, but truly, the only way I can do my duty to Atticus is by doing what I'm doing—making my own living and my own life. The only time Atticus'll need me is when his health fails, and I don't have to tell you what I'd do then. Don't you see?"

No, she didn't. Alexandra saw what Maycomb saw: Maycomb expected every daughter to do her duty. The duty of his only daughter to her widowed father after the death of his only son was clear: Jean Louise would return and make her home with Atticus; that was what a daughter did, and she who did not was no daughter.

"—you can get a job at the bank and go to the coast on weekends. There's a cute crowd in Maycomb now; lots of new young people. You like to paint, don't you?"

Like to paint. What the hell did Alexandra think she was doing with her evenings in New York? The same as Cousin Edgar, probably. Art Students League every weeknight at eight. Young ladies sketched, did watercolors, wrote short paragraphs of imaginative prose. To Alexandra, there was a distinct and distasteful difference between one who paints and a painter, one who writes and a writer.

"—there are a lot of pretty views on the coast and you'll have weekends free."

Jehovah. She catches me when I'm nearly out of my mind and lays out the avenues of my life. How can she be his sister and not have the slightest idea what goes on in his head, my head, anybody's head? Oh Lord, why didn't you give us tongues to explain to Aunt Alexandra? "Aunty, it's easy to tell somebody what to do—"

"But very hard to make them do it. That's the cause of most trouble in this world, people not doing as they're told."

It was decided upon, definitely. Jean Louise would stay home. Alexandra would tell Atticus, and it would make him the happiest man in the world.

"Aunty, I'm not staying home, and if I did Atticus would be the saddest man in the world . . . but don't worry, Atticus understands perfectly, and I'm sure once you get started you'll make Maycomb understand."

The knife hit deep, suddenly: "Jean Louise, your brother worried about your thoughtlessness until the day he died!"

It was raining softly on his grave now, in the hot evening. You never said it, you never even thought it; if you'd thought it you'd have said it. You were like that. Rest well, Jem.

She rubbed salt into it: I'm thoughtless, all right. Selfish, self-willed, I eat too much, and I feel like the Book of Common Prayer. Lord forgive me for not doing what I should have done and for doing what I shouldn't have done—oh hell.

She returned to New York with a throbbing conscience not even Atticus could ease.

This was two years ago, and Jean Louise had long since quit worrying about how thoughtless she was, and Alexandra had disarmed her by performing the one generous act of Alexandra's life: when Atticus developed arthritis, Alexandra went to live with him. Jean Louise was humble with gratitude. Had Atticus known of the secret decision between his sister and his daughter he would have never forgiven them. He did not need anyone, but it was an excellent idea to have someone around to keep an eye on him, button his shirts when his hands were useless, and run his house. Calpurnia had done it until six months ago, but she was so old Atticus did more housekeeping than she, and she returned to the Quarters in honorable retirement.

"I'll do those, Aunty," Jean Louise said, when Alexandra collected the coffee cups. She rose and stretched. "You get sleepy when it's like this."

"Just these few cups," said Alexandra. "I can do 'em in a minute. You stay where you are."

Jean Louise stayed where she was and looked around the livingroom. The old furniture set well in the new house. She glanced toward the diningroom and saw on the sideboard her mother's heavy silver water pitcher, goblets, and tray shining against the soft green wall.

He is an incredible man, she thought. A chapter of his life comes to a close, Atticus tears down the old house and builds a new one in a new section of town. I couldn't do it. They built an ice cream parlor where the old one was. Wonder who runs it?

She went to the kitchen.

"Well, how's New York?" said Alexandra. "Want another cup before I throw this out?"

"Yessum, please."

"Oh, by the way, I'm giving a Coffee for you Monday morning."

"*Aun*ty!" Jean Louise groaned. Coffees were peculiarly Maycombian in nature. They were given for girls who came home. Such girls were placed on view at 10:30 A.M. for the express purpose of allowing the women of their age who had remained enisled in Maycomb to examine them. Childhood friendships were rarely renewed under such conditions.

Jean Louise had lost touch with nearly everyone she grew up with and did not wish particularly to rediscover the companions of her adolescence. Her schooldays were her most miserable days, she was unsentimental to the point of callousness about the women's college she had attended, nothing displeased her more than to be set in the middle of a group of people who played Remember Old So-and-So.

"I find the prospect of a Coffee infinitely horrifyin'," she said, "but I'd love one."

"I thought you would, dear."

A pang of tenderness swept over her. She would never be able to thank Alexandra enough for coming to stay with Atticus. She considered herself a heel for ever having been sarcastic to her aunt, who in spite of her corsets had a certain defenselessness plus a certain fineness Jean Louise would never have. She *is* the last of her kind, she thought. No wars had ever touched her, and she had lived through three; nothing had disturbed that world of hers, where gentlemen smoked on the porch or in hammocks, where ladies fanned themselves gently and drank cool water.

"How's Hank doing?"

"He's doing beautifully, hon. You know he was made Man of the Year by the Kiwanis Club. They gave him a lovely scroll."

"No, I didn't."

Man of the Year by the Kiwanis Club, a postwar Maycomb innovation, usually meant Young Man Going Places.

"Atticus was so proud of him. Atticus says he doesn't know the meaning of the word contract yet, but he's doing fine with taxation."

Jean Louise grinned. Her father said it took at least five years to learn law after one left law school: one practiced economy for two years, learned Alabama Pleading for two more, reread the Bible and Shakespeare for the fifth. Then one was fully equipped to hold on under any conditions.

"What would you say if Hank became your nephew?"

Alexandra stopped drying her hands on the dish-towel. She turned and looked sharply at Jean Louise. "Are you serious?"

"I might be."

"Don't be in a hurry, honey."

"Hurry? I'm twenty-six, Aunty, and I've known Hank forever."

"Yes, but—"

"What's the matter, don't you approve of him?"

"It's not that, it's—Jean Louise, dating a boy is one thing, but marrying him's another. You must take all things into account. Henry's background—"

"—is literally the same as mine. We grew up in each other's pockets."

"There's a drinking streak in that family—"

"Aunty, there's a drinking streak in every family."

Alexandra's back stiffened. "Not in the Finch family."

"You're right. We're just all crazy."

"That's untrue and you know it," said Alexandra.

"Cousin Joshua was 'round the bend, don't forget that."

"You know he got it from the other side. Jean Louise,

there's no finer boy in this county than Henry Clinton. He would make some girl a lovely husband, but—"

"But you're just saying that a Clinton's not good enough for a Finch. Aunty hon-ey, that sort of thing went out with the French Revolution, or began with it, I forget which."

"I'm not saying that at all. It's just that you should be *care*ful about things like this."

Jean Louise was smiling, and her defenses were checked and ready. It was beginning again. Lord, why did I ever even hint at it? She could have kicked herself. Aunt Alexandra, if given the chance, would pick out some nice clean cow of a girl from Wild Fork for Henry and give the children her blessing. That was Henry's place in life.

"Well, I don't know how careful you can get, Aunty. Atticus would love having Hank officially with us. You know it'd tickle him to death."

Indeed it would. Atticus Finch had watched Henry's ragged pursuit of his daughter with benign objectivity, giving advice when asked for it, but absolutely declining to become involved.

"Atticus is a man. He doesn't know much about these things."

Jean Louise's teeth began to hurt. "What things, Aunty?"

"Now look, Jean Louise, if you had a daughter what would you want for her? Nothing but the best, naturally. You don't seem to realize it, and most people your age don't seem to—how would you like to know your daughter was going to marry a man whose father deserted him and his mother and died drunk on the railroad tracks in Mobile? Cara Clinton was a good soul, and she had a sad life, and it was a sad thing, but you think about marrying the product of such a union. It's a solemn thought."

A solemn thought indeed. Jean Louise saw the glint of gold-rimmed spectacles slung across a sour face looking out from under a crooked wig, the twitter of a bony finger. She said:

"The question, gentlemen—is one of liquor;
You ask for guidance—this is my reply:
He says, when tipsy, he would thrash and kick her,
Let's make him tipsy, gentlemen, and try!"

Alexandra was not amused. She was extremely annoyed. She could not comprehend the attitudes of young people these days. Not that they needed understanding—young people were the same in every generation—but this cockiness, this refusal to take seriously the gravest questions of their lives, nettled and irritated her. Jean Louise was about to make the worst mistake of her life, and she glibly quoted those people at her, she mocked her. That girl should have had a mother. Atticus had let her run wild since she was two years old, and look what he had reaped. Now she needed bringing up to the line and bringing up sharply, before it was too late.

"Jean Louise," she said, "I would like to remind you of a few facts of life. No"—Alexandra held out her hand for silence—"I'm quite sure you know those facts already, but there are a few things you in your wise-cracking way don't know, and bless goodness I'm going to tell you. You are as innocent as a new-laid egg for all your city living. Henry is not and never will be suitable for you. We Finches do not marry the children of red-necked white trash, which is exactly what Henry's parents were when they were born and were all their lives. You can't call them anything better. The only reason Henry's like he is now is because your father took him in hand when he was a boy, and because the war came along and paid for his education. Fine a boy as he is, the trash won't wash out of him.

"Have you ever noticed how he licks his fingers when he eats cake? Trash. Have you ever seen him cough without covering his mouth? Trash. Did you know he got a girl in trouble at the University? Trash. Have you ever watched him pick at his nose when he didn't think anybody was looking? Trash—"

"That's not the trash in him, that's the man in him, Aunty," she said mildly. Inwardly, she was seething. Give her a few more minutes and she'll have worked herself into a good humor again. She can never be vulgar, as I am about to be. She can never be common, like Hank and me. I don't know what she is, but she better lay off or I'll give her something to think about—

"—and to top it all, he thinks he can make a place for himself in this town riding on your father's coat-tails. The very idea, trying to take your father's place in the Methodist Church, trying to take over his law practice, driving all around the country in his car. Why, he acts like this house was his own already, and what does Atticus do? He takes it, that's what he does. Takes it and loves it. Why, all of Maycomb's talking about Henry Clinton grabbing everything Atticus has—"

Jean Louise stopped running her fingers around the lip of a wet cup on the sink. She flicked a drop of water off her finger onto the floor and rubbed it into the linoleum with her shoe.

"Aunty," she said, cordially, "why don't you go pee in your hat?"

———————

The ritual enacted on Saturday nights between Jean Louise and her father was too old to be broken. Jean Louise walked into the livingroom and stood in front of his chair. She cleared her throat.

Atticus put down the *Mobile Press* and looked at her. She turned around slowly.

"Am I all zipped up? Stocking seams straight? Is my cowlick down?"

"Seven o'clock and all's well," said Atticus. "You've been swearing at your aunt."

"I have not."

"She told me you had."

"I was crude, but I didn't cuss her." When Jean Louise and her brother were children, Atticus had occasionally drawn them a sharp distinction between mere scatology and blasphemy. The one he could abide; he hated dragging God into it. As a result, Jean Louise and her brother never swore in his presence.

"She got my goat, Atticus."

"You shouldn't have let her. What did you say to her?"

Jean Louise told him. Atticus winced. "Well, you'd better make peace with her. Sweet, she gets on a high horse sometimes, but she's a good woman—"

"It was about Hank and she made me mad."

Atticus was a wise man, so he dropped the subject.

The Finch doorbell was a mystical instrument; it was possible to tell the state of mind of whoever pushed it. When it said *dee-ding!* Jean Louise knew Henry was outside bearing down happily. She hurried to the door.

The pleasant, remotely masculine smell of him hit her when he walked into the hall, but shaving cream, tobacco, new car, and dusty books faded at the memory of the conversation in the kitchen. Suddenly she put her arms around his waist and nuzzled her head on his chest.

"What was that for?" said Henry delightedly.

"General Principles, who fought in the Peninsular War. Let's get going."

Henry peered around the corner at Atticus in the livingroom. "I'll bring her home early, Mr. Finch." Atticus jiggled the paper at him.

When they walked out into the night, Jean Louise wondered what Alexandra would do if she knew her niece was closer to marrying trash than she had ever been in her life.

PART II

4

The town of Maycomb, Alabama, owed its location to the presence of mind of one Sinkfield, who in the early dawnings of the county operated an inn where two pig trails met, the only tavern in the territory. Governor William Wyatt Bibb, with a view to promoting the domestic tranquillity of the new county, sent out a team of surveyors to locate its exact center and there establish its seat of government: had not Sinkfield made a bold stroke to preserve his holdings, Maycomb would have sat in the middle of Winston Swamp, a place totally devoid of interest.

Instead, Maycomb grew and sprawled out from its hub, Sinkfield's Tavern, because Sinkfield made the surveyors drunk one evening, induced them to bring forward their maps and charts, lop off a little here, add a bit there, and adjust the center of the county to meet his requirements. He sent them packing the next day armed with their charts and five quarts of shinny in their saddlebags—two apiece and one for the Governor.

Jean Louise could never make up her mind whether Sinkfield's maneuver was wise; he placed the young town twenty miles away from the only kind of public transportation in those days—river-boat—and it took a man from the south end of the county two days to journey to Maycomb for store-bought goods. Consequently, the town remained the same size for over 150 years. Its primary reason for existence was government. What saved it from becoming another grubby little Alabama community was that Maycomb's proportion of professional people ran high: one went to Maycomb to have his teeth pulled, his wagon fixed, his heart listened to, his money deposited, his mules vetted, his soul saved, his mortgage extended.

New people rarely went there to live. The same families married the same families until relationships were hopelessly entangled and the members of the community looked monotonously alike. Jean Louise, until the Second World War, was related by blood or marriage to nearly everybody in the town, but this was mild compared to what went on in the northern half of Maycomb County: there was a community called Old Sarum populated by two families, separate and apart in the beginning, but unfortunately bearing the same name. The Cunninghams and the Coninghams married each other until the spelling of the names was academic— academic unless a Cunningham wished to jape with a Coningham over land titles and took to the law. The only time Jean Louise ever saw Judge Taylor at a dead standstill in open court was during a dispute of this kind. Jeems Cunningham testified that his mother spelled it Cunningham occasionally on deeds and things but she was really a Coningham, she was an uncertain speller, and she was given to looking far away sometimes when she sat on the front porch. After nine hours of listening to the vagaries of Old Sarum's inhabitants, Judge Taylor threw the case out of court on grounds of frivolous pleading and declared he hoped to God the litigants were satisfied by each having had his public say. They were. That was all they had wanted in the first place.

Maycomb did not have a paved street until 1935, courtesy of F. D. Roosevelt, and even then it was not exactly a street that was paved. For some reason the President decided that a clearing from the front door of the Maycomb Grammar School to the connecting two ruts adjoining the school property was in need of improvement, it was improved accordingly, resulting in skinned knees and cracked crania for the children and a proclamation from the principal that nobody was to play Pop-the-Whip on the pavement. Thus the seeds of states' rights were sown in the hearts of Jean Louise's generation.

The Second World War did something to Maycomb: its boys who came back returned with bizarre ideas about making money and an urgency to make up for lost time. They painted their parents' houses atrocious colors; they whitewashed Maycomb's stores and put up neon signs; they built red brick houses of their own in what were formerly corn patches and pine thickets; they ruined the old town's looks. Its streets were not only paved, they were named (Adeline Avenue, for Miss Adeline Clay), but the older residents refrained from using street names—the road that runs by the Tompkins Place was sufficient to get one's bearings. After the war young men from tenant farms all over the county flocked to Maycomb and erected matchbox wooden houses and started families. Nobody quite knew how they made a living, but they did, and they would have created a new social stratum in Maycomb had the rest of the town acknowledged their existence.

Although Maycomb's appearance had changed, the same hearts beat in new houses, over Mixmasters, in front of television sets. One could whitewash all he pleased, and put up comic neon signs, but the aged timbers stood strong under their additional burden.

"You don't like it, do you?" asked Henry. "I saw your face when you walked in the door."

"Conservative resistance to change, that's all," said Jean Louise behind a mouthful of fried shrimp. They were in the Maycomb Hotel diningroom sitting on chromium chairs at a table for two. The air-conditioning unit made its will known by a constant low rumble. "The only thing I like about it is the smell's gone."

A long table laden with many dishes, the smell of musty old room and hot grease in the kitchen. "Hank, what's Hot-Grease-in-the-Kitchen?"

"Mm?"

"It was a game or something."

"You mean Hot Peas, honey. That's jumping rope, when they turn the rope fast and try to trip you."

"No, it had something to do with Tag."

She could not remember. When she was dying, she probably would remember, but now only the faint flash of a denim sleeve caught in her mind, a quick cry, "Hotgreaseinthekit-chen!" She wondered who owned the sleeve, what had become of him. He might be raising a family out in one of those new little houses. She had an odd feeling that time had passed her by.

"Hank, let's go to the river," she said.

"Didn't think we weren't, did you?" Henry was smiling at her. He never knew why, but Jean Louise was most like her old self when she went to Finch's Landing: she seemed to breathe something out of the air—"You're a Jekyll-and-Hyde character," he said.

"You've been watching too much television."

"Sometimes I think I've got you like this"—Henry made a fist—"and just when I think I've got you, holding you tight, you go away from me."

Jean Louise raised her eyebrows. "Mr. Clinton, if you'll permit an observation from a woman of the world, your hand is showing."

"How?"

She grinned. "Don't you know how to catch a woman, honey?" She rubbed an imaginary crew cut, frowned, and said, "Women like for their men to be masterful and at the same time remote, if you can pull that trick. Make them feel helpless, especially when you know they can pick up a load of light'ud knots with no trouble. Never doubt yourself in front of them, and by no means tell them you don't understand them."

"Touché, baby," said Henry. "But I'd quibble with your last suggestion. I thought women liked to be thought strange and mysterious."

"No, they just like to look strange and mysterious.

When you get past all the boa feathers, every woman born in this world wants a strong man who knows her like a book, who's not only her lover but he who keepeth Israel. Stupid, isn't it?"

"She wants a father instead of a husband, then."

"That's what it amounts to," she said. "The books are right on that score."

Henry said, "You're being very wise this evening. Where'd you pick up all this?"

"Living in sin in New York," she said. She lighted a cigarette and inhaled deeply. "I learned it from watching sleek, Madison Avenuey young marrieds—you know that language, baby? It's lots of fun, but you need an ear for it—they go through a kind of tribal fandango, but the application's universal. It begins by the wives being bored to death because their men are so tired from making money they don't pay any attention to 'em. But when their wives start hollering, instead of trying to understand why, the men just go find a sympathetic shoulder to cry on. Then when they get tired of talking about themselves they go back to their wives. Everything's rosy for a while, but the men get tired and their wives start yellin' again and around it goes. Men in this age have turned the Other Woman into a psychiatrist's couch, and at far less expense, too."

Henry stared at her. "I've never heard you so cynical," he said. "What's the matter with you?"

Jean Louise blinked. "I'm sorry, honey." She crushed out her cigarette. "It's just that I'm so afraid of making a mess of being married to the wrong man—the wrong kind for me, I mean. I'm no different from any other woman, and the wrong man would turn me into a screamin' shrew in record time."

"What makes you so sure you'll marry the wrong man? Didn't you know I'm a wife-beater from way back?"

A black hand held out the check on a tray. The hand was familiar to her and she looked up. "Hi, Albert," she said. "They've put you in a white coat."

"Yes ma'am, Miss Scout," said Albert. "How's New York?"

"Just fine," she said, and wondered who else in Maycomb still remembered Scout Finch, juvenile desperado, hell-raiser extraordinary. Nobody but Uncle Jack, perhaps, who sometimes embarrassed her unmercifully in front of company with a tinkling recitative of her childhood felonies. She would see him at church tomorrow, and tomorrow afternoon she would have a long visit with him. Uncle Jack was one of the abiding pleasures of Maycomb.

"Why is it," said Henry deliberately, "that you never drink more than half your second cup of coffee after supper?"

She looked down at her cup, surprised. Any reference to her personal eccentricities, even from Henry, made her shy. Astute of Hank to notice that. Why had he waited fifteen years to tell her?

5

When she was getting in the car she bumped her head hard against its top. "*Damn*ation! Why don't they make these things high enough to get into?" She rubbed her forehead until her eyes focused.

"Okay, honey?"

"Yeah. I'm all right."

Henry shut the door softly, went around, and got in beside her. "Too much city living," he said. "You're never in a car up there, are you?"

"No. How long before they'll cut 'em down to one foot high? We'll be riding prone next year."

"Shot out of a cannon," said Henry. "Shot from Maycomb to Mobile in three minutes."

"I'd be content with an old square Buick. Remember them? You sat at least five feet off the ground."

Henry said, "Remember when Jem fell out of the car?"

She laughed. "That was my hold over him for weeks—anybody who couldn't get to Barker's Eddy without falling out of the car was a big wet hen."

In the dim past, Atticus had owned an old canvas-top touring car, and once when he was taking Jem, Henry, and Jean Louise swimming, the car rolled over a particularly bad hump in the road and deposited Jem without. Atticus drove serenely on until they reached Barker's Eddy, because Jean Louise had no intention of advising her father that Jem was no longer present, and she prevented Henry from doing so by catching his finger and bending it back. When they arrived at the creek bank, Atticus turned around with a hearty "Everybody out!" and the smile froze on his face: "Where's Jem?" Jean Louise said he ought to be coming along any minute now. When Jem appeared puffing, sweaty, and filthy from his enforced sprint, he ran straight past them and dived into the creek with his clothes on. Seconds later a murderous face appeared from beneath the surface, saying, "Come on in here, Scout! I dare you, Hank!" They took his dare, and once Jean Louise thought Jem would choke the life out of her, but he let her go eventually: Atticus was there.

"They've put a planing mill on the eddy," said Henry. "Can't swim in it now."

Henry drove up to the E-Lite Eat Shop and honked

the horn. "Give us two set-ups please, Bill," he said to the youth who appeared at his summons.

In Maycomb, one drank or did not drink. When one drank, one went behind the garage, turned up a pint, and drank it down; when one did not drink, one asked for set-ups at the E-Lite Eat Shop under cover of darkness: a man having a couple of drinks before or after dinner in his home or with his neighbor was unheard of. That was Social Drinking. Those who Drank Socially were not quite out of the top drawer, and because no one in Maycomb considered himself out of any drawer but the top, there was no Social Drinking.

"Make mine light, honey," she said. "Just color the water."

"Haven't you learned to hold it yet?" Henry said. He reached under the seat and came up with a brown bottle of Seagram's Seven.

"Not the hard kind," she said.

Henry colored the water in her paper cup. He poured himself a man-sized drink, stirred it with his finger, and bottle between his knees, he replaced its cap. He shoved it under the seat and started the car.

"We're off," he said.

The car tires hummed on the asphalt and made her sleepy. The one thing she liked most about Henry Clinton was that he let her be silent when she wanted to be. She did not have to entertain him.

Henry never attempted to pester her when she was thus. His attitude was Asquithian, and he knew she appreciated him for his patience. She did not know he was learning that virtue from her father. "Relax, son," Atticus had told him in one of his rare comments on her. "Don't push her. Let her go at her own speed. Push her and every mule in the county'd be easier to live with."

Henry Clinton's class in Law School at the University was composed of bright, humorless young veterans. The competition was terrific, but Henry was accustomed to hard work. Although he was able to keep up and manage very well, he learned little of practical value. Atticus Finch was right when he said the only good the University did Henry was let him make friends with Alabama's future politicians, demagogues, and statesmen. One began to get an inkling of what law was about only when the time came to practice it. Alabama and common law pleading, for instance, was a subject so ethereal in nature that Henry passed it only by memorizing the book. The bitter little man who taught the course was the lone professor in the school who had guts enough to try to teach it, and even he evinced the rigidity of imperfect understanding. "Mr.

Clinton," he had said, when Henry ventured to inquire about a particularly ambiguous examination, "you may write until doomsday for all I care, but if your answers do not coincide with my answers they are wrong. Wrong, sir." No wonder Atticus confounded Henry in the early days of their association by saying, "Pleading's little more than putting on paper what you want to say." Patiently and unobtrusively Atticus had taught him everything Henry knew about his craft, but Henry sometimes wondered if he would be as old as Atticus before he reduced law to his possession. *Tom, Tom, the chimney sweep's son.* Was that the old bailment case? No, the first of the treasure trove cases: possession holds good against all comers except the true owner. The boy found a brooch. He looked down at Jean Louise. She was dozing.

He was her true owner, that was clear to him. From the time she threw rocks at him; when she almost blew her head off playing with gunpowder; when she would spring upon him from behind, catch him in a hard half nelson, and make him say Calf Rope; when she was ill and delirious one summer yelling for him and Jem and Dill—Henry wondered where Dill was. Jean Louise would know, she kept in touch.

"Honey, where's Dill?"

Jean Louise opened her eyes. "Italy, last time I heard."

She stirred. Charles Baker Harris. Dill, the friend of her heart. She yawned and watched the front of the car consume the white line in the highway. "Where are we?"

"Ten more miles to go yet."

She said, "You can feel the river already."

"You must be half alligator," said Henry. "I can't."

"Is Two-Toed Tom still around?"

Two-Toed Tom lived wherever there was a river. He was a genius: he made tunnels beneath Maycomb and ate people's chickens at night; he was once tracked from Demopolis to Tensas. He was as old as Maycomb County.

"We might see him tonight."

"What made you think of Dill?" she asked.

"I don't know. Just thought of him."

"You never liked him, did you?"

Henry smiled. "I was jealous of him. He had you and Jem to himself all summer long, while I had to go home the day school was out. There was nobody at home to fool around with."

She was silent. Time stopped, shifted, and went lazily in reverse. Somehow, then, it was always summer. Hank was down at his mother's and unavailable, and Jem had to make do with his younger sister for company. The days were long, Jem was eleven, and the pattern was set:

They were on the sleeping porch, the coolest part of the house. They slept there every night from the beginning of May to the end of September. Jem, who had been lying on his cot reading since daybreak, thrust a football magazine in her face, pointed to a picture, and said, "Who's this, Scout?"

"Johnny Mack Brown. Let's play a story."

Jem rattled the page at her. "Who's this then?"

"You," she said.

"Okay. Call Dill."

It was unnecessary to call Dill. The cabbages trembled in Miss Rachel's garden, the back fence groaned, and Dill was with them. Dill was a curiosity because he was from Meridian, Mississippi, and was wise in the ways of the world. He spent every summer in Maycomb with his great-aunt, who lived next door to the Finches. He was a short, square-built, cotton-headed individual with the face of an angel and the cunning of a stoat. He was a year older than she, but she was a head taller.

"Hey," said Dill. "Let's play Tarzan today. I'm gonna be Tarzan."

"You can't be Tarzan," said Jem.

"I'm Jane," she said.

"Well, I'm not going to be the ape again," said Dill. "I always have to be the ape."

"You want to be Jane, then?" asked Jem. He stretched, pulled on his pants, and said, "We'll play Tom Swift. I'm Tom."

"I'm Ned," said Dill and she together. "No you're not," she said to Dill.

Dill's face reddened. "Scout, you always have to be second-best. I never am the second-best."

"You want to do something about it?" she asked politely, clenching her fists.

Jem said, "You can be Mr. Damon, Dill. He's always funny and he saves everybody in the end. You know, he always blesses everything."

"Bless my insurance policy," said Dill, hooking his thumbs through invisible suspenders. "Oh all right."

"What's it gonna be," said Jem, "His Ocean Airport or His Flying Machine?"

"I'm tired of those," she said. "Make us up one."

"Okay. Scout, you're Ned Newton. Dill, you're Mr. Damon. Now, one day Tom's in his laboratory working on a machine that can see through a brick wall when this man comes in and says, 'Mr. Swift?' I'm Tom, so I say, 'Yessir?'—"

"Can't anything see through a brick wall," said Dill.

"This thing could. Anyway, this man comes in and says, 'Mr. Swift?'"

"Jem," she said, "if there's gonna be this man we'll need somebody else. Want me to run get Bennett?"

"No, this man doesn't last long, so I'll just tell his part. You've got to begin a story, Scout—"

This man's part consisted of advising the young inventor that a valuable professor had been lost in the Belgian Congo for thirty years and it was high time somebody tried to get him out. Naturally he had come to seek the services of Tom Swift and his friends, and Tom leaped at the prospect of adventure.

The three climbed into His Flying Machine, which was composed of wide boards they had long ago nailed across the chinaberry tree's heaviest branches.

"It's awful hot up here," said Dill. "Huh-huh-huh."

"What?" said Jem.

"I say it's awful hot up here so close to the sun. Bless my long underwear."

"You can't say that, Dill. The higher you go the colder it gets."

"I reckon it gets hotter."

"Well, it doesn't. The higher it is the colder it is because the air gets thinner. Now Scout, you say, 'Tom, where are we going?'"

"I thought we were going to Belgium," said Dill.

"You've got to say where are we going because the man told me, he didn't tell you, and I haven't told you yet, see?"

They saw.

When Jem explained their mission, Dill said, "If he's been lost for that long, how do they know he's alive?"

Jem said, "This man said he'd got a signal from the Gold Coast that Professor Wiggins was—"

"If he'd just heard from him, how come he's lost?" she said.

"—was among a lost tribe of headhunters," continued Jem, ignoring her. "Ned, do you have the rifle with the X-ray Sight? Now you say yes."

She said, "Yes, Tom."

"Mr. Damon, have you stocked the Flying Machine with enough provisions? *Mister Damon!*"

Dill jerked to attention. "Bless my rolling pin, Tom. Yessiree! Huh-huh-huh!"

They made a three-point landing on the outskirts of Capetown, and she told Jem he hadn't given her anything to say for ten minutes and she wasn't going to play any more if he didn't.

"Okay. Scout, you say, 'Tom, there's no time to lose. Let's head for the jungle.'"

She said it.

They marched around the back yard, slashing at foliage, occasionally pausing to pick off a stray elephant or fight a tribe of cannibals. Jem led the way. Sometimes he shouted, "Get back!" and they fell flat on their bellies in the warm sand. Once he rescued Mr. Damon from Victoria Falls while she stood around and sulked because all she had to do was hold the rope that held Jem.

Presently Jem cried, "We're almost there, so come on!"

They rushed forward to the carhouse, a village of headhunters. Jem dropped to his knees and began behaving like a snake healer.

"What are you doing?" she said.

"Shh! Making a sacrifice."

"You look afflicted," said Dill. "What's a sacrifice?"

"You make it to keep the headhunters off you. Look, there they are!" Jem made a low humming noise, said something like "*buja-buja-buja,*" and the carhouse came alive with savages.

Dill rolled his eyes up in their sockets in a nauseating way, stiffened, and fell to the ground.

"They've got Mr. Damon!" cried Jem.

They carried Dill, stiff as a light-pole, out into the sun. They gathered fig leaves and placed them in a row down Dill from his head to his feet.

"Think it'll work, Tom?" she said.

"Might. Can't tell yet. Mr. Damon? Mr. Damon, wake up!" Jem hit him on the head.

Dill rose up scattering fig leaves. "Now stop it, Jem Finch," he said, and resumed his spread-eagle position. "I'm not gonna stay here much longer. It's getting hot."

Jem made mysterious papal passes over Dill's head and said, "Look, Ned. He's coming to."

Dill's eyelids fluttered and opened. He got up and reeled around the yard muttering, "Where am I?"

"Right here, Dill," she said, in some alarm.

Jem scowled. "You know that's not right. You say, 'Mr. Damon, you're lost in the Belgian Congo where you have been put under a spell. I am Ned and this is Tom.'"

"Are we lost, too?" said Dill.

"We were all the time you were hexed but we're not any more," said Jem. "Professor Wiggins is staked out in a hut over yonder and we've got to get him—"

For all she knew, Professor Wiggins was still staked out. Calpurnia broke everybody's spell by sticking her head out the back door and screaming, "Yawl want any lemonade? It's ten-thirty. You all better come get some or you'll be boiled alive in that sun!"

Calpurnia had placed three tumblers and a big pitcher full of lemonade inside the door on the back porch, an arrangement to ensure their staying in the shade for at least five minutes. Lemonade in the middle of the morning was a daily occurrence in the summertime. They downed three glasses apiece and found the remainder of the morning lying emptily before them.

"Want to go out in Dobbs Pasture?" asked Dill.

No.

"How about let's make a kite?" she said. "We can get some flour from Calpurnia . . ."

"Can't fly a kite in the summertime," said Jem. "There's not a breath of air blowing."

The thermometer on the back porch stood at ninety-two, the carhouse shimmered faintly in the distance, and the giant twin chinaberry trees were deadly still.

"*I* know what," said Dill. "Let's have a revival."

The three looked at one another. There was merit in this.

Dog days in Maycomb meant at least one revival, and one was in progress that week. It was customary for the town's three churches—Methodist, Baptist, and Presbyterian—to unite and listen to one visiting minister, but occasionally when the churches could not agree on a preacher or his salary, each congregation held its own revival with an open invitation to all; sometimes, therefore, the populace was assured of three weeks' spiritual reawakening. Revival time was a time of war: war on sin, Coca-Cola, picture shows, hunting on Sunday; war on the increasing tendency of young women to paint themselves and smoke in public; war on drinking whiskey—in this connection at least fifty children per summer went to the altar and swore they would not drink, smoke, or curse until they were twenty-one; war on something so nebulous Jean Louise never could figure out what it was, except there was nothing to swear concerning it; and war among the town's ladies over who could set the best table for the evangelist. Maycomb's regular pastors ate free for a week also, and it was hinted in disrespectful quarters that the local clergy deliberately led their churches into holding separate services, thereby gaining two more weeks' honoraria. This, however, was a lie.

That week, for three nights, Jem, Dill, and she had sat in the children's section of the Baptist Church (the Baptists were hosts this time) and listened to the messages of the Reverend James Edward Moorehead, a renowned speaker from north Georgia. At least that is what they were told; they understood little of what he said except his observations on hell. Hell was and would always be as far as she was concerned, a lake of fire exactly the size of Maycomb, Alabama, surrounded by a brick wall two hundred feet high. Sinners were pitchforked over this wall by Satan, and they simmered throughout eternity in a sort of broth of liquid sulfur.

Reverend Moorehead was a tall sad man with a stoop and a tendency to give his sermons startling titles. (*Would You Speak to Jesus If You Met Him on the Street?* Reverend Moorehead doubted that you could even if you wanted to, because Jesus probably spoke Aramaic.) The second night he preached, his topic was *The Wages of Sin*. At that time the local movie house was featuring a film of the same title (persons under sixteen not admitted): Maycomb thought Reverend Moorehead was going to preach on the movie, and the whole town turned out to hear him. Reverend Moorehead did nothing of the kind. He split hairs for three-quarters of an hour on the grammatical accuracy of his text. (Which was correct—the wages of sin *is* death or the wages of sin *are* death? It made a difference, and Reverend Moorehead drew distinctions of such profundity that not even Atticus Finch could tell what he was driving at.)

Jem, Dill, and she would have been bored stiff had not Reverend Moorehead possessed a singular talent for fascinating children. He was a whistler. There was a gap between his two front teeth (Dill swore they were false, they were just made that way to look natural) which produced a disastrously satisfying sound when he said a word containing one *s* or more. *Sin, Jesus, Christ, sorrow, salvation, success,* were key words they listened for each night, and their attention was rewarded in two ways: in those days no minister could get through a sermon without using them all, and they were assured of muffled paroxysms of muffled delight at least seven times an evening; secondly, because they paid such strict attention to Reverend Moorehead, Jem, Dill, and she were thought to be the best-behaved children in the congregation.

The third night of the revival when the three went forward with several other children and accepted Christ as their personal Savior, they looked hard at the floor during the ceremony because Reverend Moorehead folded his hands over their heads and said among other things, "Blessed is he who sitteth not in the seat of the scornful." Dill was seized with a bad whooping spell, and Reverend Moorehead whispered to Jem, "Take the child out into the air. He is overcome."

Jem said, "I tell you what, we can have it over in your yard by the fishpool."

Dill said that would be fine. "Yeah, Jem. We can get some boxes for a pulpit."

A gravel driveway divided the Finch yard from Miss Rachel's. The fishpool was in Miss Rachel's side yard, and it was surrounded by azalea bushes, rose bushes, camellia bushes, and cape jessamine bushes. Some old fat goldfish lived in the pool with several frogs and water lizards, shaded by wide lily pads and ivy. A great fig tree spread its poisonous leaves over the surrounding area, making it the coolest in the neighborhood. Miss Rachel had put some yard furniture around the pool, and there was a sawbuck table under the fig tree.

They found two empty crates in Miss Rachel's smokehouse and set up an altar in front of the pool. Dill stationed himself behind it.

"I'm Mr. Moorehead," he said.

"I'm Mr. Moorehead," said Jem. "I'm the oldest."

"Oh all right," said Dill.

"You and Scout can be the congregation."

"We won't have anything to do," she said, "and I swannee if I'll sit here for an hour and listen to you, Jem Finch."

"You and Dill can take up collection," said Jem. "You can be the choir, too."

The congregation drew up two yard chairs and sat facing the altar.

Jem said, "Now you all sing something."

She and Dill sang:

"Amazing grace how sweet thuh sound
That saved a wretch like me;
I once was lost but now I'm found,
Was blind, but now I see. A-men."

Jem wrapped his arms around the pulpit, leaned over, and said in confidential tones, "My, it looks good to see you all this morning. This *is* a beautiful morning."

Dill said, "A-men."

"Does anybody this morning feel like opening up wide and singin' his heart out?" asked Jem.

"Yes-s sir," said Dill. Dill, whose square construction and lack of height doomed him forever to play the character man, rose, and before their eyes became a one-man choir:

"When the trumpet of the Lord shall sound, and time
*   shall be no more,*
And the morning breaks, eternal, bright and fair;
When the saved of earth shall gather over on the other
*   shore,*
And the roll is called up yonder, I'll be there."

The minister and the congregation joined in the chorus. While they were singing, she heard Calpurnia calling in the dim distance. She batted the gnatlike sound away from her ear.

Dill, red in the face from his exertions, sat down and filled the Amen Corner.

Jem clipped invisible pince-nez to his nose, cleared his throat, and said, "The text for the day, my brethren, is from the Psalms: 'Make a joyful noise unto the Lord, O ye gates.'"

Jem detached his pince-nez, and while wiping them repeated in a deep voice, "Make a joyful noise unto the Lord."

Dill said, "It's time to take up collection," and hit her for the two nickels she had in her pocket.

"You give 'em back after church, Dill," she said.

"You all hush," said Jem. "It's time for the sermon."

Jem preached the longest, most tedious sermon she ever heard in her life. He said that sin was about the most sinful thing he could think of, and no one who sinned could be a success, and blessed was he who sat in the seat of the scornful; in short, he repeated his own version of everything they had heard for the past three nights. His voice sank to its lowest register; it would rise to a squeak and he would clutch at the air as though the ground were opening beneath his feet. He once asked, "Where is the Devil?" and pointed straight at the congregation. "Right here in Maycomb, Alabama."

He started on hell, but she said, "Now cut it out, Jem." Reverend Moorehead's description of it was enough to last her a lifetime. Jem reversed his field and tackled heaven: heaven was full of bananas (Dill's love) and scalloped potatoes (her favorite), and when they died they would go there and eat good things until Judgement Day, but on Judgement Day, God, having written down everything they did in a book from the day they were born, would cast them into hell.

Jem drew the service to a close by asking all who wished to be united with Christ to step forward. She went.

Jem put his hand on her head and said, "Young lady, do you repent?"

"Yes sir," she said.

"Have you been baptized?"

"No sir," she said.

"Well—" Jem dipped his hand into the black water of the fishpool and laid it on her head. "I baptize you—"

"Hey, wait a minute!" shouted Dill. "That's not right!"

"I reckon it is," said Jem. "Scout and me are Methodists."

"Yeah, but we're having a Baptist revival. You've got to duck her. I think I'll be baptized, too." The ramifications of the ceremony were dawning on Dill, and he fought hard for the role. "I'm the one," he insisted. "I'm the Baptist so I reckon I'm the one to be baptized."

"Now listen here, Dill Pickle Harris," she said menacingly. "I haven't done a blessed thing this whole morning. You've been the Amen Corner, you sang a solo, and you took up collection. It's my time, now."

Her fists were clenched, her left arm cocked, and her toes gripped the ground.

Dill backed away. "Now cut it out, Scout."

"She's right, Dill," Jem said. "You can be my assistant."

Jem looked at her. "Scout, you better take your clothes off. They'll get wet."

She divested herself of her overalls, her only garment. "Don't you hold me under," she said, "and don't forget to hold my nose."

She stood on the cement edge of the pool. An ancient goldfish surfaced and looked balefully at her, then disappeared beneath the dark water.

"How deep's this thing?" she asked.

"Only about two feet," said Jem, and turned to Dill for confirmation. But Dill had left them. They saw him going like a streak toward Miss Rachel's house.

"Reckon he's mad?" she asked.

"I don't know. Let's wait and see if he comes back."

Jem said they had better shoo the fish down to one

side of the pool lest they hurt one, and they were leaning over the side rustling the water when an ominous
voice behind them said, "Whoo—"

"Whoo—" said Dill from beneath a double-bed
sheet, in which he had cut eyeholes. He raised his arms
above his head and lunged at her. "Are you ready?" he
said. "Hurry up, Jem. I'm getting hot."

"For crying out loud," said Jem. "What are you
up to?"

"I'm the Holy Ghost," said Dill modestly.

Jem took her by the hand and guided her into the
pool. The water was warm and slimy, and the bottom
was slippery. "Don't you duck me but once," she said.

Jem stood on the edge of the pool. The figure beneath the sheet joined him and flapped its arms wildly.
Jem held her back and pushed her under. As her head
went beneath the surface she heard Jem intoning, "Jean
Louise Finch, I baptize you in the name of—"

Whap!

Miss Rachel's switch made perfect contact with
the sacred apparition's behind. Since he would not go
backward into the hail of blows Dill stepped forward
at a brisk pace and joined her in the pool. Miss Rachel
flailed relentlessly at a heaving tangle of lily pads, bed
sheet, legs and arms, and twining ivy.

"Get out of there!" Miss Rachel screamed. "I'll Holy

Ghost you, Charles Baker Harris! Rip the sheets off my best bed, will you? Cut holes in 'em, will you? Take the Lord's name in vain, will you? Come on, get out of there!"

"Cut it out, Aunt Rachel!" burbled Dill, his head half under water. "Gimme a chance!"

Dill's efforts to disentangle himself with dignity were only moderately successful: he rose from the pool like a small fantastical water monster, covered with green slime and dripping sheet. A tendril of ivy curled around his head and neck. He shook his head violently to free himself, and Miss Rachel stepped back to avoid the spray of water.

Jean Louise followed him out. Her nose tingled horribly from the water in it, and when she sniffed it hurt.

Miss Rachel would not touch Dill, but waved him on with her switch, saying, "March!"

She and Jem watched the two until they disappeared inside Miss Rachel's house. She could not help feeling sorry for Dill.

"Let's go home," Jem said. "It must be dinnertime."

They turned in the direction of their house and looked straight into the eyes of their father. He was standing in the driveway.

Beside him stood a lady they did not know and Reverend James Edward Moorehead. They looked like they had been standing there for some time.

Atticus came toward them, taking his coat off. Her throat closed tight and her knees shook. When he dropped his coat over her shoulders she realized she was standing stark naked in the presence of a preacher. She tried to run, but Atticus caught her by the scruff of the neck and said, "Go to Calpurnia. Go in the back door."

Calpurnia scrubbed her viciously in the bathtub, muttering, "Mr. Finch called this morning and said he was bringing the preacher and his wife home for dinner. I yelled till I was blue in the face for you all. Why'nt you answer me?"

"Didn't hear you," she lied.

"Well, it was either get that cake in the oven or round you up. I couldn't do both. Ought to be ashamed of yourselves, mortifyin' your daddy like that!"

She thought Calpurnia's bony finger would go through her ear. "Stop it," she said.

"If he dudn't whale the tar out of both of you, I will," Calpurnia promised. "Now get out of that tub."

Calpurnia nearly took the skin off her with the rough towel, and commanded her to raise her hands above her head. Calpurnia thrust her into a stiffly starched pink dress, held her chin firmly between thumb and forefinger, and raked her hair with a sharp-toothed comb. Calpurnia threw down a pair of patent leather shoes at her feet.

"Put 'em on."

"I can't button 'em," she said. Calpurnia banged down the toilet seat and sat her on it. She watched big scarecrow fingers perform the intricate business of pushing pearl buttons through holes too small for them, and she marveled at the power in Calpurnia's hands.

"Now go to your daddy."

"Where's Jem?" she said.

"He's cleaning up in Mr. Finch's bathroom. I can trust him."

In the livingroom, she and Jem sat quietly on the sofa. Atticus and Reverend Moorehead made uninteresting conversation, and Mrs. Moorehead frankly stared at the children. Jem looked at Mrs. Moorehead and smiled. His smile was not returned, so he gave up.

To the relief of everyone, Calpurnia rang the dinnerbell. At the table, they sat for a moment in uneasy silence, and Atticus asked Reverend Moorehead to return thanks. Reverend Moorehead, instead of asking an impersonal blessing, seized the opportunity to advise the Lord of Jem's and her misdeeds. By the time Reverend Moorehead got around to explaining that these were

motherless children she felt one inch high. She peeked
at Jem: his nose was almost in his plate and his ears
were red. She doubted if Atticus would ever be able to
raise his head again, and her suspicion was confirmed
when Reverend Moorehead finally said Amen and Atticus looked up. Two big tears had run from beneath
his glasses down the sides of his cheeks. They had hurt
him badly this time. Suddenly he said, "Excuse me,"
rose abruptly, and disappeared into the kitchen.

Calpurnia came in carefully, bearing a heavily laden
tray. With company came Calpurnia's company manners: although she could speak Jeff Davis's English as
well as anybody, she dropped her verbs in the presence
of guests; she haughtily passed dishes of vegetables; she
seemed to inhale steadily. When Calpurnia was at her
side Jean Louise said, "Excuse me, please," reached up,
and brought Calpurnia's head to the level of her own.
"Cal," she whispered, "is Atticus real upset?"

Calpurnia straightened up, looked down at her, and
said to the table at large, "Mr. Finch? Nawm, Miss
Scout. He on the back porch laughin'!"

Mr. Finch? He laughin'. Car wheels running from pavement to dirt roused her. She ran her fingers through
her hair. She opened the glove compartment, found

a package of cigarettes, took one out of the pack, and lighted it.

"We're almost there," said Henry. "Where were you? Back in New York with your boyfriend?"

"Just woolgathering," she said. "I was thinking about the time we held a revival. You missed that one."

"Thank goodness. That's one of Dr. Finch's favorites."

She laughed. "Uncle Jack's told me that one for nearly twenty years, and it still embarrasses me. You know, Dill was the one person we forgot to tell when Jem died. Somebody sent him a newspaper clipping. He found out like that."

Henry said, "Always happens that way. You forget the oldest ones. Think he'll ever come back?"

Jean Louise shook her head. When the Army sent Dill to Europe, Dill stayed. He was born a wanderer. He was like a small panther when confined with the same people and surroundings for any length of time. She wondered where he would be when his life ended. Not on the sidewalk in Maycomb, that was for sure.

Cool river air cut through the hot night.

"Finch's Landing, madam," said Henry.

Finch's Landing consisted of three hundred and sixty-six steps going down a high bluff and ending in a wide jetty jutting out into the river. One approached it by way of a great clearing some three hundred yards wide extending from the bluff's edge back into the woods. A two-rut road ran from the far end of the clearing and vanished among dark trees. At the end of the road was a two-storied white house with porches extending around its four sides, upstairs and downstairs.

Far from being in an advanced stage of decay, the Old Finch House was in an excellent state of repair: it was a hunting club. Some businessmen from Mobile had leased the land around it, bought the house, and established what Maycomb thought was a private gambling hell. It was not: the rooms of the old house rang on winter nights with male cheer, and occasionally a shotgun would be let off, not in anger but in excessive high spirits. Let them play poker and carouse all they wanted, all Jean Louise wanted was for the old house to be taken care of.

The house had a routine history for the South: it was bought by Atticus Finch's grandfather from the uncle of a renowned lady poisoner who operated on both sides of the Atlantic but who came from a fine old Alabama family. Atticus's father was born in the house, and so were Atticus, Alexandra, Caroline (who married a Mobile man), and John Hale Finch. The clearing was used for family reunions until they went out of style, which was well within Jean Louise's recollection.

Atticus Finch's great-great-grandfather, an English Methodist, settled by the river near Claiborne and produced seven daughters and one son. They married the children of Colonel Maycomb's troops, were fruitful, and established what the county called the Eight Families. Through the years, when the descendants gathered annually, it would become necessary for the Finch in residence at the Landing to hack away more of the woods for picnic grounds, thus accounting for the clearing's present size. It was used for more things than family reunions, however: Negroes played basketball there, the Klan met there in its halcyon days, and a great tournament was held in Atticus's time in which the gentlemen of the county jousted for the honor of carrying their ladies into Maycomb for a great banquet. (Alexandra said watching Uncle Jimmy drive a pole through a ring at full gallop was what made her marry him.)

Atticus's time also was when the Finches moved to town: Atticus read law in Montgomery and returned to practice in Maycomb; Alexandra, overcome by Uncle Jimmy's dexterity, went with him to Maycomb; John Hale Finch went to Mobile to study medicine; and Caroline eloped at seventeen. When their father died they rented out the land, but their mother would not budge from the old place. She stayed on, watching the land rented and sold piece by piece from around her. When she died, all that was left was the house, the clearing, and the landing. The house stayed empty until the gentlemen from Mobile bought it.

Jean Louise thought she remembered her grandmother, but was not sure. When she saw her first Rembrandt, a woman in a cap and ruff, she said, "There's Grandma." Atticus said no, it didn't even look like her. But Jean Louise had an impression that somewhere in the old house she had been taken into a faintly lighted room, and in the middle of the room sat an old, old, lady dressed in black, wearing a white lace collar.

The steps to the Landing were called, of course, the Leap-Year Steps, and when Jean Louise was a child and attended the annual reunions, she and multitudes of cousins would drive their parents to the brink of the bluff worrying about them playing on the steps until the children were caught and divided into two categories, swimmers and nonswimmers. Those who could not swim were relegated to the forest side of the clearing and made to play innocuous games; swimmers had the run of the steps, supervised casually by two Negro youths.

The hunting club had kept the steps in decent repair, and used the jetty as a dock for their boats. They were lazy men; it was easier to drift downstream and row over to Winston Swamp than to thrash through under-brush and pine slashes. Farther downstream, beyond the bluff, were traces of the old cotton landing where Finch Negroes loaded bales and produce, and unloaded blocks of ice, flour and sugar, farm equipment, and ladies' things. Finch's Landing was used only by trav-elers: the steps gave the ladies an excellent excuse to swoon; their luggage was left at the cotton landing—to debark there in front of the Negroes was unthinkable.

"Think they're safe?"

Henry said, "Sure. The club keeps 'em up. We're trespassing, you know."

"Trespassing, hell. I'd like to see the day when a Finch can't walk over his own land." She paused. "What do you mean?"

"They sold the last of it five months ago."

Jean Louise said, "They didn't say word one to me about it."

The tone of her voice made Henry stop. "You don't care, do you?"

"No, not really. I just wish they'd told me."

Henry was not convinced. "For heaven's sake, Jean Louise, what good was it to Mr. Finch and them?"

"None whatever, with taxes and things. I just wish they'd told me. I don't like surprises."

Henry laughed. He stooped down and brought up a

handful of gray sand. "Going Southern on us? Want me to do a Gerald O'Hara?"

"Quit it, Hank." Her voice was pleasant.

Henry said, "I believe you are the worst of the lot. Mr. Finch is seventy-two years young and you're a hundred years old when it comes to something like this."

"I just don't like my world disturbed without some warning. Let's go down to the landing."

"You up to it?"

"I can beat you down any day."

They raced to the steps. When Jean Louise started the swift descent her fingers brushed cold metal. She stopped. They had put an iron-pipe railing on the steps since last year. Hank was too far ahead to catch, but she tried.

When she reached the landing, out of breath, Henry was already sprawled out on the boards. "Careful of the tar, hon," he said.

"I'm getting old," she said.

They smoked in silence. Henry put his arm under her neck and occasionally turned and kissed her. She looked at the sky. "You can almost reach up and touch it, it's so low."

Henry said, "Were you serious a minute ago when you said you didn't like your world disturbed?"

"Hm?" She did not know. She supposed she was.

She tried to explain: "It's just that every time I've come home for the past five years—before that, even. From college—something's changed a little more . . ."

"—and you're not sure you like it, eh?" Henry was grinning in the moonlight and she could see him.

She sat up. "I don't know if I can tell you, honey. When you live in New York, you often have the feeling that New York's not the world. I mean this: every time I come home, I feel like I'm coming back to the world, and when I leave Maycomb it's like leaving the world. It's silly. I can't explain it, and what makes it sillier is that I'd go stark raving living in Maycomb."

Henry said, "You wouldn't, you know. I don't mean to press you for an answer—don't move—but you've got to make up your mind to one thing, Jean Louise. You're gonna see change, you're gonna see Maycomb change its face completely in our lifetime. Your trouble, now, you want to have your cake and eat it: you want to stop the clock, but you can't. Sooner or later you'll have to decide whether it's Maycomb or New York."

He so nearly understood. *I'll marry you, Hank, if you bring me to live here at the Landing. I'll swap New York for this place but not for Maycomb.*

She looked out at the river. The Maycomb County side was high bluffs; Abbott County was flat. When it rained the river overflowed and one could row a boat over cotton fields. She looked upstream. The Canoe Fight was up there, she thought. Sam Dale fit the Indians and Red Eagle jumped off the bluff.

And then he thinks he knows
The hills where his life rose,
And the Sea where it goes.

"Did you say something?" said Henry.

"Nothing. Just being romantic," she said. "By the way, Aunty doesn't approve of you."

"I've known that all my life. Do you?"

"Yep."

"Then marry me."

"Make me an offer."

Henry got up and sat beside her. They dangled their feet over the edge of the landing. "Where are my shoes?" she said suddenly.

"Back by the car where you kicked 'em off. Jean Louise, I can support us both now. I can keep us well in a few years if things keep on booming. The South's the land of opportunity now. There's enough money right here in Maycomb County to sink a—how would you like to have a husband in the legislature?"

Jean Louise was surprised. "You running?"

"I'm thinking about it."

"Against the machine?"

"Yep. It's about ready to fall of its own weight, and if I get in on the ground floor . . ."

"Decent government in Maycomb County'd be such a shock I don't think the citizens could stand it," she said. "What does Atticus think?"

"He thinks the time is ripe."

"You won't have it as easy as he did." Her father, after making his initial campaign, served in the state legislature for as long as he wished, without opposition. He was unique in the history of the county: no machines opposed Atticus Finch, no machines supported him, and no one ran against him. After he retired, the machine gobbled up the one independent office left.

"No, but I can give 'em a run for their money. The Courthouse Crowd are pretty well asleep at the switch now, and a hard campaign might just beat 'em."

"Baby, you won't have a helpmate," she said. "Politics bores me to distraction."

"Anyway, you won't campaign against me. That's a relief in itself."

"A rising young man, aren't you? Why didn't you tell me you were Man of the Year?"

"I was afraid you'd laugh," Henry said.

"Laugh at you, Hank?"

"Yeah. You seem to be half laughing at me all the time."

What could she say? How many times had she hurt his feelings? She said, "You know I've never been exactly tactful, but I swear to God I've never laughed at you, Hank. In my heart I haven't."

She took his head in her arms. She could feel his crew cut under her chin; it was like black velvet. Henry, kissing her, drew her down to him on the floor of the landing.

Some time later, Jean Louise broke it up: "We'd better be going, Hank."

"Not yet."

"Yes."

Hank said wearily, "The thing I hate most about this place is you always have to climb back up."

"I have a friend in New York who always runs up stairs a mile a minute. Says it keeps him from getting out of breath. Why don't you try it?"

"He your boyfriend?"

"Don't be silly," she said.

"You've said that once today."

"Go to hell, then," she said.

"You've said that once today."

Jean Louise put her hands on her hips. "How would you like to go swimming with your clothes on? I haven't said that once today. Right now I'd just as soon push you in as look at you."

"You know, I think you'd do it."

"I'd just as soon," she nodded.

Henry grabbed her shoulder. "If I go you go with me."

"I'll make one concession," she said. "You have until five to empty your pockets."

"This is insane, Jean Louise," he said, pulling out money, keys, billfold, cigarettes. He stepped out of his loafers.

They eyed one another like game roosters. Henry got the jump on her, but when she was falling she snatched at his shirt and took him with her. They swam swiftly in silence to the middle of the river, turned, and swam slowly to the landing. "Give me a hand up," she said.

Dripping, their clothes clinging to them, they made their way up the steps. "We'll be almost dry when we get to the car," he said.

"There was a current out there tonight," she said.

"Too much dissipation."

"Careful I don't push you off this bluff. I mean that." She giggled. "Remember how Mrs. Merriweather used to do poor old Mr. Merriweather? When we're married I'm gonna do you the same way."

It was hard on Mr. Merriweather if he happened to quarrel with his wife while on a public highway. Mr. Merriweather could not drive, and if their dissension reached the acrimonious, Mrs. Merriweather would stop the car and hitchhike to town. Once they disagreed in a narrow lane, and Mr. Merriweather was abandoned for seven hours. Finally he hitched a ride on a passing wagon.

"When I'm in the legislature we can't take midnight plunges," said Henry.

"Then don't run."

The car hummed on. Gradually, the cool air receded and it was stifling again. Jean Louise saw the reflection of headlights behind them in the windshield, and a car passed. Soon another came by, and another. Maycomb was near.

With her head on his shoulder, Jean Louise was content. It might work after all, she thought. But I am not domestic. I don't even know how to run a cook. What do ladies say to each other when they go visiting? I'd have to wear a hat. I'd drop the babies and kill 'em.

Something that looked like a giant black bee whooshed by them and careened around the curve ahead. She sat up, startled. "What was that?"

"Carload of Negroes."

"Mercy, what do they think they're doing?"

"That's the way they assert themselves these days,"

Henry said. "They've got enough money to buy used cars, and they get out on the highway like ninety-to-nothing. They're a public menace."

"Driver's licenses?"

"Not many. No insurance, either."

"Golly, what if something happens?"

"It's just too sad."

At the door, Henry kissed her gently and let her go. "Tomorrow night?" he said.

She nodded. "Goodnight, sweet."

Shoes in hand, she tiptoed into the front bedroom and turned on the light. She undressed, put on her pajama tops, and sneaked quietly into the livingroom. She turned on a lamp and went to the bookshelves. Oh murder, she thought. She ran her finger along the volumes of military history, lingered at *The Second Punic War*, and stopped at *The Reason Why*. Might as well bone up for Uncle Jack, she thought. She returned to her bedroom, snapped off the ceiling light, groped for the lamp, and switched it on. She climbed into the bed she was born in, read three pages, and fell asleep with the light on.

PART III

6

"J ean Louise, Jean Louise, wake up!"

Alexandra's voice penetrated her unconsciousness, and she struggled to meet the morning. She opened her eyes and saw Alexandra standing over her. "Wh—" she said.

"Jean Louise, what do you mean—what do you and Henry Clinton *mean*—by going swimming last night naked?"

Jean Louise sat up in bed. "Hnh?"

"I said, what do you and Henry Clinton mean by going swimming in the river last night naked? It's all over Maycomb this morning."

Jean Louise put her head on her knees and tried to wake up. "Who told you that, Aunty?"

"Mary Webster called at the crack of dawn. Said you two were seen stark in the middle of the river last night at one o'clock!"

"Anybody with eyes that good was up to no good." Jean Louise shrugged her shoulders. "Well, Aunty, I suppose I've got to marry Hank now, haven't I?"

"I—I don't know what to think of you, Jean Louise. Your father will die, simply die, when he finds out. You'd better tell him before he finds out on the street corner."

Atticus was standing in the door with his hands in his pockets. "Good morning," he said. "What'll kill me?"

Alexandra said, "I'm not going to tell him, Jean Louise. It's up to you."

Jean Louise silently signaled her father; her message was received and understood. Atticus looked grave. "What's the matter?" he said.

"Mary Webster was on the blower. Her advance agents saw Hank and me swimming in the middle of the river last night with no clothes on."

"H'rm," said Atticus. He touched his glasses. "I hope you weren't doing the backstroke."

"Atticus!" said Alexandra.

"Sorry, Zandra," said Atticus. "Is that true, Jean Louise?"

"Partly. Have I disgraced us beyond repair?"

"We might survive it."

Alexandra sat down on the bed. "Then it is true,"

she said. "Jean Louise, I don't know what you were doing at the Landing last night in the first place—"

"—but you do know. Mary Webster told you everything, Aunty. Didn't she tell you what happened afterwards? Throw me my negligee, please sir."

Atticus threw her pajama bottoms at her. She put them on beneath the sheet, kicked the sheet back, and stretched her legs.

"Jean Louise—" said Alexandra, and stopped. Atticus was holding up a rough-dried cotton dress. He put it on the bed and went to the chair. He picked up a rough-dried half slip, held it up, and dropped it on top of the dress.

"Quit tormenting your aunt, Jean Louise. These your swimming togs?"

"Yes sir. Reckon we ought to take 'em through town on a pole?"

Alexandra, puzzled, fingered Jean Louise's garments and said, "But what possessed you to go in with your clothes on?"

When her brother and niece laughed, she said, "It's not funny at all. Even if you did go in with your clothes on, Maycomb won't give you credit for it. You might as well have gone in naked. I cannot imagine what put it in your heads to do such a thing."

"I can't either," said Jean Louise. "Besides, if it's

any comfort to you, Aunty, it wasn't that much fun. We just started teasing each other and I dared Hank and he couldn't back out, and then I couldn't back out, and the next thing you know we were in the water."

Alexandra was not impressed: "At your ages, Jean Louise, such conduct is most unbecoming."

Jean Louise sighed and got out of bed. "Well, I'm sorry," she said. "Is there any coffee?"

"There's a potful waiting for you."

Jean Louise joined her father in the kitchen. She went to the stove, poured herself a cup of coffee, and sat down at the table. "How can you drink ice-cold milk for breakfast?"

Atticus gulped. "Tastes better than coffee."

"Calpurnia used to say, when Jem and I'd beg her for coffee, that it'd turn us black like her. Are you worn with me?"

Atticus snorted. "Of course not. But I can think of several more interesting things to do in the middle of the night than pull a trick like that. You'd better get ready for Sunday School."

Alexandra's Sunday corset was even more formidable than her everyday ones. She stood in the door of Jean

Louise's room enarmored, hatted, gloved, perfumed, and ready.

Sunday was Alexandra's day: in the moments before and after Sunday School she and fifteen other Methodist ladies sat together in the church auditorium and conducted a symposium Jean Louise called "The News of the Week in Review." Jean Louise regretted that she had deprived her aunt of her Sabbath pleasure; today Alexandra would be on the defensive, but Jean Louise was confident that Alexandra could wage a defensive war with little less tactical genius than her forward thrusts, that she would emerge and listen to the sermon with her niece's reputation intact.

"Jean Louise, are you ready?"

"Almost," she answered. She swiped at her mouth with a lipstick, patted down her cowlick, eased her shoulders, and turned. "How do I look?" she said.

"I've never seen you completely dressed in your life. Where is your hat?"

"Aunty, you know good and well if I walked in church today with a hat on they'd think somebody was dead."

The one time she wore a hat was to Jem's funeral. She didn't know why she did it, but before the funeral she made Mr. Ginsberg open his store for her and she picked one out and clapped it on her head, fully aware that Jem would have laughed had he been able to see her, but somehow it made her feel better.

Her Uncle Jack was standing on the church steps when they arrived.

Dr. John Hale Finch was no taller than his niece, who was five seven. His father had given him a high-bridged nose, a stern nether lip, and high cheekbones. He looked like his sister Alexandra, but their physical resemblance ended at the neck: Dr. Finch was spare, almost spidery; his sister was of firmer proportions. He was the reason Atticus did not marry until he was forty—when the time came for John Hale Finch to choose a profession, he chose medicine. He chose to study it at a time when cotton was one cent a pound and the Finches had everything but money. Atticus, not yet secure in his profession, spent and borrowed every nickel he could find to put on his brother's education; in due time it was returned with interest.

Dr. Finch became a bone man, practiced in Nashville, played the stock market with shrewdness, and by the time he was forty-five he had accumulated enough money to retire and devote all his time to his first and abiding love, Victorian literature, a pursuit that in itself earned him the reputation of being Maycomb County's most learned licensed eccentric.

Dr. Finch had drunk so long and so deep of his heady brew that his being was shot through with curious mannerisms and odd exclamations. He punctuated his speech with little "hah"s and "hum"s and archaic expressions, on top of which his penchant for modern slang teetered precariously. His wit was hatpin sharp; he was absentminded; he was a bachelor but gave the impression of harboring amusing memories; he possessed a yellow cat nineteen years old; he was incomprehensible to most of Maycomb County because his conversation was colored with subtle allusions to Victorian obscurities.

He gave strangers the idea that he was a borderline case, but those who were tuned to his wavelength knew Dr. Finch to be of a mind so sound, especially when it came to market manipulation, that his friends often risked lengthy lectures on the poetry of Mackworth Praed to seek his advice. From long and close association (in her solitary teens Dr. Finch had tried to make a scholar of her) Jean Louise had developed enough understanding of his subjects to follow him most of the time, and she reveled in his conversation. When he did not have her in silent hysterics, she was bewitched by his bear-trap memory and vast restless mind.

"Good morning, daughter of Nereus!" said her uncle, as he kissed her on the cheek. One of Dr. Finch's concessions to the twentieth century was a telephone. He held his niece at arm's length and regarded her with amused interest.

"Home for nineteen hours and you've already indulged your predilection for ablutionary excesses, hah! A classic example of Watsonian Behaviorism—think I'll write you up and send you to the *AMA Journal.*"

"Hush, you old quack," whispered Jean Louise between clenched teeth. "I'm coming to see you this afternoon."

"You and Hank mollockin' around in the river—hah!—ought to be ashamed of yourselves—disgrace to the family—have fun?"

Sunday School was beginning, and Dr. Finch bowed her in the door: "Your guilty lover's waitin' within," he said.

Jean Louise gave her uncle a look which withered him not at all and marched into the church with as much dignity as she could muster. She smiled and greeted the Maycomb Methodists, and in her old classroom she settled herself by the window and slept with her eyes open through the lesson, as was her custom.

7

There's nothing like a blood-curdling hymn to make you feel at home, thought Jean Louise. Any sense of isolation she may have had withered and died in the presence of some two hundred sinners earnestly requesting to be plunged beneath a red, redeeming flood. While offering to the Lord the results of Mr. Cowper's hallucination, or declaring it was Love that lifted her, Jean Louise shared the warmness that prevails among diverse individuals who find themselves in the same boat for one hour each week.

She was sitting beside her aunt in the middle pew on the right side of the auditorium; her father and Dr. Finch sat side by side on the left, third row from the front. Why they did it was a mystery to her, but they had sat there together ever since Dr. Finch returned to Maycomb. Nobody would take them for brothers, she thought. It's hard to believe he's ten years older than Uncle Jack.

Atticus Finch looked like his mother; Alexandra and John Hale Finch looked like their father. Atticus was a head taller than his brother, his face was broad and open with a straight nose and wide thin mouth, but something about the three marked them as kin. Uncle Jack and Atticus are getting white in the same places and their eyes are alike, thought Jean Louise: that's what it is. She was correct. All the Finches had straight incisive eyebrows and heavy-lidded eyes; when they looked slant-wise, up, or straight ahead, a disinterested observer would catch a glimpse of what Maycomb called Family Resemblance.

Her meditations were interrupted by Henry Clinton. He had passed one collection plate down the pew behind her, and while waiting for its mate to return via the row she was sitting on, he winked openly and solemnly at her. Alexandra saw him and looked blue murder. Henry and his fellow usher walked up the center aisle and stood reverently in front of the altar.

Immediately after collection, Maycomb Methodists sang what they called the Doxology in lieu of the minister praying over the collection plate to spare him the rigors involved in inventing yet another prayer, since by that time he had uttered three healthy invocations. From the time of Jean Louise's earliest ecclesiastical recollection, Maycomb had sung the Doxology in one way and in one way only:

Praise—God—from—whom—all—blessings—flow,

a rendition as much a tradition of Southern Methodism as Pounding the Preacher. That Sunday, Jean Louise and the congregation were in all innocence clearing their throats to drag it accordingly when out of a cloudless sky Mrs. Clyde Haskins crashed down on the organ

PraiseGodfromwhomall Bles—sings—Flo—w
PraiseHimallcreatures He—re Bee—low
PraiseHimaboveye Heav'n—ly Ho—st
PraiseFatherSonand Ho—ly Gho—st!

In the confusion that followed, if the Archbishop of Canterbury had materialized in full regalia Jean Louise would not have been in the least surprised: the congregation had failed to notice any change in Mrs. Haskins's lifelong interpretation, and they intoned the Doxology to its bitter end as they had been reared to do, while Mrs. Haskins romped madly ahead like something out of Salisbury Cathedral.

Jean Louise's first thought was that Herbert Jemson had lost his mind. Herbert Jemson had been music director of the Maycomb Methodist Church for as long as she could remember. He was a big, good man with a soft baritone, who ruled with easy tact a choir of repressed soloists, and who had an unerring memory for the favorite hymns of District Superintendents. In the sundry church wars that were a living part of Maycomb Methodism, Herbert could be counted on as the one person to keep his head, talk sense, and reconcile the more primitive elements of the congregation with the Young Turk faction. He had devoted thirty years' spare time to his church, and his church had recently rewarded him with a trip to a Methodist music camp in South Carolina.

Jean Louise's second impulse was to blame it on the minister. He was a young man, a Mr. Stone by name, with what Dr. Finch called the greatest talent for dullness he had ever seen in a man on the near side of fifty. There was nothing whatever wrong with Mr. Stone, except that he possessed all the necessary qualifications for a certified public accountant: he did not like people, he was quick with numbers, he had no sense of humor, and he was butt-headed.

Because Maycomb's church had for years not been large enough for a good minister but too big for a mediocre one, Maycomb was delighted when, at the last Church Conference, the authorities decided to send its Methodists an energetic young one. But after less than a year the young minister had impressed his congregation to a degree that moved Dr. Finch to observe absently and audibly one Sunday: "We asked for bread and they gave us a Stone."

Mr. Stone had long been suspected of liberal tendencies; he was too friendly, some thought, with his Yankee brethren; he had recently emerged partially damaged from a controversy over the Apostles' Creed; and worst of all, he was thought to be ambitious. Jean Louise was building up an airtight case against him when she remembered Mr. Stone was tone deaf.

Unruffled by Herbert Jemson's breach of allegiance, because he had not heard it, Mr. Stone rose and walked to the pulpit with Bible in hand. He opened it and said, "My text for today is taken from the twenty-first chapter of Isaiah, verse six:

> *For thus hath the Lord said unto me,*
> *Go, set a watchman, let him declare what he seeth."*

Jean Louise made a sincere effort to listen to what Mr. Stone's watchman saw, but in spite of her efforts to quell it, she felt amusement turning into indignant displeasure and she stared straight at Herbert Jemson throughout the service. How dare he change it? Was he trying to lead them back to the Mother Church? Had she allowed reason to rule, she would have realized that Herbert Jemson was Methodist of the whole cloth: he was notoriously short on theology and a mile long on good works.

The Doxology's gone, they'll be having incense next—*orthodoxy's my doxy*. Did Uncle Jack say that or was it one of his old bishops? She looked across the aisle toward him and saw the sharp edge of his profile: he's in a snit, she thought.

Mr. Stone droned . . . a Christian can rid himself of the frustrations of modern living by . . . coming to Family Night every Wednesday and bringing a covered dish . . . abide with you now and forevermore, Amen.

Mr. Stone had pronounced the benediction and was on his way to the front door when she went down the aisle to corner Herbert, who had remained behind to shut the windows. Dr. Finch was faster on the draw:

"—shouldn't sing it like that, Herbert," he was saying. "We are Methodists after all, D.V."

"Don't look at me, Dr. Finch." Herbert threw up his hands as if to ward off whatever was coming. "It's the way they told us to sing it at Camp Charles Wesley."

"You aren't going to take something like that lying down, are you? Who told you to do that?" Dr. Finch screwed up his under lip until it was almost invisible and released it with a snap.

"The music instructor. He taught a course in what was wrong with Southern church music. He was from New Jersey," said Herbert.

"He did, did he?"

"Yes sir."

"What'd he say was wrong with it?"

Herbert said: "He said we might as well be singing 'Stick your snout under the spout where the Gospel comes out' as most of the hymns we sing. Said they ought to ban Fanny Crosby by church law and that *Rock of Ages* was an abomination unto the Lord."

"Indeed?"

"He said we ought to pep up the Doxology."

"Pep it up? How?"

"Like we sang it today."

Dr. Finch sat down in the front pew. He slung his arm across the back and moved his fingers meditatively. He looked up at Herbert.

"Apparently," he said, "apparently our brethren in the Northland are not content merely with the Supreme Court's activities. They are now trying to change our hymns on us."

Herbert said, "He told us we ought to get rid of the Southern hymns and learn some other ones. I don't like it—ones he thought were pretty don't even have tunes."

Dr. Finch's "Hah!" was crisper than usual, a sure sign that his temper was going. He retrieved it sufficiently to say, "Southern hymns, Herbert? Southern hymns?"

Dr. Finch put his hands on his knees and straightened his spine to an upright position.

"Now, Herbert," he said, "let us sit quietly in this sanctuary and analyze this calmly. I believe your man wishes us to sing the Doxology down the line with nothing less than the Church of England, yet he reverses himself—reverses himself—and wants to throw out . . . *Abide with Me*?"

"Right."

"Lyte."

"Er—sir?"

"Lyte, sir. Lyte. What about *When I Survey the Wondrous Cross*?"

"That's another one," said Herbert. "He gave us a list."

"Gave you a list, did he? I suppose *Onward, Christian Soldiers* is on it?"

"At the top."

"Hur!" said Dr. Finch. "H. F. Lyte, Isaac Watts, Sabine Baring-Gould."

Dr. Finch rolled out the last name in Maycomb County accents: long *a*'s, *i*'s, and a pause between syllables.

"Every one an Englishman, Herbert, good and true," he said. "Wants to throw them out, yet tries to make us sing the Doxology like we were all in Westminster Abbey, does he? Well, let me tell you something—"

Jean Louise looked at Herbert, who was nodding agreement, and at her uncle, who was looking like Theobald Pontifex.

"—your man's a snob, Herbert, and that's a fact."

"He was sort of a sissy," said Herbert.

"I'll bet he was. Are you going along with all this nonsense?"

"Heavens no," said Herbert. "I thought I'd try it once, just to make sure of what I'd already guessed. Congregation'll never learn it. Besides, I like the old ones."

"So do I, Herbert," said Dr. Finch. He rose and hooked his arm through Jean Louise's. "I'll see you this time next Sunday, and if I find this church risen one foot off the ground I'll hold you personally responsible."

Something in Dr. Finch's eyes told Herbert that this was a joke. He laughed and said, "Don't worry, sir."

Dr. Finch walked his niece to the car, where Atticus and Alexandra were waiting. "Want a lift?" she said.

"Of course not," said Dr. Finch. It was his habit to walk to and from church every Sunday, and this he did, undeterred by tempests, boiling sun, or freezing weather.

As he turned to go, Jean Louise called to him. "Uncle Jack," she said. "What does D.V. mean?"

Dr. Finch sighed his you-have-no-education-young-woman sigh, raised his eyebrows, and said: "*Deo volente*. 'God willin',' child. 'God willin'.' A reliable Catholic utterance."

8

With the same suddenness that a barbarous boy yanks the larva of an ant lion from its hole to leave it struggling in the sun, Jean Louise was snatched from her quiet realm and left alone to protect her sensitive epidermis as best she could, on a humid Sunday afternoon at precisely 2:28 P.M. The circumstances leading to the event were these:

After dinner, at which time Jean Louise regaled her household with Dr. Finch's observations on stylish hymn-singing, Atticus sat in his corner of the livingroom reading the Sunday papers, and Jean Louise was looking forward to an afternoon's hilarity with her uncle, complete with teacakes and the strongest coffee in Maycomb.

The doorbell rang. She heard Atticus call, "Come in!" and Henry's voice answer him, "Ready, Mr. Finch?"

She threw down the dishtowel; before she could leave the kitchen Henry stuck his head in the door and said, "Hey."

Alexandra pinned him to the wall in no time flat: "Henry Clinton, you ought to be ashamed of yourself."

Henry, whose charms were not inconsiderable, turned them full force on Alexandra, who showed no signs of melting. "Now, Miss Alexandra," he said. "You can't stay mad with us long even if you try."

Alexandra said, "I got you two out of it this time, but I may not be around next time."

"Miss Alexandra, we appreciate that more than anything." He turned to Jean Louise. "Seven-thirty tonight and no Landing. We'll go to the show."

"Okay. Where're you all going?"

"Courthouse. Meeting."

"On Sunday?"

"Yep."

"That's right, I keep forgetting all the politicking's done on Sunday in these parts."

Atticus called for Henry to come on. "Bye, baby," he said.

Jean Louise followed him into the livingroom. When the front door slammed behind her father and Henry, she went to her father's chair to tidy up the papers he had left on the floor beside it. She picked them up, arranged them in sectional order, and put them on the sofa in a neat pile. She crossed the room again to straighten the stack of books on his lamp table, and was doing so when a pamphlet the size of a business envelope caught her eye.

On its cover was a drawing of an anthropophagous Negro; above the drawing was printed *The Black Plague*. Its author was somebody with several academic degrees after his name. She opened the pamphlet, sat down in her father's chair, and began reading. When she had finished, she took the pamphlet by one of its corners, held it like she would hold a dead rat by the tail, and walked into the kitchen. She held the pamphlet in front of her aunt.

"What is this thing?" she said.

Alexandra looked over her glasses at it. "Something of your father's."

Jean Louise stepped on the garbage can trigger and threw the pamphlet in.

"Don't do that," said Alexandra. "They're hard to come by these days."

Jean Louise opened her mouth, shut it, and opened it again. "Aunty, have you read that thing? Do you know what's in it?"

"Certainly."

If Alexandra had uttered an obscenity in her face, Jean Louise would have been less surprised.

"You—Aunty, do you know the stuff in that thing makes Dr. Goebbels look like a naive little country boy?"

"I don't know what you're talking about, Jean Louise. There are a lot of truths in that book."

"Yes indeedy," said Jean Louise wryly. "I especially liked the part where the Negroes, bless their hearts, couldn't help being inferior to the white race because their skulls are thicker and their brain-pans shallower—whatever that means—so we must all be very kind to them and not let them do anything to hurt themselves and keep them in their places. Good God, Aunty—"

Alexandra was ramrod straight. "Well?" she said.

Jean Louise said, "It's just that I never knew you went in for salacious reading material, Aunty."

Her aunt was silent, and Jean Louise continued: "I was real impressed with the parable where since the dawn of history the rulers of the world have always been white, except Genghis Khan or somebody—the author was real fair about that—and he made a killin' point about even the Pharaohs were white and their subjects were either black or Jews—"

"That's true, isn't it?"

"Sure, but what's that got to do with the case?"

When Jean Louise felt apprehensive, expectant, or on edge, especially when confronting her aunt, her brain clicked to the meter of Gilbertian tomfoolery. Three sprightly figures whirled madly in her head—hours filled with Uncle Jack and Dill dancing to preposterous measures blacked out the coming of tomorrow with tomorrow's troubles.

Alexandra was talking to her: "I told you. It's something your father brought home from a citizens' council meeting."

"From a what?"

"From the Maycomb County Citizens' Council. Didn't you know we have one?"

"I did not."

"Well, your father's on the board of directors and Henry's one of the staunchest members." Alexandra sighed. "Not that we really need one. Nothing's happened here in Maycomb yet, but it's always wise to be prepared. That's where they are this minute."

"Citizens' council? In Maycomb?" Jean Louise heard herself repeating fatuously. "Atticus?"

Alexandra said, "Jean Louise, I don't think you fully realize what's been going on down here—"

Jean Louise turned on her heel, walked to the front door, out of it, across the broad front yard, down the street toward town as fast as she could go, Alexandra's "you aren't going to town Like That" echoing behind her. She had forgotten that there was a car in good running condition in the garage, that its keys were on the hall table. She walked swiftly, keeping time to the absurd jingle running through her head.

Here's a how-de-do!
If I marry you,
When your time has come to perish
Then the maiden whom you cherish
Must be slaughtered, too!
Here's a how-de-do!

What were Hank and Atticus up to? What was going on? She did not know, but before the sun went down she would find out.

It had something to do with that pamphlet she found in the house—sitting there before God and everybody—something to do with citizens' councils. She knew about them, all right. New York papers full of it. She wished she had paid more attention to them, but only one glance down a column of print was enough to tell her a familiar story: same people who were the Invisible Empire, who hated Catholics; ignorant, fear-ridden, red-faced, boorish, law-abiding, one hundred per cent red-blooded Anglo-Saxons, her fellow Americans—trash.

Atticus and Hank were pulling something, they were there merely to keep an eye on things—Aunty said Atticus was on the board of directors. She was wrong. It was all a mistake; Aunty got mixed up on her facts sometimes. . . .

She slowed up when she came to the town. It was deserted; only two cars were in front of the drugstore. The old courthouse stood white in the afternoon glare. A black hound loped down the street in the distance, the monkey puzzles bristled silently on the corners of the square.

When she went to the north side entrance she saw empty cars standing in a double row the length of the building.

When she went up the courthouse steps she missed the elderly men who loitered there, she missed the water cooler that stood inside the door, missed the cane-bottom chairs in the hallway; she did not miss the dank urine-sweet odor of sunless county cubbyholes. She walked past the offices of the tax collector, tax assessor, county clerk, registrar, judge of probate, up old unpainted stairs to the courtroom floor, up a small covered stairway to the Colored balcony, walked out into it, and took her old place in the corner of the front row, where she and her brother had sat when they went to court to watch their father.

Below her, on rough benches, sat not only most of the trash in Maycomb County, but the county's most respectable men.

She looked toward the far end of the room, and behind the railing that separated court from spectators, at a long table, sat her father, Henry Clinton, several men she knew only too well, and a man she did not know.

At the end of the table, sitting like a great dropsical gray slug, was William Willoughby, the political symbol of everything her father and men like him despised. He's the last of *his* kind, she thought. Atticus'd scarcely give him the time of day, and there he is at the same . . .

William Willoughby was indeed the last of his kind, for a while, at least. He was bleeding slowly to death in the midst of abundance, for his life's blood was poverty. Every county in the Deep South had a Willoughby, each so like the other that they constituted a category called He, the Great Big Man, the Little Man, allowing for minor territorial differences. He, or whatever his subjects called him, occupied the leading administrative office in his county—usually he was sheriff or judge or probate—but there were mutations, like Maycomb's

Willoughby, who chose to grace no public office. Willoughby was rare—his preference to remain behind the scenes implied the absence of vast personal conceit, a trait essential for two-penny despots.

Willoughby chose to run the county not in its most comfortable office, but in what was best described as a hutch—a small, dark, evil-smelling room with his name on the door, containing nothing more than a telephone, a kitchen table, and unpainted captain's chairs of rich patina. Wherever Willoughby went, there followed axiomatically a coterie of passive, mostly negative characters known as the Courthouse Crowd, specimens Willoughby had put into the various county and municipal offices to do as they were told.

Sitting at the table by Willoughby was one of them, Tom-Carl Joyner, his right-hand man and justly proud: wasn't he in with Willoughby from the beginning? Did he not do all of Willoughby's legwork? Did he not, in the old days during the Depression, knock on tenant-cabin doors at midnight, did he not drum it into the head of every ignorant hungry wretch who accepted public assistance, whether job or relief money, that his vote was Willoughby's? No votee, no eatee. Like his lesser satellites, over the years Tom-Carl had assumed an ill-fitting air of respectability and did not care to be reminded of his nefarious beginnings. Tom-Carl sat that Sunday secure in the knowledge that the small empire he had lost so much sleep building would be his when Willoughby lost interest or died. Nothing in Tom-Carl's face indicated that he might have a rude surprise coming to him: already, prosperity-bred independence had undermined his kingdom until it was foundering; two more elections and it would crumble into thesis material for a sociology major. Jean Louise watched his self-important little face and almost laughed when she reflected that the South was indeed pitiless to reward its public servants with extinction.

She looked down on rows of familiar heads—white hair, brown hair, hair carefully combed to hide no hair—and she remembered how, long ago when court was dull, she would quietly aim spitballs at the shining domes below. Judge Taylor caught her at it one day and threatened her with a bench warrant.

The courthouse clock creaked, strained, said, "Phlugh!" and struck the hour. Two. When the sound shivered away she saw her father rise and address the assembly in his dry courtroom voice:

"Gentlemen, our speaker for today is Mr. Grady O'Hanlon. He needs no introduction. Mr. O'Hanlon."

Mr. O'Hanlon rose and said, "As the cow said to the milkman on a cold morning, 'Thank you for the warm hand.'"

She had never seen or heard of Mr. O'Hanlon in her life. From the gist of his introductory remarks, however, Mr. O'Hanlon made plain to her who he was—he was an ordinary, God-fearing man just like any ordinary man, who had quit his job to devote his full time to the preservation of segregation. Well, some people have strange fancies, she thought.

Mr. O'Hanlon had light-brown hair, blue eyes, a mulish face, a shocking necktie, and no coat. He unbuttoned his collar, untied his tie, blinked his eyes, ran his hand through his hair, and got down to business:

Mr. O'Hanlon was born and bred in the South, went to school there, married a Southern lady, lived all his life there, and his main interest today was to uphold the Southern Way of Life and no niggers and no Supreme Court was going to tell him or anybody else what to do . . . a race as hammerheaded as . . . essential inferiority . . . kinky woolly heads . . . still in the trees . . . greasy smelly . . . marry your daughters . . . mongrelize the race . . . mongrelize . . . *mongrelize* . . . save the South . . . Black Monday . . . lower than cockroaches . . . God made the races . . . nobody knows why but He intended for 'em to stay apart . . . if He hadn't He'd've made us all one color . . . back to Africa . . .

She heard her father's voice, a tiny voice talking in the warm comfortable past. *Gentlemen, if there's one slogan in this world I believe, it is this: equal rights for all, special privileges for none.*

These top-water nigger preachers . . . like apes . . . mouths like Number 2 cans . . . twist the Gospel . . . the court prefers to listen to Communists . . . take 'em all out and shoot 'em for treason . . .

Against Mr. O'Hanlon's humming harangue, a memory was rising to dispute him: the courtroom shifted imperceptibly, in it she looked down on the same heads. When she looked across the room a jury sat in the box, Judge Taylor was on the bench, his pilot fish sat below in front of him writing steadily; her father was on his feet: he had risen from a table at which she could see the back of a kinky woolly head. . . .

Atticus Finch rarely took a criminal case; he had no taste for criminal law. The only reason he took this one was because he knew his client to be innocent of the charge, and he could not for the life of him let the black boy go to prison because of a half-hearted, court-appointed defense. The boy had come to him by way of Calpurnia, told him his story, and had told him the truth. The truth was ugly.

Atticus took his career in his hands, made good use of a careless indictment, took his stand before a jury, and accomplished what was never before or afterwards done in Maycomb County: he won an acquittal for a colored boy on a rape charge. The chief witness for the prosecution was a white girl.

Atticus had two weighty advantages: although the white girl was fourteen years of age the defendant was not indicted for statutory rape, therefore Atticus could and did prove consent. Consent was easier to prove than under normal conditions—the defendant had only one arm. The other was chopped off in a sawmill accident.

Atticus pursued the case to its conclusion with every spark of his ability and with an instinctive distaste so bitter only his knowledge that he could live peacefully with himself was able to wash it away. After the verdict, he walked out of the courtroom in the middle of the day, walked home, and took a steaming bath. He never counted what it cost him; he never looked back. He never knew two pairs of eyes like his own were watching him from the balcony.

. . . not the question of whether snot-nosed niggers will go to school with your children or ride the front of the bus . . . it's whether Christian civilization will continue to be or whether we will be slaves of the Communists . . . nigger lawyers . . . stomped on the Constitution . . . our Jewish friends . . . killed Jesus . . . voted the nigger . . . our granddaddies . . . nigger judges and sheriffs . . . separate is equal . . . ninety-five per cent of the tax money . . . for the nigger and the old hound dog . . . following the golden calf . . . preach the Gospel . . . old lady Roosevelt . . . nigger-lover . . . entertains forty-five niggers but not one fresh white Southern virgin . . . Huey Long, that Christian gentleman . . . black as burnt light'ud knots . . . bribed the Supreme Court . . . decent white Christians . . . was Jesus crucified for the nigger . . .

Jean Louise's hand slipped. She removed it from the balcony railing and looked at it. It was dripping wet. A wet place on the railing mirrored thin light coming through the upper windows. She stared at her father sitting to the right of Mr. O'Hanlon, and she did not believe what she saw. She stared at Henry sitting to the left of Mr. O'Hanlon, and she did not believe what she saw . . .

. . . but they were sitting all over the courtroom. Men of substance and character, responsible men, good men. Men of all varieties and reputations . . . it seemed that the only man in the county not present was Uncle Jack. Uncle Jack—she was supposed to go see him sometime. When?

She knew little of the affairs of men, but she knew that her father's presence at the table with a man who spewed filth from his mouth—did that make it less filthy? No. It condoned.

She felt sick. Her stomach shut, she began to tremble.

Hank.

Every nerve in her body shrieked, then died. She was numb.

She pulled herself to her feet clumsily, and stumbled from the balcony down the covered staircase. She did not hear her feet scraping down the broad stairs, or the courthouse clock laboriously strike two-thirty; she did not feel the dank air of the first floor.

The glaring sun pierced her eyes with pain, and she put her hands to her face. When she took them down slowly to adjust her eyes from dark to light, she saw Maycomb with no people in it, shimmering in the steaming afternoon.

She walked down the steps and into the shade of a live oak. She put her arm out and leaned against the trunk. She looked at Maycomb, and her throat tightened: Maycomb was looking back at her.

Go away, the old buildings said. There is no place for you here. You are not wanted. We have secrets.

In obedience to them, in the silent heat she walked down Maycomb's main thoroughfare, a highway leading to Montgomery. She walked on, past houses with wide front yards in which moved green-thumbed ladies and slow large men. She thought she heard Mrs. Wheeler yelling to Miss Maudie Atkinson across the street, and if Miss Maudie saw her she would say come in and have some cake, I've just made a big one for the Doctor and a little one for you. She counted the cracks in the sidewalk, steeled herself for Mrs. Henry Lafayette Dubose's onslaught—*Don't you say hey to me, Jean Louise Finch, you say good afternoon!*—hurried by the old steep-roofed house, past Miss Rachel's, and found herself home.

HOME-MADE ICE CREAM.

She blinked hard. I'm losing my mind, she thought.

She tried to walk on but it was too late. The square, squat, modern ice cream shop where her old home had been was open, and a man was peering out the window at her. She dug in the pockets of her slacks and came up with a quarter.

"Could I have a cone of vanilla, please?"

"Don't come in cones no more. I can give you a—"

"That's all right. Give me whatever it comes in," she said to the man.

"Jean Louise Finch, ain'tcha?" he said.

"Yes."

"Used to live right here, didn'tcha?"

"Yes."

"Matter of fact, born here, weren'tcha?"

"Yes."

"Been livin' in New York, haven'tcha?"

"Yes."

"Maycomb's changed, ain't it?"

"Yes."

"Don't remember who I am, do you?"

"No."

"Well I ain't gonna tell you. You can just sit there and eat your ice cream and try to figure out who I am, and if you can I'll give you another helpin' free of charge."

"Thank you sir," she said. "Do you mind if I go around in the back—"

"Sure. There's tables and chairs out in the back. Folks set out there at night and eat their ice cream."

The back yard was strewn over with white gravel. How small it looks with no house, no carhouse, no chinaberry trees, she thought. She sat down at a table and put the container of ice cream on it. I've got to think.

It happened so quickly that her stomach was still heaving. She breathed deeply to quieten it, but it would not stay still. She felt herself turning green with nausea, and she put her head down; try as she might she could not think, she only knew, and what she knew was this:

The one human being she had ever fully and whole-heartedly trusted had failed her; the only man she had ever known to whom she could point and say with expert knowledge, "He is a gentleman, in his heart he is a gentleman," had betrayed her, publicly, grossly, and shamelessly.

9

Integrity, humor, and patience were the three words for Atticus Finch. There was also a phrase for him: pick at random any citizen from Maycomb County and its environs, ask him what he thought of Atticus Finch, and the answer would most likely be, "I never had a better friend."

Atticus Finch's secret of living was so simple it was deeply complex: where most men had codes and tried to live up to them, Atticus lived his to the letter with no fuss, no fanfare, and no soul-searching. His private character was his public character. His code was simple New Testament ethic, its rewards were the respect and devotion of all who knew him. Even his enemies loved him, because Atticus never acknowledged that they were his enemies. He was never a rich man, but he was the richest man his children ever knew.

His children were in a position to know as children

seldom are: when Atticus was in the legislature he met, loved, and married a Montgomery girl some fifteen years his junior; he brought her home to Maycomb and they lived in a new-bought house on the town's main street. When Atticus was forty-two their son was born, and they named him Jeremy Atticus, for his father and his father's father. Four years later their daughter was born, and they named her Jean Louise for her mother and her mother's mother. Two years after that Atticus came home from work one evening and found his wife on the floor of the front porch dead, cut off from view by the wisteria vine that made the corner of the porch a cool private retreat. She had not been dead long; the chair from which she had fallen was still rocking. Jean Graham Finch had brought to the family the heart that killed her son twenty-two years later on the sidewalk in front of his father's office.

At forty-eight, Atticus was left with two small children and a Negro cook named Calpurnia. It is doubtful that he ever sought for meanings; he merely reared his children as best he could, and in terms of the affection his children felt for him, his best was indeed good: he was never too tired to play Keep-Away; he was never too busy to invent marvelous stories; he was never too absorbed in his own problems to listen earnestly to a tale of woe; every night he read aloud to them until his voice cracked.

Atticus killed several birds with one stone when he read to his children, and would probably have caused a child psychologist considerable dismay: he read to Jem and Jean Louise whatever he happened to be reading, and the children grew up possessed of an obscure erudition. They cut their back teeth on military history, Bills to Be Enacted into Laws, *True Detective Mysteries*, *The Code of Alabama*, the Bible, and Palgrave's *Golden Treasury*.

Wherever Atticus went, Jem and Jean Louise would most of the time follow. He took them to Montgomery with him if the legislature was in summer session; he took them to football games, to political meetings, to church, to the office at night if he had to work late. After the sun went down, Atticus was seldom seen in public without his children in tow.

Jean Louise had never known her mother, and she never knew what a mother was, but she rarely felt the need of one. In her childhood her father had never misinterpreted her, nor bobbled once, except when she was eleven and came home to dinner from school one day and found that her blood had begun to flow.

She thought she was dying and she began to scream. Calpurnia and Atticus and Jem came running, and when they saw her plight, Atticus and Jem looked helplessly at Calpurnia, and Calpurnia took her in hand.

It had never fully occurred to Jean Louise that she was a girl: her life had been one of reckless, pummeling activity; fighting, football, climbing, keeping up with Jem, and besting anyone her own age in any contest requiring physical prowess.

When she was calm enough to listen, she considered that a cruel practical joke had been played upon her: she must now go into a world of femininity, a world she despised, could not comprehend nor defend herself against, a world that did not want her.

Jem left her when he was sixteen. He began slicking back his hair with water and dating girls, and her only friend was Atticus. Then Dr. Finch came home.

The two aging men saw her through her loneliest and most difficult hours, through the malignant limbo of turning from a howling tomboy into a young woman. Atticus took her air rifle from her hand and put a golf club in it, Dr. Finch taught her—Dr. Finch taught her what he was most interested in. She gave lip service to the world: she went through the motions of complying with the regulations governing the behavior of teenaged girls from good families; she developed a halfway interest in clothes, boys, hairdos, gossip, and female aspirations; but she was uneasy all the time she was away from the security of those who she knew loved her.

Atticus sent her to a women's college in Georgia; when she finished he said it was high time she started shifting for herself and why didn't she go to New York or somewhere. She was vaguely insulted and felt she was being turned out of her own house, but as the years passed she recognized the full value of Atticus's wisdom; he was growing old and he wanted to die safe in the knowledge that his daughter could fend for herself.

She did not stand alone, but what stood behind her, the most potent moral force in her life, was the love of her father. She never questioned it, never thought about it, never even realized that before she made any decision of importance the reflex, "What would Atticus do?" passed through her unconscious; she never realized what made her dig in her feet and stand firm whenever she did was her father; that whatever was decent and of good report in her character was put there by her father; she did not know that she worshiped him.

All she knew was that she felt sorry for the people her age who railed against their parents for not giving them this and cheating them out of that. She felt sorry

for middle-aged matrons who after much analysis discovered that the seat of their anxiety was in their seats;
she felt sorry for persons who called their fathers My
Old Man, denoting that they were raffish, probably
boozy ineffective creatures who had disappointed their
children dreadfully and unforgivably somewhere along
the line.

She was extravagant with her pity, and complacent
in her snug world.

10

Jean Louise got up from the yard chair she was sitting in, walked to the corner of the lot, and vomited up her Sunday dinner. Her fingers caught the strands of a wire fence, the fence that separated Miss Rachel's garden from the Finch back yard. If Dill were here he would leap over the fence to her, bring her head down to his, kiss her, and hold her hand, and together they would take their stand when there was trouble in the house. But Dill had long since gone from her.

Her nausea returned with redoubled violence when she remembered the scene in the courthouse, but she had nothing left to part with.

If you had only spat in my face . . .

It could be, might be, still was, a horrible mistake. Her mind refused to register what her eyes and ears told it. She returned to her chair and sat staring at a pool of melted vanilla ice cream working its way slowly to the edge of the table. It spread, paused, dribbled and dripped. Drip, drip, drip, into the white gravel until, saturated, it could no longer receive and a second tiny pool appeared.

You did that. You did it as sure as you were sitting there.

"Guessed my name yet? Why looka yonder, you've wasted your ice cream."

She raised her head. The man in the shop was leaning out the back window, less than five feet from her. He withdrew and reappeared with a limp rag. As he wiped the mess away he said, "What's my name?"

Rumpelstiltskin.

"Oh, I am sorry." She looked at the man carefully. "Are you one of the *cee-oh* Coninghams?"

The man grinned broadly. "Almost. I'm one of the *cee-you*'s. How'd you know?"

"Family resemblance. What got you out of the woods?"

"Mamma left me some timber and I sold it. Put up this shop here."

"What time is it?" she asked.

"Gettin' on to four-thirty," said Mr. Cunningham.

She rose, smiled goodbye, and said she would be coming back soon. She made her way to the sidewalk.

Two solid hours and I didn't know where I was. I am so tired.

She did not return by town. She walked the long way round, through a schoolyard, down a street lined with pecan trees, across another schoolyard, across a football field on which Jem in a daze had once tackled his own man. I am so tired.

Alexandra was standing in the doorway. She stepped aside to let Jean Louise pass. "Where have you been?" she said. "Jack called ages ago and asked after you. Have you been visiting out of the family Like That?"

"I—I don't know."

"What do you mean you don't know? Jean Louise, talk some sense and go phone your uncle."

She went wearily to the telephone and said, "One one nine." Dr. Finch's voice said, "Dr. Finch." She said softly, "I'm sorry. See you tomorrow?" Dr. Finch said, "Right."

She was too tired to be amused at her uncle's telephone manners: he viewed such instruments with deep anger and his conversations were monosyllabic at best.

When she turned around Alexandra said, "You look right puny. What's the matter?"

Madam, my father has left me flopping like a flounder at low tide and you say what's the matter. "Stomach," she said.

"There's a lot of that going around now. Does it hurt?"

Yes it hurts. Like hell. It hurts so much I can't stand it. "No ma'am, just upset."

"Then why don't you take an Alka-Seltzer?"

Jean Louise said she would, and the day dawned for Alexandra: "Jean Louise, did you go to that meeting with all those men there?"

"Yes'm."

"Like That?"

"Yes'm."

"Where did you sit?"

"In the balcony. They didn't see me. I watched from the balcony. Aunty, when Hank comes tonight tell him I'm . . . indisposed."

"Indisposed?"

She could not stand there another minute. "Yes, Aunty. I'm gonna do what every Christian young white fresh Southern virgin does when she's indisposed."

"And what might that be?"

"I'm takin' to my bed."

Jean Louise went to her room, shut the door, unbuttoned her blouse, unzipped the fly of her slacks, and fell across her mother's lacy wrought-iron bed. She groped blindly for a pillow and pushed it under her face. In one minute she was asleep.

Had she been able to think, Jean Louise might have prevented events to come by considering the day's occurrences in terms of a recurring story as old as time: the chapter which concerned her began two hundred years ago and was played out in a proud society the bloodiest war and harshest peace in modern history could not destroy, returning, to be played out again on private ground in the twilight of a civilization no wars and no peace could save.

Had she insight, could she have pierced the barriers of her highly selective, insular world, she may have discovered that all her life she had been with a visual defect which had gone unnoticed and neglected by herself and by those closest to her: she was born color blind.

PART IV

11

There was a time, long ago, when the only peaceful moments of her existence were those from the time she opened her eyes in the morning until she attained full consciousness, a matter of seconds until when finally roused she entered the day's wakeful nightmare.

She was in the sixth grade, a grade memorable for the things she learned in class and out. That year the small group of town children were swamped temporarily by a collection of elderly pupils shipped in from Old Sarum because somebody had set fire to the school there. The oldest boy in Miss Blunt's sixth grade was nearly nineteen, and he had three contemporaries. There were several girls of sixteen, voluptuous, happy creatures who thought school something of a holiday from chopping cotton and feeding livestock. Miss Blunt was equal to them all: she was as tall as the tallest boy in the class and twice as wide.

Jean Louise took to the Old Sarum newcomers immediately. After holding the class's undivided attention by deliberately introducing Gaston B. Means into a discussion on the natural resources of South Africa, and proving her accuracy with a rubberband gun during recess, she enjoyed the confidence of the Old Sarum crowd.

With rough gentleness the big boys taught her to shoot craps and chew tobacco without losing it. The big girls giggled behind their hands most of the time and whispered among themselves a great deal, but Jean Louise considered them useful when choosing sides for a volleyball match. All in all, it was turning out to be a wonderful year.

Wonderful, until she went home for dinner one day. She did not return to school that afternoon, but spent the afternoon on her bed crying with rage and trying to understand the terrible information she had received from Calpurnia.

The next day she returned to school walking with extreme dignity, not prideful, but encumbered by accoutrements hitherto unfamiliar to her. She was positive everybody knew what was the matter with her, that she was being looked at, but she was puzzled that she had never heard it spoken of before in all her years.

Maybe nobody knows anything about it, she thought. If that was so, she had news, all right.

At recess, when George Hill asked her to be It for Hot-Grease-in-the-Kitchen, she shook her head.

"I can't do anything any more," she said, and she sat on the steps and watched the boys tumble in the dust. "I can't even walk."

When she could bear it no longer, she joined the knot of girls under the live oak in a corner of the schoolyard.

Ada Belle Stevens laughed and made room for her on the long cement bench. "Why ain'tcha playin'?" she asked.

"Don't wanta," said Jean Louise.

Ada Belle's eyes narrowed and her white brows twitched. "I bet I know what's the matter with you."

"What?"

"You've got the Curse."

"The what?"

"The Curse. Curse o' Eve. If Eve hadn't et the apple we wouldn't have it. You feel bad?"

"No," said Jean Louise, silently cursing Eve. "How'd you know it?"

"You walk like you was ridin' a bay mare," said Ada Belle. "You'll get used to it. I've had it for years."

"I'll never get used to it."

It was difficult. When her activities were limited Jean Louise confined herself to gambling for small sums behind a coal pile in the rear of the school building. The inherent dangerousness of the enterprise appealed to her far more than the game itself; she was not good enough at arithmetic to care whether she won or lost, there was no real joy in trying to beat the law of averages, but she derived some pleasure from deceiving Miss Blunt. Her companions were the lazier of the Old Sarum boys, the laziest of whom was one Albert Coningham, a slow thinker to whom Jean Louise had rendered invaluable service during six-weeks' tests.

One day, as the taking-in bell rang, Albert, beating coal dust from his breeches, said, "Wait a minute, Jean Louise."

She waited. When they were alone, Albert said, "I want you to know I made a C-minus this time in geography."

"That's real good, Albert," she said.

"I just wanted to thank you."

"You're welcome, Albert."

Albert blushed to his hairline, caught her to him, and kissed her. She felt his wet, warm tongue on her lips, and she drew back. She had never been kissed like that before. Albert let her go and shuffled toward the school building. Jean Louise followed, bemused and faintly annoyed.

She only suffered a kinsman to kiss her on the cheek and then she secretly wiped it off; Atticus kissed her vaguely wherever he happened to land; Jem kissed her not at all. She thought Albert had somehow miscalculated, and she soon forgot.

As the year passed, often as not recess would find her with the girls under the tree, sitting in the middle of the crowd, resigned to her fate, but watching the boys play their seasonal games in the schoolyard. One morning, arriving late to the scene, she found the girls giggling more surreptitiously than usual and she demanded to know the reason.

"It's Francine Owen," one said.

"Francine Owen? She's been absent a couple of days," said Jean Louise.

"Know why?" said Ada Belle.

"Nope."

"It's her sister. The welfare's got 'em both."

Jean Louise nudged Ada Belle, who made room for her on the bench.

"What's wrong with her?"

"She's pregnant, and you know who did it? Her daddy."

Jean Louise said, "What's pregnant?"

A groan went up from the circle of girls. "Gonna have a baby, stupid," said one.

Jean Louise assimilated the definition and said, "But what's her daddy got to do with it?"

Ada Belle sighed, "Her daddy's the daddy."

Jean Louise laughed. "Come on, Ada Belle—"

"That's a fact, Jean Louise. Betcha the only reason Francine ain't is she ain't started yet."

"Started what?"

"Started ministratin'," said Ada Belle impatiently. "I bet he did it with both of 'em."

"Did what?" Jean Louise was now totally confused.

The girls shrieked. Ada Belle said, "You don't know one thing, Jean Louise Finch. First of all you—then if you do it after that, after you start, that is, you'll have a solid baby."

"Do *what*, Ada Belle?"

Ada Belle glanced up at the circle and winked. "Well, first of all it takes a boy. Then he hugs you tight and breathes real hard and then he French-kisses you. That's when he kisses you and opens his mouth and sticks his tongue in your mouth—"

A ringing noise in her ears obliterated Ada Belle's narrative. She felt the blood leave her face. Her palms grew sweaty and she tried to swallow. She would not leave. If she left they would know it. She stood up, trying to smile, but her lips were trembling. She clamped her mouth shut and clenched her teeth.

"—an' that's all there is to it. What's the matter, Jean Louise? You're white as a hain't. Ain't scared'ja, have I?" Ada Belle smirked.

"No," said Jean Louise. "I just don't feel so hot. Think I'll go inside."

She prayed they would not see her knees shaking as she walked across the schoolyard. Inside the girls' bathroom she leaned over a washbasin and vomited.

There was no mistaking it, Albert had stuck out his tongue at her. She was pregnant.

Jean Louise's gleanings of adult morals and mores to date were few, but enough: it was possible to have a baby without being married, she knew that. Until today she neither knew nor cared how, because the subject was uninteresting, but if someone had a baby without being married, her family was plunged into deep disgrace. She had heard Alexandra go on at length about Disgraces to Families: disgrace involved being sent to Mobile and shut up in a Home away from decent people. One's family was never able to hold up their heads again. Something had happened once, down the street toward Montgomery, and the ladies at the other end of the street whispered and clucked about it for weeks.

She hated herself, she hated everybody. She had done nobody any harm. She was overwhelmed by the unfairness of it: she had meant no harm.

She crept away from the school building, walked around the corner to the house, sneaked to the back yard, climbed the chinaberry tree, and sat there until dinnertime.

Dinner was long and silent. She was barely conscious of Jem and Atticus at the table. After dinner she returned to the tree and sat there until twilight, when she heard Atticus call her.

"Come down from there," he said. She was too miserable to react to the ice in his voice.

"Miss Blunt called and said you left school at recess and didn't come back. Where were you?"

"Up the tree."

"Are you sick? You know if you're sick you're to go straight to Cal."

"No sir."

"Then if you aren't sick what favorable construction can you put upon your behavior? Any excuse for it?"

"No sir."

"Well, let me tell you something. If this happens again it will be Hail Columbia."

"Yes sir."

It was on the tip of her tongue to tell him, to shift her burden to him, but she was silent.

"You sure you're feeling all right?"

"Yes sir."

"Then come on in the house."

At the supper table, she wanted to throw her plate fully loaded at Jem, a superior fifteen in adult communication with their father. From time to time Jem would cast scornful glances at her. I'll get you back, don't you worry, she promised him. But I can't now.

Every morning she awakened full of catlike energy and the best intentions, every morning the dull dread returned; every morning she looked for the baby. During the day it was never far from her immediate consciousness, intermittently returning at unsuspected moments, whispering and taunting her.

She looked under *baby* in the dictionary and found little; she looked under *birth* and found less. She came upon an ancient book in the house called *Devils, Drugs, and Doctors* and was frightened to mute hysteria by pictures of medieval labor chairs, delivery instruments, and the information that women were sometimes thrown repeatedly against walls to induce birth. Gradually she assembled data from her friends at school, carefully spacing her questions weeks apart so as not to arouse suspicion.

She avoided Calpurnia for as long as she could, because she thought Cal had lied to her. Cal had told her all girls had it, it was natural as breathing, it was a sign they were growing up, and they had it until they were in their fifties. At the time, Jean Louise was so overcome with despair at the prospect of being too old to enjoy anything when it would finally be over, she refrained from pursuing the subject. Cal had said nothing about babies and French-kissing.

Eventually she sounded out Calpurnia by way of the Owen family. Cal said she didn't want to talk about that Mr. Owen because he wasn't fit to associate with humans. They were going to keep him in jail a long time. Yes, Francine's sister had been sent to Mobile, poor little girl. Francine was at the Baptist Orphans' Home in Abbott County. Jean Louise was not to occupy her head thinking about those folks. Calpurnia was becoming furious, and Jean Louise let matters rest.

When she discovered that she had nine months to go before the baby came, she felt like a reprieved criminal. She counted the weeks by marking them off on a calendar, but she failed to take into consideration that four months had passed before she began her calculations. As the time drew near she spent her days in helpless panic lest she wake up and find a baby in bed with her. They grew in one's stomach, of that she was sure.

The idea had been in the back of her mind for a long time, but she recoiled from it instinctively: the suggestion of a final separation was unbearable to her, but she knew that a day would come when there would be no putting off, no concealment. Although her relations with Atticus and Jem had reached their lowest ebb ("You're downright addled these days, Jean Louise," her father had said. "Can't you concentrate on anything five minutes?"), the thought of any existence without them, no matter how nice heaven was, was untenable. But being sent to Mobile and causing her family to live thereafter with bowed heads was worse: she didn't even wish that on Alexandra.

According to her calculations, the baby would come with October, and on the thirtieth day of September she would kill herself.

Autumn comes late in Alabama. On Halloween, even, one may hide porch chairs unencumbered by one's heavy coat. Twilights are long, but darkness comes suddenly; the sky turns from dull orange to blue-black before one can take five steps, and with the light goes the last ray of the day's heat, leaving livingroom weather.

Autumn was her happiest season. There was an expectancy about its sounds and shapes: the distant *thunk* pomp of leather and young bodies on the practice field near her house made her think of bands and cold Coca-Colas, parched peanuts and the sight of people's breath in the air. There was even something to look forward to when school started— renewals of old feuds and friendships, weeks of learning again what one half forgot in the long summer. Fall was hot-supper time with everything to eat one missed in the morning when too sleepy to enjoy it. Her world was at its best when her time came to leave it.

She was now twelve and in the seventh grade. Her capacity to savor the change from grammar school was limited; she did not revel in going to different classrooms during the day and being taught by different teachers, nor in knowing that she had a hero for a brother somewhere in the remote senior school. Atticus was away in Montgomery in the legislature, Jem might as well have been with him for all she saw of him.

On the thirtieth of September she sat through school and learned nothing. After classes, she went to the library and stayed until the janitor came in and told her to leave. She walked to town slowly, to be with it as long as possible. Daylight was fading when she walked across the old sawmill tracks to the ice-house. Theodore the ice-man said hey to her as she passed, and she walked down the street and looked back at him until he went inside.

The town water-tank was in a field by the ice-house. It was the tallest thing she had ever seen. A tiny ladder ran from the ground to a small porch encircling the tank.

She threw down her books and began climbing. When she had climbed higher than the chinaberry trees in her back yard she looked down, was dizzy, and looked up the rest of the way.

All of Maycomb was beneath her. She thought she could see her house: Calpurnia would be making biscuits, before long Jem would be coming in from football practice. She looked across the square and was sure she saw Henry Clinton come out of the Jitney Jungle carrying an armload of groceries. He put them in the back seat of someone's car. All the streetlights came on at once, and she smiled with sudden delight.

She sat on the narrow porch and dangled her feet over the side. She lost one shoe, then the other. She wondered what kind of funeral she would have: old Mrs. Duff would sit up all night and make people sign a book. Would Jem cry? If so, it would be the first time.

She wondered if she should do a swan dive or just slip off the edge. If she hit the ground on her back perhaps it would not hurt so much. She wondered if they would ever know how much she loved them.

Someone grabbed her. She stiffened when she felt hands pinning her arms to her sides. They were Henry's, stained green from vegetables. Wordlessly he pulled her to her feet and propelled her down the steep ladder.

When they reached the bottom, Henry jerked her hair: "I swear to God if I don't tell Mr. Finch on you this time!" he bawled. "I swear, Scout! Haven't you got any sense playing on this tank? You might have killed yourself!"

He pulled her hair again, taking some with him: he shook her; he unwound his white apron, rolled it into a wad, and threw it viciously at the ground. "Don't you know you could've killed yourself. Haven't you got any sense?"

Jean Louise stared blankly at him.

"Theodore saw you up yonder and ran for Mr. Finch, and when he couldn't find him he got me. God Almighty—!"

When he saw her trembling he knew she had not been playing. He took her lightly by the back of the neck; on the way home he tried to find out what was bothering her, but she would say nothing. He left her in the livingroom and went to the kitchen.

"Baby, what have you been doing?"

When speaking to her, Calpurnia's voice was always a mixture of grudging affection and mild disapproval. "Mr. Hank," she said. "You better go back to the store. Mr. Fred'll be wondering what happened to you."

Calpurnia, resolutely chewing on a sweetgum stick, looked down at Jean Louise. "What have you been up to?" she said. "What were you doing on that water-tank?"

Jean Louise was still.

"If you tell me I won't tell Mr. Finch. What's got you so upset, baby?"

Calpurnia sat down beside her. Calpurnia was past middle age and her body had thickened a little, her kinky hair was graying, and she squinted from myopia. She spread her hands in her lap and examined them. "Ain't anything in this world so bad you can't tell it," she said.

Jean Louise flung herself into Calpurnia's lap. She felt rough hands kneading her shoulders and back.

"I'm going to have a baby!" she sobbed.

"When?"

"Tomorrow!"

Calpurnia pulled her up and wiped her face with an

apron corner. "Where in the name of sense did you get a notion like that?"

Between gulps, Jean Louise told her shame, omitting nothing, and begging that she not be sent to Mobile, stretched, or thrown against a wall. "Couldn't I go out to your house? Please, Cal." She begged that Calpurnia see her through in secret; they could take the baby away by night when it came.

"You been totin' all this around with you all this time? Why didn't you say somethin' about it?"

She felt Calpurnia's heavy arm around her, comforting when there was no comfort. She heard Calpurnia muttering:

". . . no business fillin' your head full of stories . . . kill 'em if I could get my hands on 'em."

"Cal, you will help me, won't you?" she said timidly.

Calpurnia said, "As sure as the sweet Jesus was born, baby. Get this in your head right now, you ain't pregnant and you never were. That ain't the way it is."

"Well if I ain't, then what am I?"

"With all your book learnin', you are the most ignorant child I ever did see . . ." Her voice trailed off. ". . . but I don't reckon you really ever had a chance."

Slowly and deliberately Calpurnia told her the simple story. As Jean Louise listened, her year's collection of revolting information fell into a fresh crystal design; as

Calpurnia's husky voice drove out her year's accumulation of terror, Jean Louise felt life return. She breathed deeply and felt cool autumn in her throat. She heard sausages hissing in the kitchen, saw her brother's collection of sports magazines on the livingroom table, smelled the bittersweet odor of Calpurnia's hairdressing.

"Cal," she said. "Why didn't I know all this before?"

Calpurnia frowned and sought an answer. "You're sort of 'hind f'omus, Miss Scout. You sort of haven't caught up with yourself . . . now if you'd been raised on a farm you'da known it before you could walk, or if there'd been any women around—if your mamma had lived you'da known it—"

"Mamma?"

"Yessum. You'da seen things like your daddy kissin' your mamma and you'da asked questions soon as you learned to talk, I bet."

"Did they do all that?"

Calpurnia revealed her gold-crowned molars. "Bless your heart, how do you think you got here? Sure they did."

"Well I don't think they would."

"Baby, you'll have to grow some more before this makes sense to you, but your daddy and your mamma loved each other something fierce, and when you love somebody like that, Miss Scout, why that's what you want to do. That's what everybody wants to do when they love like that. They want to get married, they want to kiss and hug and carry on and have babies all the time."

"I don't think Aunty and Uncle Jimmy do."

Calpurnia picked at her apron. "Miss Scout, different folks get married for different kinds of reasons. Miss Alexandra, I think she got married to keep house." Calpurnia scratched her head. "But that's not anything you need to study about, that's not any of your concern. Don't you study about other folks's business till you take care of your own."

Calpurnia got to her feet. "Right now your business is not to give any heed to what those folks from Old Sarum tell you—you ain't called upon to contradict 'em, just don't pay 'em any attention—and if you want to know somethin', you just run to old Cal."

"Why didn't you tell me all this to start with?"

"'Cause things started for you a mite early, and you didn't seem to take to it so much, and we didn't think you'd take to the rest of it any better. Mr. Finch said wait a while till you got used to the idea, but we didn't count on you finding out so quick and so wrong, Miss Scout."

Jean Louise stretched luxuriously and yawned, delighted with her existence. She was becoming sleepy and was not sure she could stay awake until supper. "We having hot biscuits tonight, Cal?"

"Yes ma'am."

She heard the front door slam and Jem clump down the hall. He was headed for the kitchen, where he would open the refrigerator and swallow a quart of milk to quench his football-practice thirst. Before she dozed off, it occurred to her that for the first time in her life Calpurnia had said "Yes ma'am" and "Miss Scout" to her, forms of address usually reserved for the presence of high company. I must be getting old, she thought.

Jem wakened her when he snapped on the overhead light. She saw him walking toward her, the big maroon *M* standing out starkly on his white sweater.

"Are you awake, Little Three-Eyes?"

"Don't be sarcastic," she said. If Henry or Calpurnia had told on her she would die, but she would take them with her.

She stared at her brother. His hair was damp and he smelled of the strong soap in the schoolhouse locker rooms. Better start it first, she thought.

"Huh, you've been smoking," she said. "Smell it a mile."

"Haven't."

"Don't see how you can play in the line anyway. You're too skinny."

Jem smiled and declined her gambit. They've told him, she thought.

Jem patted his *M*. "Old Never-Miss-'Em-Finch, that's me. Caught seven out of ten this afternoon," he said.

He went to the table and picked up a football magazine, opened it, thumbed through it, and was thumbing through it again when he said: "Scout, if there's ever anything that happens to you or something—you know—something you might not want to tell Atticus about—"

"Huh?"

"You know, if you get in trouble at school or anything—you just let me know. I'll take care of you."

Jem sauntered from the livingroom, leaving Jean Louise wide-eyed and wondering if she were fully awake.

12

Sunlight roused her. She looked at her watch. Five o'clock. Someone had covered her up during the night. She threw off the spread, put her feet to the floor, and sat gazing at her long legs, startled to find them twenty-six years old. Her loafers were standing at attention where she had stepped out of them twelve hours ago. One sock was lying beside her shoes and she discovered its mate on her foot. She removed the sock and padded softly to the dressing table, where she caught sight of herself in the mirror.

She looked ruefully at her reflection. You have had what Mr. Burgess would call "The 'Orrors," she told it. Golly, I haven't waked up like this for fifteen years. Today is Monday, I've been home since Saturday, I have eleven days of my vacation left, and I wake up with the screamin' meemies. She laughed at herself: well, it *was* the longest on record—longer than elephants and nothing to show for it.

She picked up a package of cigarettes and three kitchen matches, stuffed the matches behind the cellophane wrapper, and walked quietly into the hall. She opened the wooden door, then the screen door.

On any other day she would have stood barefoot on the wet grass listening to the mockingbirds' early service; she would have pondered over the meaninglessness of silent, austere beauty renewing itself with every sunrise and going ungazed at by half the world. She would have walked beneath yellow-ringed pines rising to a brilliant eastern sky, and her senses would have succumbed to the joy of the morning.

It was waiting to receive her, but she neither looked nor listened. She had two minutes of peace before yesterday returned: nothing can kill the pleasure of one's first cigarette on a new morning. Jean Louise blew smoke carefully into the still air.

She touched yesterday cautiously, then withdrew. I don't dare think about it now, until it goes far enough away. It is weird, she thought, this must be like physical pain. They say when you can't stand it your body is its own defense, you black out and you don't feel any more. The Lord never sends you more than you can bear—

That was an ancient Maycomb phrase employed by

its fragile ladies who sat up with corpses, supposed to be profoundly comforting to the bereaved. Very well, she would be comforted. She would sit out her two weeks home in polite detachment, saying nothing, asking nothing, blaming not. She would do as well as could be expected under the circumstances.

She put her arms on her knees and her head in her arms. I wish to God I had caught you both at a jook with two sleazy women—the lawn needs mowing.

Jean Louise walked to the garage and raised the sliding door. She rolled out the gasoline motor, unscrewed the fuel cap, and inspected the tank. She replaced the cap, flicked a tiny lever, placed one foot on the mower, braced the other firmly in the grass, and yanked the cord quickly. The motor choked twice and died.

Damn it to hell, I've flooded it.

She wheeled the mower into the sun and returned to the garage where she armed herself with heavy hedge clippers. She went to the culvert at the entrance to the driveway and snipped the sturdier grass growing at its two mouths. Something moved at her feet, and she closed her cupped left hand over a cricket. She edged her right hand beneath the creature and scooped it up. The cricket beat frantically against her palms and she let it down again. "You were out too late," she said. "Go home to your mamma."

A truck drove up the hill and stopped in front of her. A Negro boy jumped from the running-board and handed her three quarts of milk. She carried the milk to the front steps, and on her way back to the culvert she gave the mower another tug. This time it started.

She glanced with satisfaction at the neat swath behind her. The grass lay crisply cut and smelled like a creek bank. The course of English Literature would have been decidedly different had Mr. Wordsworth owned a power mower, she thought.

Something invaded her line of vision and she looked up. Alexandra was standing at the front door making come-here-this-minute gestures. I believe she's got on a corset. I wonder if she ever turns over in bed at night.

Alexandra showed little evidence of such activity as she stood waiting for her niece: her thick gray hair was neatly arranged, as usual; she had on no makeup and it made no difference. I wonder if she has ever really felt anything in her life. Francis probably hurt her when he appeared, but I wonder if anything has ever touched her.

"Jean Louise!" hissed Alexandra. "You're waking up this whole side of town with that thing! You've already waked your father, and he didn't get two winks last night. Stop it right now!"

Jean Louise kicked off the motor, and the sudden silence broke her truce with them.

"You ought to know better than to run that thing barefooted. Fink Sewell got three toes chopped off that way, and Atticus killed a snake three feet long in the back yard just last fall. Honestly, the way you behave sometimes, anybody'd think you were behind the pale!"

In spite of herself, Jean Louise grinned. Alexandra could be relied upon to produce a malapropism on occasions, the most notable being her comment on the gulosity displayed by the youngest member of a Mobile Jewish family upon completing his thirteenth year: Alexandra declared that Aaron Stein was the greediest boy she had ever seen, that he ate fourteen ears of corn at his Menopause.

"Why didn't you bring in the milk? It's probably clabber by now."

"I didn't want to wake you all up, Aunty."

"Well, we are up," she said grimly. "Do you want any breakfast?"

"Just coffee, please."

"I want you to get dressed and go to town for me this morning. You'll have to drive Atticus. He's pretty crippled today."

She wished she had stayed in bed until he had left

the house, but he would have waked her anyway to drive him to town.

She went into the house, went to the kitchen, and sat down at the table. She looked at the grotesque eating equipment Alexandra had put by his plate. Atticus drew the line at having someone feed him, and Dr. Finch solved the problem by jamming the handles of a fork, knife, and spoon into the ends of big wooden spools.

"Good morning."

Jean Louise heard her father enter the room. She looked at her plate. "Good morning, sir."

"I heard you weren't feeling good. I looked in on you when I got home and you were sound asleep. All right this morning?"

"Yes sir."

"Don't sound it."

Atticus asked the Lord to give them grateful hearts for these and all their blessings, picked up his glass, and spilled its contents over the table. The milk ran into his lap.

"I'm sorry," he said. "It takes me a while to get going some mornings."

"Don't move, I'll fix it." Jean Louise jumped up and went to the sink. She threw two dishtowels over the milk, got a fresh one from a drawer of the cabinet, and blotted the milk from her father's trousers and shirt front.

"I have a whopping cleaning bill these days," he said.

"Yes sir."

Alexandra served Atticus bacon and eggs and toast. His attention upon his breakfast, Jean Louise thought it would be safe to have a look at him.

He had not changed. His face was the same as always. I don't know why I expected him to be looking like Dorian Gray or somebody.

She jumped when the telephone rang.

Jean Louise was unable to readjust herself to calls at six in the morning, Mary Webster's Hour. Alexandra answered it and returned to the kitchen.

"It's for you, Atticus. It's the sheriff."

"Ask him what he wants, please, Zandra."

Alexandra reappeared saying, "Something about somebody asked him to call you—"

"Tell him to call Hank, Zandra. He can tell Hank whatever he wants to tell me." He turned to Jean Louise. "I'm glad I have a junior partner as well as a sister. What one misses the other doesn't. Wonder what the sheriff wants at this hour?"

"So do I," she said flatly.

"Sweet, I think you ought to let Allen have a look at you today. You're offish."

"Yes sir."

Secretly, she watched her father eat his breakfast. He managed the cumbersome tableware as if it were its normal size and shape. She stole a glance at his face and saw it covered with white stubble. If he had a beard it would be white, but his hair's just turning and his eyebrows are still jet. Uncle Jack's already white to his forehead, and Aunty's gray all over. When I begin to go, where will I start? Why am I thinking these things?

She said, "Excuse me," and took her coffee to the livingroom. She put her cup on a lamp table and was opening the blinds when she saw Henry's car turn into the driveway. He found her standing by the window.

"Good morning. You look like pale blue sin," he said.

"Thank you. Atticus is in the kitchen."

Henry looked the same as ever. After a night's sleep, his scar was less vivid. "You in a snit about something?" he said. "I waved at you in the balcony yesterday but you didn't see me."

"You saw me?"

"Yeah. I was hoping you'd be waiting outside for us, but you weren't. Feeling better today?"

"Yes."

"Well, don't bite my head off."

She drank her coffee, told herself she wanted another cup, and followed Henry into the kitchen. He leaned against the sink, twirling his car keys on his forefinger. He is nearly as tall as the cabinets, she thought. I shall never be able to speak one lucid sentence to him again.

"—happened all right," Henry was saying. "It was bound to sooner or later."

"Was he drinking?" asked Atticus.

"Not drinking, drunk. He was coming in from an all-night boozing down at that jook they have."

"What's the matter?" said Jean Louise.

"Zeebo's boy," said Henry. "Sheriff said he has him in jail—he'd asked him to call Mr. Finch to come get him out—huh."

"Why?"

"Honey, Zeebo's boy was coming out of the Quarters at daybreak this morning splittin' the wind, and he ran over old Mr. Healy crossing the road and killed him dead."

"Oh no—"

"Whose car was it?" asked Atticus.

"Zeebo's, I reckon."

"What'd you tell the sheriff?" asked Atticus.

"Told him to tell Zeebo's boy you wouldn't touch the case."

Atticus leaned his elbows against the table and pushed himself back.

"You shouldn't've done that, Hank," he said mildly. "Of course we'll take it."

Thank you, God. Jean Louise sighed softly and rubbed her eyes. Zeebo's boy was Calpurnia's grandson. Atticus may forget a lot of things, but he would never forget them. Yesterday was fast dissolving into a bad night. Poor Mr. Healy, he was probably so loaded he never knew what hit him.

"But Mr. Finch," Henry said. "I thought none of the—"

Atticus eased his arm on the corner of the chair. When concentrating it was his practice to finger his watch-chain and rummage abstractedly in his watch-pocket. Today his hands were still.

"Hank, I suspect when we know all the facts in the case the best that can be done for the boy is for him to plead guilty. Now, isn't it better for us to stand up with him in court than to have him fall into the wrong hands?"

A smile spread slowly across Henry's face. "I see what you mean, Mr. Finch."

"Well, I don't," said Jean Louise. "What wrong hands?"

Atticus turned to her. "Scout, you probably don't

know it, but the NAACP-paid lawyers are standing around like buzzards down here waiting for things like this to happen—"

"You mean colored lawyers?"

Atticus nodded. "Yep. We've got three or four in the state now. They're mostly in Birmingham and places like that, but circuit by circuit they watch and wait, just for some felony committed by a Negro against a white person—you'd be surprised how quick they find out—in they come and . . . well, in terms you can understand, they demand Negroes on the juries in such cases. They subpoena the jury commissioners, they ask the judge to step down, they raise every legal trick in their books—and they have 'em aplenty—they try to force the judge into error. Above all else, they try to get the case into a Federal court where they know the cards are stacked in their favor. It's already happened in our next-door-neighbor circuit, and there's nothing in the books that says it won't happen here."

Atticus turned to Henry. "So that's why I say we'll take his case if he wants us."

"I thought the NAACP was forbidden to do business in Alabama," said Jean Louise.

Atticus and Henry looked at her and laughed.

"Honey," said Henry, "you don't know what went on in Abbott County when something just like this happened. This spring we thought there'd be real trouble for a while. People across the river here even, bought up all the ammunition they could find—"

Jean Louise left the room.

In the livingroom, she heard Atticus's even voice:

". . . stem the tide a little bit this way . . . good thing he asked for one of the Maycomb lawyers. . . ."

She would keep her coffee down come hell or high water. Who were the people Calpurnia's tribe turned to first and always? How many divorces had Atticus gotten for Zeebo? Five, at least. Which boy was this one? He was in real dutch this time, he needed real help and what do they do but sit in the kitchen and talk NAACP . . . not long ago, Atticus would have done it simply from his goodness, he would have done it for Cal. I must go to see her this morning without fail. . . .

What was this blight that had come down over the people she loved? Did she see it in stark relief because she had been away from it? Had it percolated gradually through the years until now? Had it always been under her nose for her to see if she had only looked? No, not the last. What turned ordinary men into screaming dirt at the top of their voices, what made her kind of people harden and say "nigger" when the word had never crossed their lips before?

"—keep them in their places, I hope," Alexandra

said, as she entered the livingroom with Atticus and Henry.

"There's nothing to fret about," said Henry. "We'll come out all right. Seven-thirty tonight, hon?"

"Yes."

"Well, you might show some enthusiasm about it."

Atticus chuckled. "She's already tired of you, Hank."

"Can I take you to town, Mr. Finch? It's powerfully early, but I think I'll run down and tend to some things in the cool of the morning."

"Thanks, but Scout'll run me down later."

His use of her childhood name crashed on her ears. Don't you ever call me that again. You who called me Scout are dead and in your grave.

Alexandra said, "I've got a list of things for you to get at the Jitney Jungle, Jean Louise. Now go change your clothes. You can run to town now—it's open—and come back for your father."

Jean Louise went to the bathroom and turned on the hot water tap in the tub. She went to her room, pulled out a cotton dress from the closet, and slung it over her arm. She found some flat-heeled shoes in her suitcase, picked up a pair of panties, and took them all into the bathroom.

She looked at herself in the medicine-cabinet mirror. Who's Dorian now?

There were blue-brown shadows under her eyes, and the lines from her nostrils to the corners of her mouth were definite. No doubt about them, she thought. She pulled her cheek to one side and peered at the tiny mother line. I couldn't care less. By the time I'm ready to get married I'll be ninety and then it'll be too late. Who'll bury me? I'm the youngest by far—that's one reason for having children.

She cut the hot water with cold, and when she could stand it she got into the tub, scrubbed herself soberly, released the water, rubbed herself dry, and dressed quickly. She gave the tub a rinse, dried her hands, spread the towel on the rack, and left the bathroom.

"Put on some lipstick," said her aunt, meeting her in the hall. Alexandra went to the closet and dragged out the vacuum cleaner.

"I'll do that when I come back," said Jean Louise.

"It'll be done when you get back."

The sun had not yet blistered the sidewalks of Maycomb, but it soon would. She parked the car in front of the grocery store and went in.

Mr. Fred shook hands with her, said he was glad to see her, drew out a wet Coke from the machine, wiped it on his apron, and gave it to her.

This is one good thing about life that never changes, she thought. As long as he lived, as long as she returned, Mr. Fred would be here with his . . . simple welcome. What was that? Alice? Brer Rabbit? It was Mole. Mole, when he returned from some long journey, desperately tired, had found the familiar waiting for him with its simple welcome.

"I'll rassle up these groceries for you and you can enjoy your Coke," said Mr. Fred.

"Thank you, sir," she said. Jean Louise glanced at the list and her eyes widened. "Aunty's gettin' more like Cousin Joshua all the time. What does she want with cocktail napkins?"

Mr. Fred chuckled. "I reckon she means party napkins. I've never heard of a cocktail passing her lips."

"You never will, either."

Mr. Fred went about his business, and presently he called from the back of the store. "Hear about Mr. Healy?"

"Ah—um," said Jean Louise. She was a lawyer's daughter.

"Didn't know what hit him," said Mr. Fred. "Didn't know where he was going to begin with, poor old thing. He drank more jack-leg liquor than any human I ever saw. That was his one accomplishment."

"Didn't he used to play the jug?"

"Sure did," said Mr. Fred. "You remember back when they'd have talent nights at the courthouse? He'd always be there blowin' that jug. He'd bring it full and drink a bit to get the tone down, then drink some more until it was real low, and then play his solo. It was always *Old Dan Tucker*, and he always scandalized the ladies, but they never could prove anything. You know pure shinny doesn't smell much."

"How did he live?"

"Pension, I think. He was in the Spanish—to tell you the truth he was in some war but I can't remember what it was. Here's your groceries."

"Thanks, Mr. Fred," Jean Louise said. "Good Lord, I've forgot my money. Can I leave the slip on Atticus's desk? He'll be down before long."

"Sure, honey. How's your daddy?"

"He's grim today, but he'll be at the office come the Flood."

"Why don't you stay home this time?"

She lowered her guard when she saw nothing but incurious good humor in Mr. Fred's face: "I will, someday."

"You know, I was in the First War," said Mr. Fred. "I didn't go overseas, but I saw a lot of this country. I didn't have the itch to get back, so after the war I stayed away for ten years, but the longer I stayed away the more I missed Maycomb. I got to the point where I felt like I had to come back or die. You never get it out of your bones."

"Mr. Fred, Maycomb's just like any other little town. You take a cross-section—"

"It's not, Jean Louise. You know that."

"You're right," she nodded.

It was not because this was where your life began. It was because this was where people were born and born and born until finally the result was you, drinking a Coke in the Jitney Jungle.

Now she was aware of a sharp apartness, a separation, not from Atticus and Henry merely. All of Maycomb and Maycomb County were leaving her as the hours passed, and she automatically blamed herself.

She bumped her head getting into the car. I shall never become accustomed to these things. Uncle Jack has a few major points in his philosophy.

Alexandra took the groceries from the back seat. Jean Louise leaned over and opened the door for her father; she reached across him and shut it.

"Want the car this morning, Aunty?"

"No, dear. Going somewhere?"

"Yessum. I won't be gone long."

She watched the street closely. I can do anything but look at him and listen to him and talk to him.

When she stopped in front of the barbershop she said, "Ask Mr. Fred how much we owe him. I forgot to take the slip out of the sack. Said you'd pay him."

When she opened the door for him, he stepped into the street.

"Be careful!"

Atticus waved to the driver of the passing car. "It didn't hit me," he said.

She drove around the square and out the Meridian highway until she came to a fork in the road. This is where it must have happened, she thought.

There were dark patches in the red gravel where the pavement ended, and she drove the car over Mr. Healy's blood. When she came to a fork in the dirt road she turned right, and drove down a lane so narrow the big car left no room on either side. She went on until she could go no farther.

The road was blocked by a line of cars standing aslant halfway in the ditch. She parked behind the last one and got out. She walked down the row past a 1939 Ford, a Chevrolet of ambiguous vintage, a Willys, and a robin's-egg blue hearse with the words HEAVENLY REST picked out in a chromium semicircle on its front door. She was startled, and she peered inside: in the back there were rows of chairs screwed to the floor and no place for a recumbent body, quick or dead. This is a taxi, she thought.

She pulled a wire ring off the gatepost and went inside. Calpurnia's was a swept yard: Jean Louise could tell it had been swept recently, brushbroom scratches were still visible between smooth footprints.

She looked up, and on the porch of Calpurnia's little house stood Negroes in various states of public attire: a couple of women wore their best, one had on a calico apron, one was dressed in her field clothes. Jean Louise identified one of the men as Professor Chester Sumpter, principal of the Mt. Sinai Trade Institute, Maycomb County's largest Negro school. Professor Sumpter was clad, as he always was, in black. The other black-suited man was a stranger to her, but Jean Louise knew he was a minister. Zeebo wore his work clothes.

When they saw her, they stood straight and retreated from the edge of the porch, becoming as one. The men removed their hats and caps, the woman wearing the apron folded her hands beneath it.

"Morning, Zeebo," said Jean Louise.

Zeebo broke the pattern by stepping forward. "Howdy do, Miss Jean Louise. We didn't know you was home."

Jean Louise was acutely conscious that the Negroes

were watching her. They stood silent, respectful, and were watching her intently. She said, "Is Calpurnia home?"

"Yessum, Miss Jean Louise, Mamma in the house. Want me to fetch her?"

"May I go in, Zeebo?"

"Yessum."

The black people parted for her to enter the front door. Zeebo, unsure of protocol, opened the door and stood back to let her enter. "Lead the way, Zeebo," she said.

She followed him into a dark parlor to which clung the musky sweet smell of clean Negro, snuff, and Hearts of Love hairdressing. Several shadowy forms rose when she entered.

"This way, Miss Jean Louise."

They walked down a tiny hallway, and Zeebo tapped at an unpainted pine door. "Mamma," he said. "Miss Jean Louise here."

The door opened softly, and Zeebo's wife's head appeared around it. She came out into the hall, which was scarcely large enough to contain the three of them.

"Hello, Helen," said Jean Louise. "How is Calpurnia?"

"She taking it mighty hard, Miss Jean Louise. Frank, he never had any trouble before. . . ."

So, it was Frank. Of all her multifarious descendants, Calpurnia took most pride in Frank. He was on the waiting list for Tuskegee Institute. He was a born plumber, could fix anything water ran through.

Helen, heavy with a pendulous stomach from having carried so many children, leaned against the wall. She was barefooted.

"Zeebo," said Jean Louise, "you and Helen living together again?"

"Yessum," said Helen placidly. "He's done got old."

Jean Louise smiled at Zeebo, who looked sheepish. For the life of her, Jean Louise could not disentangle Zeebo's domestic history. She thought Helen must be Frank's mother, but she was not sure. She was positive Helen was Zeebo's first wife, and was equally sure she was his present wife, but how many were there in between?

She remembered Atticus telling of the pair in his office, years ago when they appeared seeking a divorce. Atticus, trying to reconcile them, asked Helen would she take her husband back. "Naw sir, Mr. Finch," was her slow reply. "Zeebo, he been goin' around enjoyin' other women. He don't enjoy me none, and I don't want no man who don't enjoy his wife."

"Could I see Calpurnia, Helen?"

"Yessum, go right in."

Calpurnia was sitting in a wooden rocking chair in a corner of the room by the fireplace. The room contained an iron bedstead covered with a faded quilt of a Double Wedding Ring pattern. There were three huge gilt-framed photographs of Negroes and a Coca-Cola calendar on the wall. A rough mantelpiece teemed with small bright objets d'art made of plaster, porcelain, clay, and milk glass. A naked light bulb burned on a cord swinging from the ceiling, casting sharp shadows on the wall behind the mantelpiece, and in the corner where Calpurnia sat.

How small she looks, thought Jean Louise. She used to be so tall.

Calpurnia was old and she was bony. Her sight was failing, and she wore a pair of black-rimmed glasses which stood out in harsh contrast to her warm brown skin. Her big hands were resting in her lap, and she raised them and spread her fingers when Jean Louise entered.

Jean Louise's throat tightened when she caught sight of Calpurnia's bony fingers, fingers so gentle when Jean Louise was ill and hard as ebony when she was bad, fingers that had performed long-ago tasks of loving intricacy. Jean Louise held them to her mouth.

"Cal," she said.

"Sit down, baby," said Calpurnia. "Is there a chair?"

"Yes, Cal." Jean Louise drew up a chair and sat in front of her old friend.

"Cal, I came to tell you—I came to tell you that if there's anything I can do for you, you must let me know."

"Thank you, ma'am," said Calpurnia. "I don't know of anything."

"I want to tell you that Mr. Finch got word of it early this morning. Frank had the sheriff call him and Mr. Finch'll . . . help him."

The words died on her lips. Day before yesterday she would have said "Mr. Finch'll help him" confident that Atticus would turn dark to daylight.

Calpurnia nodded. Her head was up and she looked straight before her. She cannot see me well, thought Jean Louise. I wonder how old she is. I never knew exactly, and I doubt if she ever did.

Jean Louise said, "Don't worry, Cal. Atticus'll do his best."

Calpurnia said, "I know he will, Miss Scout. He always do his best. He always do right."

Jean Louise stared open-mouthed at the old woman. Calpurnia was sitting in a haughty dignity that appeared on state occasions, and with it appeared erratic grammar. Had the earth stopped turning, had the trees frozen, had the sea given up its dead, Jean Louise would not have noticed.

"Cal*pur*nia!"

She barely heard Calpurnia talking: "Frank, he do wrong . . . he pay for it . . . my grandson. I love him . . . but he go to jail with or without Mr. Finch. . . ."

"Calpurnia, stop it!"

Jean Louise was on her feet. She felt the tears come and she walked blindly to the window.

The old woman had not moved. Jean Louise turned and saw her sitting there, seeming to inhale steadily.

Calpurnia was wearing her company manners.

Jean Louise sat down again in front of her. "Cal," she cried, "Cal, Cal, Cal, what are you doing to me? What's the matter? I'm your baby, have you forgotten me? Why are you shutting me out? What are you doing to me?"

Calpurnia lifted her hands and brought them down softly on the arms of the rocker. Her face was a million tiny wrinkles, and her eyes were dim behind thick lenses.

"What are you all doing to us?" she said.

"Us?"

"Yessum. Us."

Jean Louise said slowly, more to herself than to Calpurnia: "As long as I've lived I never remotely dreamed that anything like this could happen. And here it is. I cannot talk to the one human who raised me from the time I was two years old . . . it is happening as I sit here and I cannot believe it. Talk to me, Cal. For God's sake talk to me right. Don't sit there like that!"

She looked into the old woman's face and she knew it was hopeless. Calpurnia was watching her, and in Calpurnia's eyes was no hint of compassion.

Jean Louise rose to go. "Tell me one thing, Cal," she said, "just one thing before I go—please, I've got to know. Did you hate us?"

The old woman sat silent, bearing the burden of her years. Jean Louise waited.

Finally, Calpurnia shook her head.

"Zeebo," said Jean Louise. "If there's anything I can do, for goodness' sake call on me."

"Yessum," the big man said. "But it don't look like there's anything. Frank, he sho' killed him, and there's nothing nobody can do. Mr. Finch, he can't do nothing about sump'n like that. Is there anything I can do for you while you're home, ma'am?"

They were standing on the porch in the path cleared for them. Jean Louise sighed. "Yes, Zeebo, right now.

You can come help me turn my car around. I'd be in the corn patch before long."

"Yessum, Miss Jean Louise."

She watched Zeebo manipulate the car in the narrow confine of the road. I hope I can get back home, she thought. "Thank you, Zeebo," she said wearily. "Remember now." The Negro touched his hatbrim and walked back to his mother's house.

Jean Louise sat in the car, staring at the steering wheel. Why is it that everything I have ever loved on this earth has gone away from me in two days' time? Would Jem turn his back on me? She loved us, I swear she loved us. She sat there in front of me and she didn't see me, she saw white folks. She raised me, and she doesn't care.

It was not always like this, I swear it wasn't. People used to trust each other for some reason, I've forgotten why. They didn't watch each other like hawks then. I wouldn't get looks like that going up those steps ten years ago. She never wore her company manners with one of us . . . when Jem died, her precious Jem, it nearly killed her. . . .

Jean Louise remembered going to Calpurnia's house late one afternoon two years ago. She was sitting in her room, as she was today, her glasses down on her nose. She had been crying. "Always so easy to fix for," Calpurnia said. "Never a day's trouble in his life, my boy. He brought me a present home from the war, he brought me an electric coat." When she smiled Calpurnia's face broke into its million wrinkles. She went to the bed, and from under it pulled out a wide box. She opened the box and held up an enormous expanse of black leather. It was a German flying officer's coat. "See?" she said. "It turns on." Jean Louise examined the coat and found tiny wires running through it. There was a pocket containing batteries. "Mr. Jem said it'd keep my bones warm in the wintertime. He said for me not to be scared of it, but to be careful when it was lightning." Calpurnia in her electric coat was the envy of her friends and neighbors. "Cal," Jean Louise had said. "Please come back. I can't go back to New York easy in my mind if you aren't there." That seemed to help: Calpurnia straightened up and nodded. "Yes ma'am," she said. "I'm coming back. Don't you worry."

Jean Louise pressed the drive button and the car moved slowly down the road. *Eeny, meeny, miny, moe. Catch a nigger by his toe. When he hollers let him go . . .* God help me.

PART V

13

Alexandra was at the kitchen table absorbed in culinary rites. Jean Louise tiptoed past her to no avail.

"Come look here."

Alexandra stepped back from the table and revealed several cut-glass platters stacked three-deep with delicate sandwiches.

"Is that Atticus's dinner?"

"No, he's going to try to eat downtown today. You know how he hates barging in on a bunch of women."

Holy Moses King of the Jews. The Coffee.

"Sweet, why don't you get the livingroom ready. They'll be here in an hour."

"Who've you invited?"

Alexandra called out a guest list so preposterous that Jean Louise sighed heavily. Half the women were younger than she, half were older; they had shared no experience that she could recall, except one female with whom she had quarreled steadily all through grammar school. "Where's everybody in my class?" she said.

"About, I suppose."

Ah yes. About, in Old Sarum and points deeper in the woods. She wondered what had become of them.

"Did you go visiting this morning?" asked Alexandra.

"Went to see Cal."

Alexandra's knife clattered on the table. "Jean Louise!"

"*Now* what the hell's the matter?" This is the last round I will ever have with her, so help me God. I have never been able to do anything right in my life as far as she's concerned.

"Calm down, Miss." Alexandra's voice was cold. "Jean Louise, nobody in Maycomb goes to see Negroes any more, not after what they've been doing to us. Besides being shiftless now they look at you sometimes with open insolence, and as far as depending on them goes, why that's out.

"That NAACP's come down here and filled 'em with poison till it runs out of their ears. It's simply because we've got a strong sheriff that we haven't had bad trouble in this county so far. You do not *realize* what is going on. We've been good to 'em, we've bailed 'em out of jail and out of debt since the beginning of time, we've made work for 'em when there was no work, we've encouraged 'em to better themselves, they've gotten civilized, but my dear— that veneer of civilization's so thin that a bunch of uppity Yankee Negroes can shatter a hundred years' progress in five. . . .

"No ma'am, after the thanks they've given us for looking after 'em, nobody in Maycomb feels much inclined to help 'em when they get in trouble now. All they do is bite the hands that feed 'em. No sir, not any more—they can shift for themselves, now."

She had slept twelve hours, and her shoulders ached from weariness.

"Mary Webster's Sarah's carried a card for years— so's everybody's cook in this town. When Calpurnia left I simply couldn't be bothered with another one, not for just Atticus and me. Keeping a nigger happy these days is like catering to a king—"

My Sainted Aunt is talking like Mr. Grady O'Hanlon, who left his job to devote his full time to the preservation of segregation.

"—you have to fetch and tote for them until you wonder who's waiting on who. It's just not worth the trouble these days—where are you going?"

"To get the livingroom ready."

She sank into a deep armchair and considered how

all occasions had made her poor indeed. My aunt is a hostile stranger, my Calpurnia won't have anything to do with me, Hank is insane, and Atticus—something's wrong with me, it's something about me. It has to be because all these people cannot have changed.

Why doesn't their flesh creep? How can they devoutly believe everything they hear in church and then say the things they do and listen to the things they hear without throwing up? I thought I was a Christian but I'm not. I'm something else and I don't know what. Everything I have ever taken for right and wrong these people have taught me—these same, these very people. So it's me, it's not them. Something has happened to me.

They are all trying to tell me in some weird, echoing way that it's all on account of the Negroes . . . but it's no more the Negroes than I can fly and God knows, I might fly out the window any time, now.

"Haven't you done the livingroom?" Alexandra was standing in front of her.

Jean Louise got up and did the livingroom.

The magpies arrived at 10:30, on schedule. Jean Louise stood on the front steps and greeted them one by one as they entered. They wore gloves and hats, and smelled to high heaven of attars, perfumes, eaus, and bath powder. Their makeup would have put an Egyptian draftsman to shame, and their clothes—particularly their shoes—had definitely been purchased in Montgomery or Mobile: Jean Louise spotted A. Nachman, Gayfer's, Levy's, Hammel's, on all sides of the living-room.

What do they talk about these days? Jean Louise had lost her ear, but she presently recovered it. The Newlyweds chattered smugly of their Bobs and Michaels, of how they had been married to Bob and Michael for four months and Bob and Michael had gained twenty pounds apiece. Jean Louise crushed the temptation to enlighten her young guests upon the probable clinical reasons for their loved ones' rapid growth, and she turned her attention to the Diaper Set, which distressed her beyond measure:

When Jerry was two months old he looked up at me and said . . . toilet training should really begin when . . . he was christened he grabbed Mr. Stone by the hair and Mr. Stone . . . wets the bed now. I broke her of that the same time I broke her from sucking her finger, with . . . the cu-utest, absolutely the *cutest* sweatshirt you've ever seen: it's got a little red elephant and "Crimson Tide" written right across the front . . . and it cost us five dollars to get it yanked out.

The Light Brigade sat to the left of her: in their early and middle thirties, they devoted most of their free time to the Amanuensis Club, bridge, and getting one-up on each other in the matter of electrical appliances:

John says . . . Calvin says it's the . . . kidneys, but Allen took me off fried things . . . when I got caught in that zipper I like to have never . . . wonder what on earth makes her think she can get away with it . . . poor thing, if I were in her place I'd take . . . shock treatments, that's what she had. They say she . . . kicks back the rug every Saturday night when Lawrence Welk comes on . . . and laugh, I thought I'd die! There he was, in . . . my old wedding dress, and you know, I can still wear it.

Jean Louise looked at the three Perennial Hopefuls on her right. They were jolly Maycomb girls of excellent character who had never made the grade. They were patronized by their married contemporaries, they were vaguely felt sorry for, and were produced to date any stray extra man who happened to be visiting their friends. Jean Louise looked at one of them with acid amusement: when Jean Louise was ten, she made her only attempt to join a crowd, and she asked Sarah Finley one day, "Can I come to see you this afternoon?" "No," said Sarah, "Mamma says you're too rough."

Now we are both lonely, for entirely different reasons, but it feels the same, doesn't it?

The Perennial Hopefuls talked quietly among themselves:

longest day I ever had . . . in the back of the bank building . . . a new house out on the road by . . . the Training Union, add it all up and you spend four hours every Sunday in church . . . times I've told Mr. Fred I like my tomatoes . . . boiling hot. I told 'em if they didn't get air-conditioning in that office I'd . . . throw up the whole game. Now who'd want to pull a trick like that?

Jean Louise threw herself into the breach: "Still at the bank, Sarah?"

"Goodness yes. Be there till I drop."

Um. "Ah, what ever happened to Jane—what was her last name? You know, your high school friend?" Sarah and Jane What-Was-Her-Last-Name were once inseparable.

"Oh her. She got married to a right peculiar boy during the war and now she rolls her *ah*'s so, you'd never recognize her."

"Oh? Where's she living now?"

"Mobile. She went to Washington during the war and got this hideous accent. Everybody thought she was puttin' on so bad, but nobody had the nerve to tell her so she still does it. Remember how she used to walk with her head way up, like this? She still does."

"She does?"

"Uh hum."

Aunty has her uses, damn her, thought Jean Louise when she caught Alexandra's signal. She went to the kitchen and brought out a tray of cocktail napkins. As she passed them down the line, Jean Louise felt as if she were running down the keys of a gigantic harpsichord:

I never in all my life . . . saw that marvelous picture . . . with old Mr. Healy . . . lying on the mantelpiece in front of my eyes the whole time . . . is it? Just about eleven, I think . . . she'll wind up gettin' a divorce. After all, the way he . . . rubbed my back every hour the whole ninth month . . . would have killed you. If you could have seen him . . . piddling every five minutes during the night. I put a stop . . . to everybody in our class except that horrid girl from Old Sarum. She won't know the difference . . . between the lines, but you know ex*act*ly what he meant.

Back up the scale with the sandwiches:

Mr. Talbert looked at me and said . . . he'd never learn to sit on the pot . . . of beans every Thursday night. That's the one Yankee thing he picked up in the . . . War of the *Ro*ses? No, honey, I said Warren pro*po*ses

. . . to the garbage collector. That was all I could do after she got through . . . the rye. I just couldn't help it, it made me feel like a big . . . A-men! I'll be so glad when that's over . . . the way he's treated her . . . piles and piles of diapers, and he said why was I so tired? After all, he'd been . . . in the files the whole time, that's where it was.

Alexandra walked behind her, muffling the keys with coffee until they subsided to a gentle hum. Jean Louise decided that the Light Brigade might suit her best, and she drew up a hassock and joined them. She cut Hester Sinclair from the covey: "How's Bill?"

"Fine. Gets harder to live with every day. Wasn't that bad about old Mr. Healy this morning?"

"Certainly was."

Hester said, "Didn't that boy have something to do with you all?"

"Yes. He's our Calpurnia's grandson."

"Golly, I never know who they are these days, all the young ones. Reckon they'll try him for murder?"

"Manslaughter, I should think."

"Oh." Hester was disappointed. "Yes, I reckon that's right. He didn't mean to do it."

"No, he didn't mean to do it."

Hester laughed. "And I thought we'd have some excitement."

Jean Louise's scalp jumped. *I guess I'm losing my sense of humor, maybe that's what it is. I'm gettin' like Cousin Edgar.*

Hester was saying, "—hasn't been a good trial around here in ten years. Good nigger trial, I mean. Nothing but cuttin' and drinkin'."

"Do you like to go to court?"

"Sure. Wildest divorce case last spring you ever saw. Some yaps from Old Sarum. It's a good thing Judge Taylor's dead—you know how he hated that sort of thing, always askin' the ladies to leave the courtroom. This new one doesn't care. Well—"

"Excuse me, Hester. You need some more coffee."

Alexandra was carrying the heavy silver coffee pitcher. Jean Louise watched her pour. *She doesn't spill a drop. If Hank and I—Hank.*

She glanced down the long, low-ceilinged livingroom at the double row of women, women she had merely known all her life, and she could not talk to them five minutes without drying up stone dead. *I can't think of anything to say to them. They talk incessantly about the things they do, and I don't know how to do the things they do. If we married—if I married anybody from this town—these would be my friends, and I couldn't think of a thing to say to them. I would be*

Jean Louise the Silent. I couldn't possibly bring off one of these affairs by myself, and there's Aunty having the time of her life. I'd be churched to death, bridge-partied to death, called upon to give book reviews at the Amanuensis Club, expected to become a part of the community. It takes a lot of what I don't have to be a member of this wedding.

"—a mighty sad thing," Alexandra said, "but that's just the way they are and they can't help it. Calpurnia was the best of the lot. That Zeebo of hers, that scamp's still in the trees, but you know, Calpurnia made him marry every one of his women. Five, I think, but Calpurnia made him marry every one of 'em. That's Christianity to them."

Hester said, "You never can tell what goes on in their heads. My Sophie now, one day I asked her, 'Sophie,' I said, 'what day does Christmas come on this year?' Sophie scratched that wool of hers and said, 'Miss Hester, I thinks it comes on the twenty-fifth this year.' Laugh, I thought I'd die. I wanted to know the day of the week, not the day of the year. Thi-ick!"

Humor, humor, humor, I have lost my sense of humor. I'm gettin' like the *New York Post*.

"—but you know they're still doing it. Stoppin' 'em just made 'em go underground. Bill says he wouldn't be surprised if there was another Nat Turner Uprisin', we're sittin' on a keg of dynamite and we just might as well be ready," Hester said.

"Ahm, ah—Hester, of course I don't know much about it, but I thought that Montgomery crowd spent most of their meeting time in church praying," said Jean Louise.

"Oh my child, don't you know that was just to get sympathy up in the East? That's the oldest trick known to mankind. You know Kaiser Bill prayed to God every night of his life."

An absurd verse vibrated in Jean Louise's memory. Where had she read it?

By right Divine, my dear Augusta,
We've had another awful buster;
Ten thousand Frenchmen sent below.
Praise God from Whom all blessings flow.

She wondered where Hester had picked up her information. She could not conceive of Hester Sinclair's having read anything other than *Good Housekeeping* save under strong duress. Someone had told her. Who?

"Goin' in for history these days, Hester?"

"What? Oh, I was just sayin' what my Bill says. Bill, he's a deep reader. He says the niggers who are runnin' the thing up north are tryin' to do it like Gandhi did it, and you know what that is."

"I'm afraid I don't. What is it?"

"Communism."

"Ah—I thought the Communists were all for violent overthrow and that sort of thing."

Hester shook her head. "Where've you been, Jean Louise? They use any means they can to help themselves. They're just like the Catholics. You know how the Catholics go down to those places and practically go native themselves to get converts. Why, they'd say Saint Paul was a nigger just like them if it'd convert one black man. Bill says—he was in the war down there, you know—Bill says he couldn't figure out what was voo-doo and what was R.C. on some of those islands, that he wouldn't've been surprised if he'd seen a voo-doo man with a collar on. It's the same way with the Communists. They'll do anything, no matter what it is, to get hold of this country. They're all around you, you can't tell who's one and who isn't. Why, even here in Maycomb County—"

Jean Louise laughed. "Oh, Hester, what would the Communists want with Maycomb County?"

"I don't know, but I do know there's a cell right up the road in Tuscaloosa, and if it weren't for those boys a nigger'd be goin' to classes with the rest of 'em."

"I don't follow you, Hester."

"Didn't you read about those fancy professors asking those questions in that—that Convocation? Why, they'd've let her right in. If it hadn't been for those fraternity boys. . . ."

"Golly, Hester. I've been readin' the wrong newspaper. One I read said the mob was from that tire factory—"

"What do you read, the *Worker*?"

You are fascinated with yourself. You will say anything that occurs to you, but what I can't understand are the things that do occur to you. I should like to take your head apart, put a fact in it, and watch it go its way through the runnels of your brain until it comes out of your mouth. We were both born here, we went to the same schools, we were taught the same things. I wonder what you saw and heard.

"—everybody knows the NAACP's dedicated to the overthrow of the South . . ."

Conceived in mistrust, and dedicated to the proposition that all men are created evil.

"—they make no bones about saying they want to do away with the Negro race, and they will in four generations, Bill says, if they start with this one . . ."

I hope the world will little note nor long remember what you are saying here.

"—and anybody who thinks different's either a Communist or might as well be one. Passive resistance, my hind foot . . ."

When in the course of human events it becomes necessary for one people to dissolve the political bands which have connected them with another they are Communists.

"—they always want to marry a shade lighter than themselves, they want to mongrelize the race—"

Jean Louise interrupted. "Hester, let me ask you something. I've been home since Saturday now, and since Saturday I've heard a great deal of talk about mongrelizin' the race, and it's led me to wonder if that's not rather an unfortunate phrase, and if probably it should be discarded from Southern jargon these days. It takes two races to mongrelize a race—if that's the right word—and when we white people holler about mongrelizin', isn't that something of a reflection on ourselves as a race? The message I get from it is that if it were lawful, there'd be a wholesale rush to marry Negroes. If I were a scholar, which I ain't, I would say that kind of talk has a deep psychological significance that's not particularly flattering to the one who talks it. At its best, it denotes an alarmin' mistrust of one's own race."

Hester looked at Jean Louise. "I'm sure I don't know what you mean," she said.

"I'm not sure of what I mean, either," said Jean Louise, "except the hair curls on my head every time I hear talk like that. I guess it was because I wasn't brought up hearing it."

Hester bristled: "Are you insinuating—"

"I'm sorry," said Jean Louise. "I didn't mean that. I do beg your pardon."

"Jean Louise, when I said that I wasn't referring to *us*."

"Who were you talking about, then?"

"I was talking about the—you know, the trashy people. The men who keep Negro women and that kind of thing."

Jean Louise smiled. "That's odd. A hundred years ago the gentlemen had colored women, now the trash have them."

"That was when they owned 'em, silly. No, the trash is what the NAACP's after. They want to get the niggers married to that class and keep on until the whole social pattern's done away with."

Social pattern. Double Wedding Ring quilts. She could not have hated us, and Atticus cannot believe this kind of talk. I'm sorry, it's impossible. Since yesterday I feel like I'm being wadded down into the bottom of a deep, deep

"WELL, HOW'S NEW YORK?"

New York. New York? I'll tell you how New York is. New York has all the answers. People go to the YMHA, the English-Speaking Union, Carnegie Hall, the New School for Social Research, and find the answers. The city lives by slogans, isms, and fast sure answers. New York is saying to me right now: you, Jean Louise Finch, are not reacting according to our doctrines regarding your kind, therefore you do not exist. The best minds in the country have told us who you are. You can't escape it, and we don't blame you for it, but we do ask you to conduct yourself within the rules that those who know have laid down for your behavior, and don't try to be anything else.

She answered: please believe me, what has happened in my family is not what you think. I can say only this—that everything I learned about human decency I learned here. I learned nothing from you except how to be suspicious. I didn't know what hate was until I lived among you and saw you hating every day. They even had to pass laws to keep you from hating. I despise your quick answers, your slogans in the subways, and most of all I despise your lack of good manners: you'll never have 'em as long as you exist.

The man who could not be discourteous to a ground-squirrel had sat in the courthouse abetting the cause of grubby-minded little men. Many times she had seen him in the grocery store waiting his turn in line behind Negroes and God knows what. She had seen Mr. Fred raise his eyebrows at him, and her father shake his head in reply. He was the kind of man who instinctively waited his turn; he had manners.

Look sister, we know the facts: you spent the first twenty-one years of your life in the lynching country, in a county whose population is two-thirds agricultural Negro. So drop the act.

You will not believe me, but I will tell you: never in my life until today did I hear the word "nigger" spoken by a member of my family. Never did I learn to think in terms of The Niggers. When I grew up, and I did grow up with black people, they were Calpurnia, Zeebo the garbage collector, Tom the yard man, and whatever else their names were. There were hundreds of Negroes surrounding me, they were hands in the fields, who chopped the cotton, who worked the roads, who sawed the lumber to make our houses. They were poor, they were diseased and dirty, some were lazy and shiftless, but never in my life was I given the idea that I should despise one, should fear one, should be discourteous to one, or think that I could mistreat one and get away with it. They as a people did not enter my world, nor did I enter theirs: when I went hunting I did not trespass on a Negro's land, not because it was a Negro's, but because I was not supposed to trespass on anybody's land. I was taught never to take advantage of anybody who was less fortunate than myself, whether he be less fortunate in brains, wealth, or social position; it meant anybody, not just Negroes. I was given to understand that the reverse was to be despised. That is the way I was raised, by a black woman and a white man.

You must have lived it. If a man says to you, "This is the truth," and you believe him, and you discover what he says is not the truth, you are disappointed and you make sure you will not be caught out by him again.

But a man who has lived by truth—and you have believed in what he has lived—he does not leave you merely wary when he fails you, he leaves you with nothing. I think that is why I'm nearly out of my mind. . . .

"New York? It'll always be there." Jean Louise turned to her inquisitor, a young woman with a small hat, small features, and small sharp teeth. She was Claudine McDowell.

"Fletcher and I were up there last spring and we tried to get you day and night."

I'll bet you did. "Did you enjoy it? No, don't tell me, let me tell you: you had a marvelous time but you wouldn't dream of living there."

Claudine showed her mouse-teeth. "Absolutely! How'd you guess that?"

"I'm psychic. Did you do the town?"

"Lord yes. We went to the Latin Quarter, the Copacabana, and *The Pajama Game*. That was the first stage show we'd ever seen and we were right disappointed in it. Are they all like that?"

"Most of 'em. Did you go to the top of the you-know-what?"

"No, but we did go through Radio City. You know, people could live in that place. We saw a stage show at Radio City Music Hall, and Jean Louise, a horse came out on the stage."

Jean Louise said she wasn't surprised.

"Fletcher and I surely were glad to get back home. I don't see how you live there. Fletcher spent more money up there in two weeks than we spend in six months down here. Fletcher said he couldn't see why on earth people lived in that place when they could have a house and a yard for far less down here."

I can tell you. In New York you are your own person. You may reach out and embrace all of Manhattan in sweet aloneness, or you can go to hell if you want to.

"Well," said Jean Louise, "it takes considerable getting used to. I hated it for two years. It intimidated me daily until one morning when someone pushed me on a bus and I pushed back. After I pushed back I realized I'd become a part of it."

"Pushing, that's what they are. They have no manners up there," said Claudine.

"They have manners, Claudine. They're just different from ours. The person who pushed me on the bus expected to be pushed back. That's what I was supposed to do; it's just a game. You won't find better people than in New York."

Claudine pursed her lips. "Well, I wouldn't want to get mixed up with all those Italians and Puerto Ricans. In a drugstore one day I looked around and there was a Negro woman eating her dinner right next to me, right *next* to me. Of course I knew she could, but it did give me a shock."

"Did she hurt you in any way?"

"Reckon she didn't. I got up real quick and left."

"You know," said Jean Louise gently, "they go around loose up there, all kinds of folks."

Claudine hunched her shoulders. "I don't see how you live up there with them."

"You aren't aware of them. You work with them, eat by and with them, ride the buses with them, and you aren't aware of them unless you want to be. I don't know that a great big fat Negro man's been sitting beside me on a bus until I get up to leave. You just don't notice it."

"Well, I certainly noticed it. You must be blind or something."

Blind, that's what I am. I never opened my eyes. I never thought to look into people's hearts, I looked only in their faces. Stone blind . . . Mr. Stone. Mr. Stone set a watchman in church yesterday. He should have provided me with one. I need a watchman to lead me around and declare what he seeth every hour on the hour. I need a watchman to tell me this is what a man says but this is what he means, to draw a line down the middle and say here is this justice and there is that justice and make me understand the difference. I need a watchman to go forth and proclaim to them all that twenty-six years is too long to play a joke on anybody, no matter how funny it is.

14

A unty," said Jean Louise, when they had cleared away the rubble of the morning's devastation, "if you don't want the car I'm going around to Uncle Jack's."

"All I want's a nap. Don't you want some dinner?"

"No ma'am. Uncle Jack'll give me a sandwich or something."

"Better not count on it. He eats less and less these days."

She stopped the car in Dr. Finch's driveway, climbed the high front steps to his house, knocked on the door, and went in, singing in a raucous voice:

"Old Uncle Jack with his cane and his crutch
When he was young he boogie-woogied too much;
Put the sales tax on it—"

Dr. Finch's house was small, but the front hallway was enormous. At one time it was a dog-trot hall, but Dr. Finch had sealed it in and built bookshelves around the walls.

He called from the rear of the house, "I heard that, you vulgar girl. I'm in the kitchen."

She walked down the hall, through a door, and came to what was once an open back porch. It was now something faintly like a study, as were most of the rooms in his house. She had never seen a shelter that reflected so strongly the personality of its owner. An eerie quality of untidiness prevailed amid order: Dr. Finch kept his house militarily spotless, but books tended to pile up wherever he sat down, and because it was his habit to sit down anywhere he got ready, there were small stacks of books in odd places about the house that were a constant curse to his cleaning woman. He would not let her touch them, and he insisted on apple-pie neatness, so the poor creature was obliged to vacuum, dust, and polish around them. One unfortunate maid lost her head and lost his place in Tuckwell's *Pre-Tractarian Oxford*, and Dr. Finch shook a broom at her.

When her uncle appeared, Jean Louise thought styles may come and styles may go, but he and Atticus will cling to their vests forever. Dr. Finch was coatless, and in his arms was Rose Aylmer, his old cat.

"Where were you yesterday, in the river again?" He looked at her sharply. "Stick out your tongue."

Jean Louise stuck out her tongue, and Dr. Finch shifted Rose Aylmer to the crook of his right elbow, fished in his vest pocket, brought out a pair of half-glasses, flicked them open, and clapped them to his face.

"Well, don't leave it there. Put it back," he said. "You look like hell. Come on to the kitchen."

"I didn't know you had half-glasses, Uncle Jack," said Jean Louise.

"Hah—I discovered I was wasting money."

"How?"

"Looking over my old ones. These cost half as much."

A table stood in the center of Dr. Finch's kitchen, and on the table was a saucer containing a cracker upon which rested a solitary sardine.

Jean Louise gaped. "Is that your dinner? Honestly, Uncle Jack, can you possibly get any weirder?"

Dr. Finch drew a high stool to the table, deposited Rose Aylmer upon it, and said, "No. Yes."

Jean Louise and her uncle sat down at the table. Dr. Finch picked up the cracker and sardine and presented them to Rose Aylmer. Rose Aylmer took a small bite, put her head down, and chewed.

"She eats like a human," said Jean Louise.

"I hope I've taught her manners," said Dr. Finch. "She's so old now I have to feed her bit by bit."

"Why don't you put her to sleep?"

Dr. Finch looked indignantly at his niece. "Why should I? What's the matter with her? She's got a good ten years yet."

Jean Louise silently agreed and wished, comparatively speaking, that she would look as good as Rose Aylmer when she was as old. Rose Aylmer's yellow coat was in excellent repair; she still had her figure; her eyes were bright. She slept most of her life now, and once a day Dr. Finch walked her around the back yard on a leash.

Dr. Finch patiently persuaded the old cat to finish her lunch, and when she had done so he went to a cabinet over the sink and took out a bottle. Its cap was a medicine dropper. He drew up a mighty portion of the fluid, set the bottle down, caught the back of the cat's head, and told Rose Aylmer to open her mouth. The cat obeyed. She gulped and shook her head. Dr. Finch drew more fluid into the dropper and said, "Open your mouth," to Jean Louise.

Jean Louise gulped and spluttered. "Dear Lord, what was that?"

"Vitamin C. I want you to let Allen have a look at you."

Jean Louise said she would, and asked her uncle what was on his mind these days.

Dr. Finch, stooping at the oven, said, "Sibthorp."

"Sir?"

Dr. Finch took from the oven a wooden salad bowl filled, to Jean Louise's amazement, with greens. I hope it wasn't on.

"Sibthorp, girl. Sibthorp," he said. "Richard Waldo Sibthorp. Roman Catholic priest. Buried with full Church of England ceremonials. Tryin' to find another one like him. Highly significant."

Jean Louise was accustomed to her uncle's brand of intellectual shorthand: it was his custom to state one or two isolated facts, and a conclusion seemingly unsupported thereby. Slowly and surely, if prodded correctly, Dr. Finch would unwind the reel of his strange lore to reveal reasoning that glittered with a private light of its own.

But she was not there to be entertained with the vacillations of a minor Victorian esthete. She watched her uncle maneuver salad greens, olive oil, vinegar, and several ingredients unknown to her with the same precision and assurances he employed on a difficult osteotomy. He divided the salad into two plates and said, "Eat, child."

Dr. Finch chewed ferociously on his lunch and eyed his niece, who was arranging lettuce, hunks of avocado, green pepper, and onions in a neat row on her plate. "All right, what's the matter? Are you pregnant?"

"Gracious no, Uncle Jack."

"That's about the only thing I can think of that worries young women these days. Do you want to tell me?" His voice softened. "Come on, old Scout."

Jean Louise's eyes blurred with tears. "What's been happening, Uncle Jack? What *is* the matter with Atticus? I think Hank and Aunty have lost their minds and I know I'm losing mine."

"I haven't noticed anything the matter with them. Should I?"

"You should have seen them sitting in that meeting yesterday—"

Jean Louise looked up at her uncle, who was balancing himself dangerously on the back legs of his chair. He put his hands on the table to steady himself, his incisive features melted, his eyebrows shot up, he laughed loudly. The front legs of his chair came down with a bang, and he subsided into chuckles.

Jean Louise raged. She got up from the table, tipped over her chair, restored it, and walked to the door. "I didn't come here to be made fun of, Uncle Jack," she said.

"Oh sit down and shut up," said her uncle. He looked at her with genuine interest, as if she were something under a microscope, as though she were some medical marvel that had inadvertently materialized in his kitchen.

"As I sit here and breathe, I never thought the good God would let me live to see someone walk into the middle of a revolution, pull a lugubrious face, and say, 'What's the matter?'" He laughed again, shaking his head.

"Matter, child? I'll tell you what's the matter if you collect yourself and refrain from carrying on like—ar-um!—I wonder if your eyes and ears ever make anything save spasmodic contact with your brain." His face tightened. "You won't be pleased with some of it," he said.

"I don't care what it is, Uncle Jack, if you'll only tell me what's turned my father into a nigger-hater."

"Hold your tongue." Dr. Finch's voice was stern. "Don't you ever call your father that. I detest the sound of it as much as its matter."

"What am I to call him, then?"

Her uncle sighed at length. He went to the stove and turned on the front burner under the coffeepot. "Let us consider this calmly," he said. When he turned around

Jean Louise saw amusement banish the indignation in his eyes, then meld into an expression she could not read. She heard him mutter, "Oh dear. Oh dear me, yes. The novel must tell a story."

"What do you mean by that?" she said. She knew he was quoting at her but she didn't know what, she didn't know why, and she didn't care. Her uncle could annoy the hell out of her when he chose, apparently he was choosing to do so now, and she resented it.

"Nothing." He sat down, took off his glasses, and returned them to his vest pocket. He spoke deliberately. "Baby," he said, "all over the South your father and men like your father are fighting a sort of rearguard, delaying action to preserve a certain kind of philosophy that's almost gone down the drain—"

"If it's what I heard yesterday I say good riddance."

Dr. Finch looked up. "You're making a bad mistake if you think your daddy's dedicated to keeping the Negroes in their places."

Jean Louise raised her hands and her voice: "What the hell am I to think? It made me sick, Uncle Jack. Plain-out sick—"

Her uncle scratched his ear. "You no doubt, somewhere along the line, have had certain historical facts and nuances placed in front of you—"

"Uncle Jack, don't hand me that kind of talk now— fightin' the War has nothing to do with it."

"On the contrary, it has a great deal to do with it if you want to understand. The first thing you must realize is something—God help us, it was something—that three-fourths of a nation have failed to this day to understand. What kind of people were we, Jean Louise? What kind of people are we? Who are we still closest to in this world?"

"I thought we were just people. I have no idea."

Her uncle smiled, and an unholy light appeared in his eyes. He's gonna skate off now, she thought. I can never catch him and bring him back.

"Consider Maycomb County," said Dr. Finch. "It's typical South. Has it never struck you as being singular that nearly everybody in the county is either kin or almost kin to everybody else?"

"Uncle Jack, how can someone be almost kin to someone else?"

"Quite simple. You remember Frank Buckland, don't you?"

In spite of herself, Jean Louise felt she was being lured slowly and stealthily into Dr. Finch's web. He is a wonderful old spider, but nevertheless he is a spider. She inched toward him: "Frank Buckland?"

"The naturalist. Carried dead fish around in his suit-case and kept a jackal in his rooms."

"Yes sir?"

"You remember Matthew Arnold, don't you?"

She said she did.

"Well, Frank Buckland was Matthew Arnold's fa-ther's sister's husband's brother's son, therefore, they were almost kin. See?"

"Yes sir, but—"

Dr. Finch looked at the ceiling. "Wasn't my nephew Jem," he said slowly, "engaged to marry his great-un-cle's son's wife's second cousin?"

She put her hands over her eyes and thought furi-ously. "He was," she finally said. "Uncle Jack, I think you've made a non sequitur but I'm not at all positive."

"All the same thing, really."

"But I don't get the connection."

Dr. Finch put his hands on the table. "That's be-cause you haven't looked," he said. "You've never opened your eyes."

Jean Louise jumped.

Her uncle said, "Jean Louise, there are to this day in Maycomb County the living counterparts of every butt-headed Celt, Angle, and Saxon who ever drew a breath. You remember Dean Stanley, don't you?"

They were coming back to her, the days of the endless hours. She was in this house, in front of a warm fire, being read to from musty books. Her uncle's voice was its usual low growl, or pitched high with helpless laughter. The absentminded, fluff-haired little clergyman and his stalwart wife drifted into her memory.

"Doesn't he remind you of Fink Sewell?"

"No sir," she said.

"Think, girl. Think. Since you are not thinking, I'll give you a hint. When Stanley was Dean of Westminster he dug up nearly everybody in the Abbey looking for James the First."

"Oh my God," she said.

During the Depression, Mr. Finckney Sewell, a Maycomb resident long noted for his independence of mind, disentombed his own grandfather and extracted all his gold teeth to pay off a mortgage. When the sheriff apprehended him for grave-robbery and gold-hoarding, Mr. Fink demurred on the theory that if his own grandfather wasn't his, whose was he? The sheriff said old Mr. M. F. Sewell was in the public domain, but Mr. Fink said testily he supposed it was his cemetery lot, his granddaddy, and his teeth, and declined forthwith to be arrested. Public opinion in Maycomb was with him: Mr. Fink was an honorable man, he was trying his best to pay his debts, and the law molested him no further.

"Stanley had the highest historical motives for his excavations," mused Dr. Finch, "but their minds worked exactly alike. You can't deny he invited every heretic he could lay hands on to preach in the Abbey. I believe he once gave communion to Mrs. Annie Besant. You remember how he supported Bishop Colenso."

She remembered. Bishop Colenso, whose views on everything were considered unsound that day and are archaic in this, was the little dean's particular pet. Colenso was the object of acrimonious debate wherever the clergy gathered, and Stanley once made a ringing Convocation speech in his defense, asking that body was it aware that Colenso was the only colonial bishop who had bothered to translate the Bible into Zulu, which was rather more than the rest had done.

"Fink was just like him," said Dr. Finch. "He subscribed to the *Wall Street Journal* in the depths of the Depression and dared anybody to say a word about it." Dr. Finch chuckled. "Jake Jeddo at the post office nearly had a spasm every time he put the mail up."

Jean Louise stared at her uncle. She sat in his kitchen, in the middle of the Atomic Age, and in the deepest recesses of her consciousness she knew that Dr. Finch was outrageously correct in his comparisons.

"—just like him," Dr. Finch was saying, "or take Harriet Martineau—"

Jean Louise found herself treading water in the Lake District. She floundered to keep her head up.

"Do you remember Mrs. E. C. B. Franklin?"

She did. She groped through the years for Miss Martineau, but Mrs. E.C.B. was easy: she remembered a crocheted tam, a crocheted dress through which peeped pink crocheted drawers, and crocheted stockings. Every Saturday Mrs. E.C.B. walked three miles to town from her farm, which was called Cape Jessamine Copse. Mrs. E.C.B. wrote poetry.

Dr. Finch said, "Remember the minor women poets?"

"Yes sir," she said.

"Well?"

When she was a child she had deviled for a while at the *Maycomb Tribune* office and had witnessed several altercations, including the last, between Mrs. E.C.B. and Mr. Underwood. Mr. Underwood was an old-time printer and stood for no nonsense. He worked all day at a vast black Linotype, refreshing himself at intervals from a gallon jug containing harmless cherry wine. One Saturday Mrs. E.C.B. stalked into the office with an effusion Mr. Underwood said he refused to disgrace the *Tribune* with: it was a cow obituary in verse, beginning:

O kine no longer mine
With those big brown eyes of thine. . . .

and containing grave breaches of Christian philosophy. Mr. Underwood said, "Cows don't go to heaven," to which Mrs. E.C.B. replied, "This one did," and explained poetic license. Mr. Underwood, who in his time had published memorial verses of indeterminate variety, said he still couldn't print this because it was blasphemous and didn't scan. Furious, Mrs. E.C.B. unlocked a frame and scattered the Biggs Store ad all over the office. Mr. Underwood inhaled like a whale, drank an enormous slug of cherry wine in her face, swallowed it down, and cursed her all the way to the courthouse square. After that, Mrs. E.C.B. composed verse for her private edification. The county felt the loss.

"Now are you willing to concede that there is some faint connection, not necessarily between two eccentrics, but with a—um—general turn of mind that exists in some quarters across the water?"

Jean Louise threw in the towel.

Dr. Finch said more to himself than to his niece, "In the 1770s where did the white-hot words come from?"

"Virginia," said Jean Louise, confidently.

"And in the 1940s, before we got into it, what made

every Southerner read his newspaper and listen to newscasts with a special kind of horror? Tribal feelin', honey, at the bottom of it. They might be sons of bitches, the British, but they were our sons of bitches—"

Dr. Finch caught himself. "Go back now," he said briskly. "Go back to the early 1800s in England, before some pervert invented machinery. What was life there?"

Jean Louise answered automatically, "A society of dukes and beggars—"

"Hah! You are not so far corrupted as I thought, if you still remember Caroline Lamb, poor thing. You've almost got it, but not quite: it was mainly an agricultural society, with a handful of landowners and multitudes of tenants. Now, what was the South before the War?"

"An agricultural society with a handful of large landowners, multitudes of dirt farmers, and slaves."

"Correct. Leave the slaves out of it for a while, and what do you have? Your Wade Hamptons by the scores, and your small landowners and tenants by the thousands. The South was a little England in its heritage and social structure. Now, what is the one thing that has beat in the heart of every Anglo-Saxon— don't cringe, I know it's a dirty word these days—

no matter what his condition or status in life, no matter what the barriers of ignorance, since he stopped painting himself blue?"

"He is proud. He's sort of stubborn."

"You're damn right. What else?"

"I—I don't know."

"What was it that made the ragtag little Confederate Army the last of its kind? What made it so weak, but so powerful it worked miracles?"

"Ah—Robert E. Lee?"

"Good God, girl!" shouted her uncle. "It was an army of individuals! They walked off their farms and walked to the War!"

As if to study a rare specimen, Dr. Finch produced his glasses, put them on, tilted his head back, and looked at her. "No machine," he said, "when it's been crushed to powder, puts itself together again and ticks, but those dry bones rose up and marched and how they marched. Why?"

"I reckon it was the slaves and tariffs and things. I never thought about it much."

Dr. Finch said softly, "Jehovah God."

He made a visible effort to master his temper by going to the stove and silencing the coffeepot. He poured out two cups of blistering black brew and brought them to the table.

"Jean Louise," he said dryly, "not much more than five per cent of the South's population ever saw a slave, much less owned one. Now, something must have irritated the other ninety-five per cent."

Jean Louise looked blankly at her uncle.

"Has it never occurred to you—have you never, somewhere along the line, received vibrations to the effect—that this territory was a separate nation? No matter what its political bonds, a nation with its own people, existing within a nation? A society highly paradoxical, with alarming inequities, but with the private honor of thousands of persons winking like lightning bugs through the night? No war was ever fought for so many different reasons meeting in one reason clear as crystal. They fought to preserve their identity. Their political identity, their personal identity."

Dr. Finch's voice softened. "It seems quixotic today, with jet airplanes and overdoses of Nembutal, that a man would go through a war for something so insignificant as his state."

He blinked. "No, Scout, those ragged ignorant people fought until they were nearly exterminated to maintain something that these days seems to be the sole privilege of artists and musicians."

As it rolled by, Jean Louise made a frantic dive for

her uncle's trolley: "That's been over for a—nearly a hundred years, sir."

Dr. Finch grinned. "Has it really? It depends how you look at it. If you were sitting on the sidewalk in Paris, you'd say certainly. But look again. The remnants of that little army had children—God, how they multiplied—the South went through the Reconstruction with only one permanent political change: there was no more slavery. The people became no less than what they were to begin with—in some cases they became horrifyingly more. They were never destroyed. They were ground into the dirt and up they popped. Up popped Tobacco Road, and up popped the ugliest, most shameful aspect of it all—the breed of white man who lived in open economic competition with freed Negroes.

"For years and years all that man thought he had that made him any better than his black brothers was the color of his skin. He was just as dirty, he smelled just as bad, he was just as poor. Nowadays he's got more than he ever had in his life, he has everything but breeding, he's freed himself from every stigma, but he sits nursing his hangover of hatred. . . ."

Dr. Finch got up and poured more coffee. Jean Louise watched him. Good Lord, she thought, my own grandfather fought in it. His and Atticus's daddy. He was only a child. He saw the corpses stacked and watched the blood run in little streams down Shiloh's hill. . . .

"Now then, Scout," said her uncle. "Now, at this very minute, a political philosophy foreign to it is being pressed on the South, and the South's not ready for it—we're finding ourselves in the same deep waters. As sure as time, history is repeating itself, and as sure as man is man, history is the last place he'll look for his lessons. I hope to God it'll be a comparatively bloodless Reconstruction this time."

"I don't understand."

"Look at the rest of the country. It's long since gone by the South in its thinking. The time-honored, common-law concept of property—a man's interest in and duties to that property—has become almost extinct. People's attitudes toward the duties of a government have changed. The have-nots have risen and have demanded and received their due—sometimes more than their due. The haves are restricted from getting more. You are protected from the winter winds of old age, not by yourself voluntarily, but by a government that says we do not trust you to provide for yourself, therefore we will make you save. All kinds of strange little things like that have become part and parcel of this country's government. America's a brave new Atomic world and the South's just beginning its Industrial Revolution. Have you looked around you in the past seven or eight years and seen a new class of people down here?"

"New class?"

"Good grief, child. Where are your tenant farmers? In factories. Where are your field hands? Same place. Have you ever noticed who are in those little white houses on the other side of town? Maycomb's new class. The same boys and girls who went to school with you and grew up on tiny farms. Your own generation."

Dr. Finch pulled his nose. "Those people are the apples of the Federal Government's eye. It lends them money to build their houses, it gives them a free education for serving in its armies, it provides for their old age and assures them of several weeks' support if they lose their jobs—"

"Uncle Jack, you are a cynical old man."

"Cynical, hell. I'm a healthy old man with a constitutional mistrust of paternalism and government in large doses. Your father's the same—"

"If you tell me that power tends to corrupt and absolute power corrupts absolutely I will throw this coffee at you."

"The only thing I'm afraid of about this country is that its government will someday become so monstrous that the smallest person in it will be trampled underfoot, and then it wouldn't be worth living in. The only thing in America that is still unique in this tired world is that a man can go as far as his brains will take him or he can go to hell if he wants to, but it won't be that way much longer."

Dr. Finch grinned like a friendly weasel. "Melbourne said once, that the only real duties of government were to prevent crime and preserve contracts, to which I will add one thing since I find myself reluctantly in the twentieth century: and to provide for the common defense."

"That's a cloudy statement."

"Indeed it is. It leaves us with so much freedom."

Jean Louise put her elbows on the table and ran her fingers through her hair. Something was the matter with him. He was deliberately making some eloquent unspoken plea to her, he was deliberately keeping off the subject. He was oversimplifying here, skittering off there, dodging and feinting. She wondered why. It was so easy to listen to him, to be lulled by his gentle rain of words, that she did not miss the absence of his purposeful gestures, the shower of "hum"s and "hah"s that peppered his usual conversation. She did not know he was deeply worried.

"Uncle Jack," she said. "What's this got to do with the price of eggs in China, and you know exactly what I mean."

"Ho," he said. His cheeks became rosy. "Gettin' smart, aren't you?"

"Smart enough to know that relations between the Negroes and white people are worse than I've ever seen them in my life—by the way, you never mentioned them once—smart enough to want to know what makes your sainted sister act the way she does, smart enough to want to know what the hell has happened to my father."

Dr. Finch clenched his hands and tucked them under his chin. "Human birth is most unpleasant. It's messy, it's extremely painful, sometimes it's a risky thing. It is always bloody. So is it with civilization. The South's in its last agonizing birth pain. It's bringing forth something new and I'm not sure I like it, but I won't be here to see it. You will. Men like me and my brother are obsolete and we've got to go, but it's a pity we'll carry with us the meaningful things of this society—there were some good things in it."

"Stop woolgathering and answer me!"

Dr. Finch stood up, leaned on the table, and looked at her. The lines from his nose sprang to his mouth and made a harsh trapezoid. His eyes blazed, but his voice was still quiet:

"Jean Louise, when a man's looking down the double barrel of a shotgun, he picks up the first weapon he can find to defend himself, be it a stone or a stick of stovewood or a citizens' council."

"That is no answer!"

Dr. Finch shut his eyes, opened them, and looked down at the table.

"You've been giving me some kind of elaborate run-around, Uncle Jack, and I've never known you to do it before. You've always given me a straight answer to anything I ever asked you. Why won't you now?"

"Because I cannot. It is neither within my power nor my province to do so."

"I've never heard you talk like this."

Dr. Finch opened his mouth and clamped it shut again. He took her by the arm, led her into the next room, and stopped in front of the gilt-framed mirror.

"Look at you," he said.

She looked.

"What do you see?"

"Myself, and you." She turned toward her uncle's reflection. "You know, Uncle Jack, you're handsome in a horrible sort of way."

She saw the last hundred years possess her uncle for

an instant. He made a cross between a bow and a nod, said, "That's kind of you, ma'am," stood behind her, and gripped her shoulders. "Look at you," he said. "I can only tell you this much. Look at your eyes. Look at your nose. Look at your chin. What do you see?"

"I see myself."

"I see two people."

"You mean the tomboy and the woman?"

She saw Dr. Finch's reflection shake its head. "No-o, child. That's there all right, but it's not what I mean."

"Uncle Jack, I don't know why you elect to disappear into the mist. . . ."

Dr. Finch scratched his head and a tuft of gray hair stood up. "I'm sorry," he said. "Go ahead. Go ahead and do what you're going to do. I can't stop you and I mustn't stop you, Childe Roland. But it's such a messy, risky thing. Such a bloody business—"

"Uncle Jack, sweetie, you're not with us."

Dr. Finch faced her and held her at arm's length. "Jean Louise, I want you to listen carefully. What we've talked about today—I want to tell you something and see if you can hook it all together. It's this: what was incidental to the issue in our War Between the States is incidental to the issue in the war we're in now, and is incidental to the issue in your own private war. Now think it over and tell me what you think I mean."

Dr. Finch waited.

"You sound like one of the Minor Prophets," she said.

"I thought so. Very well, now listen again: when you can't stand it any longer, when your heart is in two, you must come to me. Do you understand? You must come to me. Promise me." He shook her. "Promise me."

"Yes sir, I promise, but—"

"Now scat," said her uncle. "Go off somewhere and play post office with Hank. I've got better things to do—"

"Than what?"

"None of your business. Git."

When Jean Louise went down the steps, she did not see Dr. Finch bite his under lip, go to his kitchen, and tug Rose Aylmer's fur, or return to his study with his hands in his pockets and walk slowly back and forth across the room until, finally, he picked up the telephone.

PART VI

PART VI

15

Mad, mad, mad as a hatter. Well, that's the way of all Finches. Difference between Uncle Jack and the rest of 'em, though, is he knows he's crazy.

She was sitting at a table behind Mr. Cunningham's ice cream shop, eating from a wax-paper container. Mr. Cunningham, a man of uncompromising rectitude, had given her a pint free of charge for having guessed his name yesterday, one of the tiny things she adored about Maycomb: people remembered their promises.

What was he driving at? *Promise me—incidental to the issue—Anglo-Saxon—dirty word—Childe Roland.* I hope he doesn't lose his sense of propriety or they will have to shut him up. He's so far out of this century he can't go to the bathroom, he goes to the water closet. But mad or not, he's the only one of 'em who hasn't done something or said something—

Why did I come back here? Just to rub it in, I suppose. Just to look at the gravel in the back yard where the trees were, where the carhouse was, and wonder if it was all a dream. Jem parked his fishing car over there, we dug earthworms by the back fence, I planted a bamboo shoot one time and we fought it for twenty years. Mr. Cunningham must have salted the earth where it grew, I don't see it any more.

Sitting in the one o'clock sun, she rebuilt her house, populated the yard with her father and brother and Calpurnia, put Henry across the street and Miss Rachel next door.

It was the last two weeks of the school year and she was going to her first dance. Traditionally, the members of the senior class invited their younger brothers and sisters to the Commencement Dance, held the night before the Junior-Senior Banquet, which was always the last Friday in May.

Jem's football sweater had grown increasingly gorgeous—he was captain of the team, the first year Maycomb beat Abbottsville in thirteen seasons. Henry was president of the Senior Debating Society, the only extracurricular activity he had time for, and Jean Louise was a fat fourteen, immersed in Victorian poetry and detective novels.

In those days when it was fashionable to court across

the river, Jem was so helplessly in love with a girl from Abbott County he seriously considered spending his senior year at Abbottsville High, but was discouraged by Atticus, who put his foot down and solaced Jem by advancing him sufficient funds to purchase a Model-A coupe. Jem painted his car bright black, achieved the effect of whitewalled tires with more paint, kept his conveyance polished to perfection, and motored to Abbottsville every Friday evening in quiet dignity, oblivious to the fact that his car sounded like an over-sized coffee mill, and that wherever he went hound dogs tended to congregate in large numbers.

Jean Louise was sure Jem had made some kind of deal with Henry to take her to the dance, but she did not mind. At first she did not want to go, but Atticus said it would look funny if everybody's sisters were there except Jem's, told her she'd have a good time, and that she could go to Ginsberg's and pick out any dress she wanted.

She found a beauty. White, with puffed sleeves and a skirt that billowed when she spun around. There was only one thing wrong: she looked like a bowling pin in it.

She consulted Calpurnia, who said nobody could do anything about her shape, that's just the way she was, which was the way all girls more or less were when they were fourteen.

"But I look so peculiar," she said, tugging at the neckline.

"You look that way all the time," said Calpurnia. "I mean you're the same in every dress you have. That'un's no different."

Jean Louise worried for three days. On the afternoon of the dance she returned to Ginsberg's and selected a pair of false bosoms, went home, and tried them on.

"Look now, Cal," she said.

Calpurnia said, "You're the right shape all right, but hadn't you better break 'em in by degrees?"

"What do you mean?"

Calpurnia muttered, "You should'a been wearing 'em for a while to get used to 'em—it's too late now."

"Oh Cal, don't be silly."

"Well, give 'em here. I'm gonna sew 'em together."

As Jean Louise handed them over, a sudden thought rooted her to the spot. "Oh golly," she whispered.

"What's the matter now?" said Calpurnia. "You've been fixin' for this thing a slap week. What did you forget?"

"Cal, I don't think I know how to dance."

Calpurnia put her hands on her hips. "Fine time to think of that," she said, looking at the kitchen clock. "Three forty-five."

Jean Louise ran to the telephone. "Six five, please," she said, and when her father answered she wailed into the mouthpiece.

"Keep calm and consult Jack," he said. "Jack was good in his day."

"He must have cut a mean minuet," she said, but called her uncle, who responded with alacrity.

Dr. Finch coached his niece to the tune of Jem's record player: "Nothing to it . . . like chess . . . just concentrate . . . no,no,no, tuck in your butt . . . you're not playing tackle . . . loathe ballroom dancing . . . too much like work . . . don't try to lead me . . . when he steps on your foot it's your own fault for not moving it . . . don't look down . . . don't,don't,don't . . . now you've got it . . . basic, so don't try anything fancy."

After one hour's intense concentration Jean Louise mastered a simple box step. She counted vigorously to herself, and admired her uncle's ability to talk and dance simultaneously.

"Relax and you'll do all right," he said.

His exertions were repaid by Calpurnia with the offer of coffee and an invitation to supper, both of which he accepted. Dr. Finch spent a solitary hour in the living-groom until Atticus and Jem arrived; his niece locked herself in the bathroom and remained there scrubbing herself and dancing. She emerged radiant, ate supper in her bathrobe, and vanished into her bedroom unconscious of her family's amusement.

While she was dressing she heard Henry's step on the front porch and thought him calling for her too early, but he walked down the hall toward Jem's room. She applied Tangee Orange to her lips, combed her hair, and stuck down her cowlick with some of Jem's Vitalis. Her father and Dr. Finch rose to their feet when she entered the livingroom.

"You look like a picture," said Atticus. He kissed her on the forehead.

"Be careful," she said. "You'll muss up my hair."

Dr. Finch said, "Shall we take a final practice turn?"

Henry found them dancing in the livingroom. He blinked when he saw Jean Louise's new figure, and he tapped Dr. Finch on the shoulder. "May I cut in, sir?

"You look plain pretty, Scout," Henry said. "I've got something for you."

"You look nice too, Hank," said Jean Louise. Henry's blue serge Sunday pants were creased to painful sharpness, his tan jacket smelled of cleaning fluid; Jean Louise recognized Jem's light-blue necktie.

"You dance well," said Henry, and Jean Louise stumbled.

"Don't look down, Scout!" snapped Dr. Finch. "I

told you it's like carrying a cup of coffee. If you look at it you spill it."

Atticus opened his watch. "Jem better get a move on if he wants to get Irene. That trap of his won't do better than thirty."

When Jem appeared Atticus sent him back to change his tie. When he reappeared, Atticus gave him the keys to the family car, some money, and a lecture on not doing over fifty.

"Say," said Jem, after duly admiring Jean Louise, "you all can go in the Ford, and you won't have to go all that way to Abbottsville with me."

Dr. Finch was fidgeting with his coat pockets. "It is immaterial to me how you go," he said. "Just go. You're making me nervous standing around in all your finery. Jean Louise is beginning to sweat. Come in, Cal."

Calpurnia was standing shyly in the hall, giving her grudging approval to the scene. She adjusted Henry's tie, picked invisible lint from Jem's coat, and desired the presence of Jean Louise in the kitchen.

"I think I ought to sew 'em in," she said doubtfully.

Henry shouted come on or Dr. Finch would have a stroke.

"I'll be okay, Cal."

Returning to the livingroom, Jean Louise found her uncle in a suppressed whirlwind of impatience, in vivid contrast to her father, who was standing casually with his hands in his pockets. "You'd better get going," said Atticus. "Alexandra'll be here in another minute—then you will be late."

They were on the front porch when Henry halted. "I forgot!" he yelped, and ran to Jem's room. He returned carrying a box, presenting it to Jean Louise with a low bow: "For you, Miss Finch," he said. Inside the box were two pink camellias.

"Ha-ank," said Jean Louise. "They're bought!"

"Sent all the way to Mobile for 'em," said Henry. "They came up on the six o'clock bus."

"Where'll I put 'em?"

"Heavenly Fathers, put 'em where they belong!" exploded Dr. Finch. "Come here!"

He snatched the camellias from Jean Louise and pinned them to her shoulder, glaring sternly at her false front. "Will you now do me the favor of leaving the premises?"

"I forgot my purse."

Dr. Finch produced his handkerchief and made a pass at his jaw. "Henry," he said, "go get that abomination cranked. I'll meet you out in front with her."

She kissed her father goodnight, and he said, "I hope you have the time of your life."

The Maycomb County High School gymnasium was

tastefully decorated with balloons and white-and-red crepe paper streamers. A long table stood at the far end; paper cups, plates of sandwiches, and napkins surrounded two punch bowls filled with a purple mixture. The gymnasium floor was freshly waxed and the basketball goals were folded to the ceiling. Greenery enveloped the stage front, and in the center, for no particular reason, were large red cardboard letters: *MCHS*.

"It's beautiful, isn't it?" said Jean Louise.

"Looks awfully nice," said Henry. "Doesn't it look bigger when there's no game going on?"

They joined a group of younger and elder brothers and sisters standing around the punch bowls. The crowd was visibly impressed with Jean Louise. Girls she saw every day asked her where she got her dress, as if they didn't all get them there: "Ginsberg's. Calpurnia took it up," she said. Several of the younger boys with whom she had been on eye-gouging terms only a few years ago made self-conscious conversation with her.

When Henry handed her a cup of punch she whispered, "If you want to go on with the seniors or anything I'll be all right."

Henry smiled at her. "You're my date, Scout."

"I know, but you shouldn't feel obliged—"

Henry laughed. "I don't feel obligated to do one thing. I wanted to bring you. Let's dance."

"Okay, but take it easy."

He swung her out to the center of the floor. The public address system blared a slow number, and counting systematically to herself, Jean Louise danced through it with only one mistake.

As the evening wore on, she realized that she was a modest success. Several boys had cut in on her, and when she showed signs of becoming stuck, Henry was never far away.

She was sensible enough to sit out jitterbug numbers and avoid music with a South American taint, and Henry said when she learned to talk and dance at the same time she'd be a hit. She hoped the evening would last forever.

Jem and Irene's entrance caused a stir. Jem had been voted Most Handsome in the senior class, a reasonable assessment: he had his mother's calflike brown eyes, the heavy Finch eyebrows, and even features. Irene was the last word in sophistication. She wore a clinging green taffeta dress and high-heeled shoes, and when she danced dozens of slave bracelets clinked on her wrists. She had cool green eyes and jet hair, a quick smile, and was the type of girl Jem fell for with monotonous regularity.

Jem danced his duty dance with Jean Louise, told her she was doing fine but her nose was shining, to which she replied he had lipstick on his mouth. The number ended and Jem left her with Henry. "I can't believe you're going in the Army in June," she said. It makes you sound so old."

Henry opened his mouth to answer, suddenly goggled, and clasped her to him in a clinch.

"What's the matter, Hank?"

"Don't you think it's hot in here? Let's go out."

Jean Louise tried to break away, but he held her close and danced her out the side door into the night.

"What's eating you, Hank? Have I said something—"

He took her hand and walked her around to the front of the school building.

"Ah—" said Henry. He held both her hands. "Honey," he said. "Look at your front."

"It's pitch dark. I can't see anything."

"Then feel."

She felt, and gasped. Her right false bosom was in the center of her chest and the other was nearly under her left armpit. She jerked them back into position and burst into tears.

She sat down on the schoolhouse steps; Henry sat beside her and put his arm around her shoulders. When she stopped crying she said, "When did you notice it?"

"Just then, I swear."

"Do you suppose they've been laughing at me long?"

Henry shook his head. "I don't think anybody noticed it, Scout. Listen, Jem danced with you just before I did, and if he'd noticed it he'da certainly told you."

"All Jem's got on his mind's Irene. He wouldn't see a cyclone if it was comin' at him." She was crying again, softly. "I'll never be able to face them again."

Henry squeezed her shoulder. "Scout, I swear they slipped when we were dancing. Be logical—if anybody'd seen they'd've told you, you know that."

"No I don't. They'd just whisper and laugh. I know how they do."

"Not the seniors," said Henry sedately. "You've been dancing with the football team ever since Jem came in."

She had. The team, one by one, had requested the pleasure: it was Jem's quiet way of making sure she had a good time.

"Besides," continued Henry, "I don't like 'em anyway. You don't look like yourself in them."

Stung, she said, "You mean I look funny in 'em? I look funny without 'em, too."

"I mean you're just not Jean Louise." He added, "You don't look funny at all, you look fine to me."

"You're nice to say that, Hank, but you're just saying it. I'm all fat in the wrong places, and—"

Henry hooted. "How old are you? Goin' on fifteen

still. You haven't even stopped growing yet. Say, you remember Gladys Grierson? Remember how they used to call her 'Happy Butt'?"

"Ha-ank!"

"Well, look at her now."

Gladys Grierson, one of the more delectable ornaments of the senior class, had been afflicted to a greater extent with Jean Louise's complaint. "She's downright slinky now, isn't she?"

Henry said masterfully, "Listen, Scout, they'll worry you the rest of the night. You better take 'em off."

"No. Let's go home."

"We're not going home, we're going back in and have a good time."

"No!"

"Damn it, Scout, I said we're going back, so take 'em off!"

"Take me home, Henry."

With furious, disinterested fingers, Henry reached beneath the neck of her dress, drew out the offending appurtenances, and flung them as far as he could into the night.

"*Now* shall we go in?"

No one seemed to notice the change in her appearance, which proved, Henry said, that she was vain as a peacock, thinking everybody was looking at her all the time.

The next day was a school day, and the dance broke up at eleven. Henry coasted the Ford down the Finch driveway and brought it to a stop under the chinaberry trees. He and Jean Louise walked to the front door, and before he opened it for her, Henry put his arms around her lightly and kissed her. She felt her cheeks grow hot.

"Once more for good luck," he said.

He kissed her again, shut the door behind her, and she heard him whistling as he ran across the street to his room.

Hungry, she tiptoed down the hall to the kitchen. Passing her father's room, she saw a strip of light under his door. She knocked and went in. Atticus was in bed reading.

"Have a good time?"

"I had a won-derful time," she said. "Atticus?"

"Hm?"

"Do you think Hank's too old for me?"

"What?"

"Nothing. Goodnight."

She sat through roll call the next morning under the weight of her crush on Henry, coming to attention only when her homeroom teacher announced that there would be a special assembly of the junior and senior schools immediately after the first-period bell.

She went to the auditorium with nothing more on her mind than the prospect of seeing Henry, and weak curiosity as to what Miss Muffett had to say. Probably another war bond drive.

The Maycomb County High School principal was a Mr. Charles Tuffett, who to compensate for his name, habitually wore an expression that made him resemble the Indian on a five-cent piece. The personality of Mr. Tuffett was less inspiring: he was a disappointed man, a frustrated professor of education with no sympathy for young people. He was from the hills of Mississippi, which placed him at a disadvantage in Maycomb: hard-headed hill folk do not understand coastal-plain dreamers, and Mr. Tuffett was no exception. When he came to Maycomb he lost no time in making known to the parents that their children were the most ill-mannered lot he had ever seen, that vocational agriculture was all they were fit to learn, that football and basketball were a waste of time, and that he, happily, had no use for clubs and extracurricular activities because school, like life, was a business proposition.

His student body, from the eldest to the youngest,

responded in kind: Mr. Tuffett was tolerated at all times, but ignored most of the time.

Jean Louise sat with her class in the middle section of the auditorium. The senior class sat in the rear across the aisle from her, and it was easy to turn and look at Henry. Jem, sitting beside him, was squint-eyed, miasmal, and mute, as he always was in the morning. When Mr. Tuffett faced them and read some announcements, Jean Louise was grateful that he was killing the first period, which meant no math. She turned around when Mr. Tuffett descended to brass tacks:

In his time he had come across all varieties of students, he said, some of which carried pistols to school, but never in his experience had he witnessed such an act of depravity as greeted him when he came up the front walk this morning.

Jean Louise exchanged glances with her neighbors. "What's eating him?" she whispered. "God knows," answered her neighbor on the left.

Did they realize the enormity of such an outrage? He would have them know this country was at war, that while our boys—our brothers and sons—were fighting and dying for us, someone directed an obscene act of defilement at them, an act the perpetrator of which was beneath contempt.

Jean Louise looked around at a sea of perplexed faces;

she could spot guilty parties easily on public occasions, but she was met with blank astonishment on all sides.

Furthermore, before they adjourned, Mr. Tuffett would say he knew who did it, and if the party wished leniency he would appear at his office not later than two o'clock with a statement in writing.

The assembly, suppressing a growl of disgust at Mr. Tuffett's indulgence in the oldest schoolmaster's trick on record, adjourned and followed him to the front of the building.

"He just loves confessions in writing," said Jean Louise to her companions. "He thinks it makes it legal."

"Yeah, he doesn't believe anything unless it's written down," said one.

"Then when it's written down he always believes every word of it," said another.

"Reckon somebody's painted swastikas on the sidewalk?" said a third.

"Been done," said Jean Louise.

They rounded the corner of the building and stood still. Nothing seemed amiss; the pavement was clean, the front doors were in place, the shrubbery had not been disturbed.

Mr. Tuffett waited until the school assembled, then pointed dramatically upward. "Look," he said. "Look, all of you!"

Mr. Tuffett was a patriot. He was chairman of every bond drive, he gave tedious and embarrassing talks in assembly on the War Effort, the project he instigated and viewed with most pride was a tremendous billboard he caused to be erected in the front schoolyard proclaiming that the following graduates of MCHS were in the service of their country. His students viewed Mr. Tuffett's billboard more darkly: he had assessed them twenty-five cents apiece and had taken the credit for it himself.

Following Mr. Tuffett's finger, Jean Louise looked at the billboard. She read, IN THE SERVICE OF THEIR COUNTR. Blocking out the last letter and fluttering softly in the morning breeze were her falsies.

"I assure you," said Mr. Tuffett, "that a signed statement had better be on my desk by two o'clock this afternoon. I was on this campus last night," he said, emphasizing each word. "Now go to your classes."

That was a thought. He always sneaked around at school dances to try and catch people necking. He looked in parked cars and beat the bushes. Maybe he saw them. Why did Hank have to throw 'em?

"He's bluffing," said Jem at recess. "But again he may not be."

They were in the school lunchroom. Jean Louise was

trying to behave inconspicuously. The school was near bursting point with laughter, horror, and curiosity.

"For the last time, you all, let me tell him," she said.

"Don't be a gump, Jean Louise. You know how he feels about it. After all, I did it," said Henry.

"Well, for heaven's sake they're mine!"

"I know how Hank feels, Scout," said Jem. "He can't let you do it."

"I fail to see why not."

"For the umpteenth time I just can't, that's all. Don't you see that?"

"No."

"Jean Louise, you were my date last night—"

"I will never understand men as long as I live," she said, no longer in love with Henry. "You don't have to protect me, Hank. I'm not your date this morning. You know you can't tell him."

"That's for sure, Hank," said Jem. "He'd hold back your diploma."

A diploma meant more to Henry than to most of his friends. It was all right for some of them to be expelled; in a pinch, they could go off to a boarding school.

"You cut him to the quick, you know," said Jem. "It'd be just like him to expel you two weeks before you graduate."

"So let me," said Jean Louise. "I'd just love being expelled." She would. School bored her intolerably.

"That's not the point, Scout. You simply can't do it. I could explain—no I couldn't, either," said Henry, as the ramifications of his impetuosity sank in. "I couldn't explain anything."

"All right," said Jem. "The situation is this. Hank, I think he's bluffing, but there's a good chance he isn't. You know he prowls around. He might have heard you all, you were practically under his office window—"

"But his office was dark," said Jean Louise.

"—he loves to sit in the dark. If Scout tells him it'll be rugged, but if you tell him he'll expel you sure as you were born, and you've got to graduate, son."

"Jem," said Jean Louise. "It's lovely to be a philosopher, but we ain't getting anywhere—"

"Your status as I see it, Hank," said Jem, tranquilly ignoring his sister, "is you'll be damned if you do and damned if you don't."

"I—"

"Oh shut up, Scout!" said Henry viciously. "Don't you see I'll never be able to hold up my head again if I let you do it?"

"Cu-u-rr, I never saw such heroes!"

Henry jumped up. "Wait a minute!" he shouted.

"Jem, give me the car keys and cover for me in study hall. I'll be back for econ."

Jem said, "Miss Muffett'll hear you leaving, Hank."

"No he won't. I'll push the car to the road. Besides, he'll be in study hall."

It was easy to be absent from a study hall Mr. Tuffett guarded. He took little personal interest in his students, knowing only the more uninhibited by name. Seats were assigned in the library, but if one made clear one's desire not to attend, the ranks closed; the person on the end of one's row set the remaining chair in the hall outside and replaced it when the period was over.

Jean Louise paid no attention to her English teacher, and fifty anxious minutes later was stopped by Henry on the way to her civics class.

"Now listen," he said tersely. "Do exactly as I tell you: you're gonna tell him. Write—" he handed her a pencil and she opened her notebook.

"Write, 'Dear Mr. Tuffett. They look like mine.' Sign your full name. Better copy it over in ink so he'll believe it. Now just before noon you go and give it to him. Got it?"

She nodded. "Just before noon."

When she went to civics she knew it was out. Groups of students were clustered in the hall mumbling and laughing. She endured grins and friendly winks with equanimity—they almost made her feel better. It's grown people who always believe the worst, she thought, confident that her contemporaries believed no more nor less than what Jem and Hank had circulated. But why did they tell it? They'd be kidded forever: they wouldn't care because they were graduating, but she would have to sit there for three more years. No, Miss Muffett would expel her and Atticus would send her off somewhere. Atticus would hit the ceiling when Miss Muffett told him the gory story. Oh well, it'd get Hank out of a mess. He and Jem were awfully gallant for a while but she was right in the end. It was the only thing to do.

She wrote out her confession in ink, and as noon drew near, her spirits flagged. Normally there was nothing she enjoyed more than a row with Miss Muffett, who was so thick one could say almost anything to him provided one was careful to maintain a grave and sorrowful countenance, but today she had no taste for dialectics. She felt nervous and she despised herself for it.

She was faintly queasy when she walked down the hall to his office. He had called it obscene and depraved in assembly; what would he say to the town? Maycomb thrived on rumors, there would be all kinds of stories getting back to Atticus—

Mr. Tuffett was sitting behind his desk, gazing testily at its top. "What do you want?" he said, without looking up.

"I wanted to give you this, sir," she said, backing away instinctively.

Mr. Tuffett took her note, wadded it up without reading it, and threw it at the wastepaper basket.

Jean Louise had the sensation of being floored by a feather.

"Ah, Mr. Tuffett," she said. "I came to tell you like you said. I—I got 'em at Ginsberg's," she added gratuitously. "I didn't mean any—"

Mr. Tuffett looked up, his face reddening with anger. "Don't you stand there and tell me what you didn't mean! Never in my experience have I come across—"

Now she was in for it.

But as she listened she received the impression that Mr. Tuffett's were general remarks directed more to the student body than to her, they were an echo of his early morning feelings. He was concluding with a précis on the unhealthy attitudes engendered by Maycomb County when she interrupted:

"Mr. Tuffett, I just want to say everybody's not to blame for what I did—you don't have to take it out on everybody."

Mr. Tuffett gripped the edge of his desk and said

between clenched teeth, "For that bit of impudence you may remain one hour after school, young lady!"

She took a deep breath. "Mr. Tuffett," she said, "I think there's been a mistake. I really don't quite—"

"You don't, do you? Then I'll show you!"

Mr. Tuffett snatched up a thick pile of loose-leaf notebook paper and waved it at her.

"You, Miss, are the hundred and fifth!"

Jean Louise examined the sheets of paper. They were all alike. On each was written "Dear Mr. Tuffett. They look like mine," and signed by every girl in the school from the ninth grade upward.

She stood for a moment in deep thought; unable to think of anything to say to help Mr. Tuffett, she stole quietly out of his office.

"He's a beaten man," said Jem, when they were riding home to dinner. Jean Louise sat between her brother and Henry, who had listened soberly to her account of Mr. Tuffett's state of mind.

"Hank, you are an absolute genius," she said. "What ever gave you the idea?"

Henry inhaled deeply on his cigarette and flicked it out the window. "I consulted my lawyer," he said grandly.

Jean Louise put her hands to her mouth.

"Naturally," said Henry. "You know he's been looking after my business since I was knee-high, so I just went to town and explained it to him. I simply asked him for advice."

"Did Atticus put you up to it?" asked Jean Louise in awe.

"No, he didn't put me up to it. It was my own idea. He balked around for a while, said it was all a question of balancin' the equities or something, that I was in an interesting but tenuous position. He swung around in his chair and looked out the window and said he always tried to put himself in his clients' shoes. . . ." Henry paused.

"Keep on."

"Well, he said owin' to the extreme delicacy of my problem, and since there was no evidence of criminal intent, he wouldn't be above throwin' a little dust in a juryman's eyes—whatever that means—and then, oh I don't know."

"Oh Hank, you do know."

"Well, he said something about safety in numbers and if he were me he wouldn't dream of connivin' at perjury but so far as he knew all falsies looked alike, and that was about all he could do for me. He said he'd bill me at the end of the month. I wasn't out of the office good before I got the idea!"

Jean Louise said, "Hank—did he say anything about what he was going to say to me?"

"Say to you?" Henry turned to her. "He won't say a darn thing to you. He can't. Don't you know everything anybody tells his lawyer's confidential?"

Thock. She flattened the paper cup into the table, shattering their images. The sun stood at two o'clock, as it had stood yesterday and would stand tomorrow.

Hell is eternal apartness. What had she done that she must spend the rest of her years reaching out with yearning for them, making secret trips to long ago, making no journey to the present? I am their blood and bones, I have dug in this ground, this is my home. But I am not their blood, the ground doesn't care who digs it, I am a stranger at a cocktail party.

16

H ank, where's Atticus?"

Henry looked up from his desk. "Hi, sweetie. He's at the post office. It's about coffee-time for me. Comin' along?"

The same thing that compelled her to leave Mr. Cunningham's and go to the office caused her to follow Henry to the sidewalk: she wished to look furtively at them again and again, to assure herself that they had not undergone some alarming physical metamorphosis as well, yet she did not wish to speak to them, to touch them, lest she cause them to commit further outrage in her presence.

As she and Henry walked side by side to the drug-store, she wondered if Maycomb was planning a fall or winter wedding for them. I'm peculiar, she thought. I cannot get into bed with a man unless I'm in some state of accord with him. Right now I can't even speak to him. Cannot speak to my oldest friend.

They sat facing each other in a booth, and Jean Louise studied the napkin container, the sugar bowl, the salt and pepper shakers.

"You're quiet," said Henry. "How was the Coffee?"

"Atrocious."

"Hester there?"

"Yes. She's about yours and Jem's age, isn't she?"

"Yeah, same class. Bill told me this morning she was pilin' on the warpaint for it."

"Hank, Bill Sinclair must be a gloomy party."

"Why?"

"All that guff he's put in Hester's head—"

"What guff?"

"Oh, the Catholics and the Communists and Lord knows what else. It seems to have run all together in her mind."

Henry laughed and said, "Honey, the sun rises and sets with that Bill of hers. Everything he says is Gospel. She loves her man."

"Is that what loving your man is?"

"Has a lot to do with it."

Jean Louise said, "You mean losing your own identity, don't you?"

"In a way, yes," said Henry.

"Then I doubt if I shall ever marry. I never met a man—"

"You're gonna marry me, remember?"

"Hank, I may as well tell you now and get it over with: I'm not going to marry you. Period and that's that."

She had not intended to say it but she could not stop herself.

"I've heard that before."

"Well, I'm telling you now that if you ever want to marry"—was it she who was talking?—"you'd best start looking around. I've never been in love with you, but you've always known I've loved you. I thought we could make a marriage with me loving you on that basis, but—"

"But what?"

"I don't even love you like that any more. I've hurt you but there it is." Yes, it was she talking, with her customary aplomb, breaking his heart in the drugstore. Well, he'd broken hers.

Henry's face became blank, reddened, and its scar leaped into prominence. "Jean Louise, you can't mean what you're saying."

"I mean every word of it."

Hurts, doesn't it? You're damn right it hurts. You know how it feels, now.

Henry reached across the table and took her hand. She pulled away. "Don't you touch me," she said.

"My darling, what is the matter?"

Matter? I'll tell you what's the matter. You won't be pleased with some of it.

"All right, Hank. It's simply this: I was at that meeting yesterday. I saw you and Atticus in your glory down there at that table with that—that scum, that dreadful man, and I tell you my stomach turned. Merely the man I was going to marry, merely my own father, merely made me so sick I threw up and haven't stopped yet! How in the name of God could you? How could you?"

"We have to do a lot of things we don't want to do, Jean Louise."

She blazed. "What kind of answer is that? I thought Uncle Jack had finally gone off his rocker but I'm not so sure now!"

"Honey," said Henry. He moved the sugar bowl to the center of the table and pushed it back again. "Look at it this way. All the Maycomb Citizens' Council is in this world is—is a protest to the Court, it's a sort of warning to the Negroes for them not to be in such a hurry, it's a—"

"—tailor-made audience for any trash who wants to get up and holler nigger. How can you be a party to such a thing, how can you?"

Henry pushed the sugar bowl toward her and brought it back. She took it away from him and banged it down in the corner.

"Jean Louise, as I said before, we have to do—"

"—a lot of things we don't—"

"—will you let me finish?—we don't want to do. No, please let me talk. I'm trying to think of something that might show you what I mean . . . you know the Klan—?"

"Yes I know the Klan."

"Now hush a minute. A long time ago the Klan was respectable, like the Masons. Almost every man of any prominence was a member, back when Mr. Finch was young. Did you know Mr. Finch joined?"

"I wouldn't be surprised at anything Mr. Finch ever joined in his life. It figures—"

"Jean Louise, shut up! Mr. Finch has no more use for the Klan than anybody, and didn't then. You know why he joined? To find out exactly what men in town were behind the masks. What men, what people. He went to one meeting, and that was enough. The Wizard happened to be the Methodist preacher—"

"That's the kind of company Atticus likes."

"Shut up, Jean Louise. I'm trying to make you see his motive: all the Klan was then was a political force, there wasn't any cross-burning, but your daddy did and still does get mighty uncomfortable around folks who cover up their faces. He had to know who he'd be fighting if the time ever came to—he had to find out who they were. . . ."

"So my esteemed father is one of the Invisible Empire."

"Jean Louise, that was forty years ago—"

"He's probably the Grand Dragon by now."

Henry said evenly, "I'm only trying to make you see beyond men's acts to their motives. A man can appear to be a part of something not-so-good on its face, but don't take it upon yourself to judge him unless you know his motives as well. A man can be boiling inside, but he knows a mild answer works better than showing his rage. A man can condemn his enemies, but it's wiser to know them. I said sometimes we have to do—"

Jean Louise said, "Are you saying go along with the crowd and then when the time comes—"

Henry checked her: "Look, honey. Have you ever considered that men, especially men, must conform to certain demands of the community they live in simply so they can be of service to it?

"Maycomb County's home to me, honey. It's the best place I know to live in. I've built up a good record here from the time I was a kid. Maycomb knows me, and I know Maycomb. Maycomb trusts me, and I trust

Maycomb. My bread and butter comes from this town, and Maycomb's given me a good living.

"But Maycomb asks certain things in return. It asks you to lead a reasonably clean life, it asks that you join the Kiwanis Club, to go to church on Sunday, it asks you to conform to its ways—"

Henry examined the salt shaker, moving his thumb up and down its grooved sides. "Remember this, honey," he said. "I've had to work like a dog for everything I ever had. I worked in that store across the square—I was so tired most of the time it was all I could do to keep up with my lessons. In the summer I worked at home in Mamma's store, and when I wasn't working there I was hammering in the house. Jean Louise, I've had to scratch since I was a kid for the things you and Jem took for granted. I've never had some of the things you take for granted and I never will. All I have to fall back on is myself—"

"That's all any of us have, Hank."

"No it isn't. Not here."

"What do you mean?"

"I mean there are some things I simply can't do that you can."

"And why am I such a privileged character?"

"You're a Finch."

"So I'm a Finch. So what?"

"So you can parade around town in your dungarees with your shirttail out and barefooted if you want to. Maycomb says, 'That's the Finch in her, that's just Her Way.' Maycomb grins and goes about its business: old Scout Finch never changes. Maycomb's delighted and perfectly ready to believe you went swimming in the river buck naked. 'Hasn't changed a bit,' it says. 'Same old Jean Louise. Remember when she—?'"

He put down the salt shaker. "But let Henry Clinton show any signs of deviatin' from the norm and Maycomb says, not 'That's the Clinton in him,' but 'That's the trash in him.'"

"Hank. That is untrue and you know it. It's unfair and it's ungenerous, but more than anything in this world it's just not true!"

"Jean Louise, it is true," said Henry gently. "You've probably never even thought about it—"

"Hank, you've got some kind of complex."

"I haven't got anything of the kind. I just know Maycomb. I'm not in the least sensitive about it, but good Lord, I'm certainly aware of it. It says to me that there are certain things I can't do and certain things I must do if I—"

"If you what?"

"Well, sweetie, I would really like to live here, and I like the things other men like. I want to keep the respect of this town, I want to serve it, I want to make a name for myself as a lawyer, I want to make money, I want to marry and have a family—"

"In that order, I suppose!"

Jean Louise got up from the booth and marched out of the drugstore. Henry followed on her heels. At the door he turned and yelled he'd get the check in a minute.

"Jean Louise, stop!"

She stopped.

"Well?"

"Honey, I'm only trying to make you see—"

"I see all right!" she said. "I see a scared little man; I see a little man who's scared not to do what Atticus tells him, who's scared not to stand on his own two feet, who's scared not to sit around with the rest of the red-blooded men—"

She started walking. She thought she was walking in the general direction of the car. She thought she had parked it in front of the office.

"Jean Louise, will you please wait a minute?"

"All right, I'm waiting."

"You know I told you there were things you'd always taken for granted—"

"Hell yes, I've been taking a lot of things for granted. The very things I've loved about you. I looked up to you like God knows what because you worked like hell for everything you ever had, for everything you've made yourself. I thought a lot of things went with it, but they obviously aren't there. I thought you had guts, I thought—"

She walked down the sidewalk, unaware that Maycomb was looking at her, that Henry was walking beside her pitifully, comically.

"Jean Louise, will you please listen to me?"

"God damn you, what?"

"I just want to ask you one thing, one thing—what the hell do you expect me to do? Tell me, what the hell do you expect me to do?"

"Do? I expect you to keep your gold-plated ass out of citizens' councils! I don't give a damn if Atticus is sitting across from you, if the King of England's on your right and the Lord Jehovah's on your left—I expect you to be a man, that's all!"

She drew in her breath sharply. "I—you go through a goddamned war, that's one kind of being scared, but you get through it, you get through it. Then you come home to be scared the rest of your life—scared of *Maycomb*! Maycomb, Alabama—oh brother!"

They had come to the door of the office.

Henry grabbed her shoulders. "Jean Louise, will you stop one second? Please? Listen to me. I know I'm not much, but think one minute. Please think. This is my life, this town, don't you understand that? God damn it, I'm part of Maycomb County's trash, but I'm part of Maycomb County. I'm a coward, I'm a little man, I'm not worth killing, but this is my *home*. What do you want me to do, go shout from the housetops that I am Henry Clinton and I'm here to tell you you're all wet? I've got to live here, Jean Louise. Don't you understand that?"

"I understand that you're a goddamned hypocrite."

"I am trying to make you see, my darling, that you are permitted a sweet luxury I'm not. You can shout to high heaven, I cannot. How can I be of any use to a town if it's against me? If I went out and—look, you will admit that I have a certain amount of education and a certain usefulness in Maycomb—you admit that? A millhand can't do my job. Now, shall I throw all that down the drain, go back down the county to the store and sell people flour when I could be helping them with what legal talent I have? Which is worth more?"

"Henry, how can you live with yourself?"

"It's comparatively easy. Sometimes I just don't vote my convictions, that's all."

"Hank, we are poles apart. I don't know much but I know one thing. I know I can't live with you. I cannot live with a hypocrite."

A dry, pleasant voice behind her said, "I don't know why you can't. Hypocrites have just as much right to live in this world as anybody."

She turned around and stared at her father. His hat was pushed back on his head; his eyebrows were raised; he was smiling at her.

17

H ank," said Atticus, "why don't you go have a long
look at the roses on the square? Estelle might
give you one if you ask her right. Looks like I'm the
only one who's asked her right today."

Atticus put his hand to his lapel, where was tucked
a fresh scarlet bud. Jean Louise glanced toward the
square and saw Estelle, black against the afternoon sun,
steadily hoeing under the bushes.

Henry held out his hand to Jean Louise, dropped it
to his side, and left without a word. She watched him
walk across the street.

"You've known all that about him?"

"Certainly."

Atticus had treated him like his own son, had given
him the love that would have been Jem's—she was suddenly aware that they were standing on the spot where
Jem died. Atticus saw her shudder.

"It's still with you, isn't it?" he said.

"Yes."

"Isn't it about time you got over that? Bury your dead, Jean Louise."

"I don't want to discuss it. I want to move somewhere else."

"Let's go in the office, then."

Her father's office had always been a source of refuge for her. It was friendly. It was a place where, if troubles did not vanish, they were made bearable. She wondered if those were the same abstracts, files, and professional impedimenta on his desk that were there when she would run in, out of breath, desperate for an ice cream cone, and request a nickel. She could see him swing around in his swivel chair and stretch his legs. He would reach down deep into his pocket, pull out a handful of change, and from it select a very special nickel for her. His door was never closed to his children.

He sat slowly and swung around toward her. She saw a flash of pain cross his face and leave it.

"You knew all that about Hank?"

"Yes."

"I don't understand men."

"We-ll, some men who cheat their wives out of grocery money wouldn't think of cheating the grocer. Men tend to carry their honesty in pigeonholes, Jean Louise. They can be perfectly honest in some ways and fool themselves in other ways. Don't be so hard on Hank, he's coming along. Jack tells me you're upset about something."

"Jack told you—"

"Called a while ago and said—among other things— that if you weren't already on the warpath you'd soon be. From what I heard, you already are."

So. Uncle Jack told him. She was accustomed now to having her family desert her one by one. Uncle Jack was the last straw and to hell with them all. Very well, she'd tell him. Tell him and go. She would not argue with him; that was useless. He always beat her: she'd never won an argument from him in her life and she did not propose to try now.

"Yes sir, I'm upset about something. That citizens' councilin' you're doing. I think it's disgusting and I'll tell you that right now."

Her father leaned back in his chair. He said, "Jean Louise, you've been reading nothing but New York papers. I've no doubt all you see is wild threats and bombings and such. The Maycomb council's not like the North Alabama and Tennessee kinds. Our council's composed of and led by our own people. I bet you saw nearly every man in the county yesterday, and you knew nearly every man there."

"Yes sir, I did. Every man from that snake Willoughby on down."

"Each man there was probably there for a different reason," said her father.

No war was ever fought for so many different reasons. Who said that? "Yeah, but they all met for one reason."

"I can tell you the two reasons I was there. The Federal Government and the NAACP. Jean Louise, what was your first reaction to the Supreme Court decision?"

That was a safe question. She would answer him.

"I was furious," she said.

She was. She had known it was coming, knew what it would be, had thought she was prepared for it, but when she bought a newspaper on the street corner and read it, she stopped at the first bar she came to and drank down a straight bourbon.

"Why?"

"Well sir, there they were, tellin' us what to do again—"

Her father grinned. "You were merely reacting according to your kind," he said. "When you started using your head, what did you think?"

"Nothing much, but it scared me. It seemed all backward—they were putting the cart way out in front of the horse."

"How so?"

He was prodding her. Let him. They were on safe ground. "Well, in trying to satisfy one amendment, it looks like they rubbed out another one. The Tenth. It's only a small amendment, only one sentence long, but it seemed to be the one that meant the most, somehow."

"Did you think this out for yourself?"

"Why, yes sir. Atticus, I don't know anything about the Constitution. . . ."

"You seem to be constitutionally sound so far. Proceed."

Proceed with what? Tell him she couldn't look him in the eye? He wanted her views on the Constitution, then he'd have 'em: "Well, it seemed that to meet the real needs of a small portion of the population, the Court set up something horrible that could—that could affect the vast majority of folks. Adversely, that is. Atticus, I don't know anything about it—all we have is the Constitution between us and anything some smart fellow wants to start, and there went the Court just breezily canceling one whole amendment, it seemed to me. We have a system of checks and balances and things, but when it comes down to it we don't have much check on the Court, so who'll bell the cat? Oh dear, I'm soundin' like the Actors Studio."

"What?"

"Nothing. I'm—I'm just trying to say that in trying to do right we've left ourselves open for something that could be truly dangerous to our set-up."

She ran her fingers through her hair. She looked at the rows of brown-and-black bound books, law reports, on the wall opposite. She looked at a faded picture of the Nine Old Men on the wall to the left of her. Is Roberts dead? she wondered. She could not remember.

Her father's voice was patient: "You were saying—?"

"Yes sir. I was saying that I—I don't know much about government and economics and all that, and I don't want to know much, but I do know that the Federal Government to me, to one small citizen, is mostly dreary hallways and waiting around. The more we have, the longer we wait and the tireder we get. Those old mossbacks on the wall up there knew it—but now, instead of going about it through Congress and the state legislatures like we should, when we tried to do right we just made it easier for them to set up more hallways and more waiting—"

Her father sat up and laughed.

"I told you I didn't know anything about it."

"Sweet, you're such a states' rightist you make me a Roosevelt Liberal by comparison."

"States' rightist?"

Atticus said, "Now that I've adjusted my ear to feminine reasoning, I think we find ourselves believing the very same things."

She had been half willing to sponge out what she had seen and heard, creep back to New York, and make him a memory. A memory of the three of them, Atticus, Jem, and her, when things were uncomplicated and people did not lie. But she would not have him compound the felony. She could not let him add hypocrisy to it:

"Atticus, if you believe all that, then why don't you do right? I mean this, that no matter how hateful the Court was, there had to be a beginning—"

"You mean because the Court said it we must take it? No ma'am. I don't see it that way. If you think I for one citizen am going to take it lying down, you're quite wrong. As you say, Jean Louise, there's only one thing higher than the Court in this country, and that's the Constitution—"

"Atticus, we are talking at cross-purposes."

"You are dodging something. What is it?"

The dark tower. Childe Roland to the dark tower came. High school lit. Uncle Jack. I remember now.

"What is it? I'm trying to say that I don't approve of the way they did it, that it scares me to death when I think about the way they did it, but they had to do it. It was put under their noses and they had to do, Atticus, the time has come when we've got to do right—"

"Do right?"

"Yes sir. Give 'em a chance."

"The Negroes? You don't think they have a chance?"

"Why, no sir."

"What's to prevent any Negro from going where he pleases in this country and finding what he wants?"

"That's a loaded question and you know it, sir! I'm so sick of this moral double-dealing I could—"

He had stung her, and she had shown him she felt it. But she could not help herself.

Her father picked up a pencil and tapped it on his desk. "Jean Louise," he said. "Have you ever considered that you can't have a set of backward people living among people advanced in one kind of civilization and have a social Arcadia?"

"You're queering the pitch on me, Atticus, so let's keep the sociology out of it for a second. Of course I know that, but I heard something once. I heard a slogan and it stuck in my head. I heard 'Equal rights for all;

special privileges for none,' and to me it didn't mean anything but what it said. It didn't mean one card off the top of the stack for the white man and one off the bottom for the Negro, it—"

"Let's look at it this way," said her father. "You realize that our Negro population is backward, don't you? You will concede that? You realize the full implications of the word 'backward,' don't you?"

"Yes sir."

"You realize that the vast majority of them here in the South are unable to share fully in the responsibilities of citizenship, and why?"

"Yes sir."

"But you want them to have all its privileges?"

"God damn it, you're twisting it up!"

"There's no point in being profane. Think this over: Abbott County, across the river, is in bad trouble. The population is almost three-fourths Negro. The voting population is almost half-and-half now, because of that big Normal School over there. If the scales were tipped over, what would you have? The county won't keep a full board of registrars, because if the Negro vote edged out the white you'd have Negroes in every county office—"

"What makes you so sure?"

"Honey," he said. "Use your head. When they vote, they vote in blocs."

"Atticus, you're like that old publisher who sent out a staff artist to cover the Spanish-American War. 'You draw the pictures. I'll make the war.' You're as cynical as he was."

"Jean Louise, I'm only trying to tell you some plain truths. You must see things as they are, as well as they should be."

"Then why didn't you show me things as they are when I sat on your lap? Why didn't you show me, why weren't you careful when you read me history and the things that I thought meant something to you that there was a fence around everything marked 'White Only'?"

"You are inconsistent," said her father mildly.

"Why so?"

"You slang the Supreme Court within an inch of its life, then you turn around and talk like the NAACP."

"Good Lord, I didn't get mad with the Court because of the Negroes. Negroes slapped the brief on the bench, all right, but that wasn't what made me furious. I was ravin' at what they were doing to the Tenth Amendment and all the fuzzy thinking. The Negroes were—"

Incidental to the issue in this war . . . to your own private war.

"You carry a card these days?"

"Why didn't you hit me instead? For God's sake, Atticus!"

Her father sighed. The lines around his mouth deepened. His hands with their swollen joints fumbled with his yellow pencil.

"Jean Louise," he said, "let me tell you something right now, as plainly as I can put it. I am old-fashioned, but this I believe with all my heart. I'm a sort of Jeffersonian Democrat. Do you know what that is?"

"Huh, I thought you voted for Eisenhower. I thought Jefferson was one of the great souls of the Democratic Party or something."

"Go back to school," her father said. "All the Democratic Party has to do with Jefferson these days is put his picture up at banquets. Jefferson believed full citizenship was a privilege to be earned by each man, that it was not something given lightly nor to be taken lightly. A man couldn't vote simply because he was a man, in Jefferson's eyes. He had to be a responsible man. A vote was, to Jefferson, a precious privilege a man attained for himself in a—a live-and-let-live economy."

"Atticus, you are rewriting history."

"No I'm not. It might benefit you to go back and have a look at what some of our founding fathers really believed, instead of relying so much on what people these days tell you they believed."

"You might be a Jeffersonian, but you're no Democrat."

"Neither was Jefferson."

"Then what are you, a snob or something?"

"Yes. I'll accept being called a snob when it comes to government. I'd like very much to be left alone to manage my own affairs in a live-and-let-live economy, I'd like for my state to be left alone to keep house without advice from the NAACP, which knows next to nothing about its business and cares less. That organization has stirred up more trouble in the past five years—"

"Atticus, the NAACP hasn't done half of what I've seen in the past two days. It's us."

"Us?"

"Yes sir, us. You. Has anybody, in all the wrangling and high words over states' rights and what kind of government we should have, thought about helping the Negroes?

"We missed the boat, Atticus. We sat back and let the NAACP come in because we were so furious at what we knew the Court was going to do, so furious at what it did, we naturally started shouting nigger. Took it out on them, because we resented the government.

"When it came we didn't give an inch, we just ran

instead. When we should have tried to help 'em live with the decision, it was like Bonaparte's retreat we ran so fast. I guess it's the first time in our history that we ever ran, and when we ran we lost. Where could they go? Who could they turn to? I think we deserve everything we've gotten from the NAACP and more."

"I don't think you mean what you're saying."

"I mean every word of it."

"Then let's put this on a practical basis right now. Do you want Negroes by the carload in our schools and churches and theaters? Do you want them in our world?"

"They're people, aren't they? We were quite willing to import them when they made money for us."

"Do you want your children going to a school that's been dragged down to accommodate Negro children?"

"The scholastic level of that school down the street, Atticus, couldn't be any lower and you know it. They're entitled to the same opportunities anyone else has, they're entitled to the same chance—"

Her father cleared his throat. "Listen, Scout, you're upset by having seen me doing something you think is wrong, but I'm trying to make you understand my position. Desperately trying. This is merely for your own information, that's all: so far in my experience, white is white and black's black. So far, I've not yet heard an argument that has convinced me otherwise. I'm seventy-two years old, but I'm still open to suggestion.

"Now think about this. What would happen if all the Negroes in the South were suddenly given full civil rights? I'll tell you. There'd be another Reconstruction. Would you want your state governments run by people who don't know how to run 'em? Do you want this town run by—now wait a minute—Willoughby's a crook, we know that, but do you know of any Negro who knows as much as Willoughby? Zeebo'd probably be Mayor of Maycomb. Would you want someone of Zeebo's capability to handle the town's money? We're outnumbered, you know.

"Honey, you do not seem to understand that the Negroes down here are still in their childhood as a people. You should know it, you've seen it all your life. They've made terrific progress in adapting themselves to white ways, but they're far from it yet. They were coming along fine, traveling at a rate they could absorb, more of 'em voting than ever before. Then the NAACP stepped in with its fantastic demands and shoddy ideas of government—can you blame the South for resenting being told what to do about its own people by people who have no idea of its daily problems?

"The NAACP doesn't care whether a Negro man owns or rents his land, how well he can farm, or whether or not he tries to learn a trade and stand on his own two feet—oh no, all the NAACP cares about is that man's vote.

"So, can you blame the South for wanting to resist an invasion by people who are apparently so ashamed of their race they want to get rid of it?

"How can you have grown up here, led the kind of life you've led, and can only see someone stomping on the Tenth Amendment? Jean Louise, they're trying to wreck us—where have you been?"

"Right here in Maycomb."

"What do you mean?"

"I mean I grew up right here in your house, and I never knew what was in your mind. I only heard what you said. You neglected to tell me that we were naturally better than the Negroes, bless their kinky heads, that they were able to go so far but so far only, you neglected to tell me what Mr. O'Hanlon told me yesterday. That was you talking down there, but you let Mr. O'Hanlon say it. You're a coward as well as a snob and a tyrant, Atticus. When you talked of justice you forgot to say that justice is something that has nothing to do with people—

"I heard you on the subject of Zeebo's boy this morning . . . nothing to do with our Calpurnia and what she's meant to us, how faithful she's been to us—you saw nigger, you saw NAACP, you balanced the equities, didn't you?

"I remember that rape case you defended, but I missed the point. You love justice, all right. Abstract justice written down item by item on a brief—nothing to do with that black boy, you just like a neat brief. His cause interfered with your orderly mind, and you had to work order out of disorder. It's a compulsion with you, and now it's coming home to you—"

She was on her feet, holding the back of the chair.

"Atticus, I'm throwing it at you and I'm gonna grind it in: you better go warn your younger friends that if they want to preserve Our Way of Life, it begins at home. It doesn't begin with the schools or the churches or anyplace but home. Tell 'em that, and use your blind, immoral, misguided, nigger-lovin' daughter as your example. Go in front of me with a bell and say, 'Unclean!' Point me out as your mistake. Point me out: Jean Louise Finch, who was exposed to all kinds of guff from the white trash she went to school with, but she might never have gone to school for all the influence it had on her. Everything that was Gospel to her she got at home from her father. You sowed the seeds in me, Atticus, and now it's coming home to you—"

"Are you finished with what you have to say?"

She sneered. "Not half through. I'll never forgive you for what you did to me. You cheated me, you've driven me out of my home and now I'm in a no-man's-land but good—there's no place for me any more in Maycomb, and I'll never be entirely at home anywhere else."

Her voice cracked. "Why in the name of God didn't you marry again? Marry some nice dim-witted Southern lady who would have raised me right? Turned me into a simpering, mealy-mouthed magnolia type who bats her eyelashes and crosses her hands and lives for nothing but her lil'ole hus-band. At least I would have been blissful. I'd have been typical one hundred per cent Maycomb; I would have lived out my little life and given you grandchildren to dote on; I would have spread out like Aunty, fanned myself on the front porch, and died happy. Why didn't you tell me the difference between justice and justice, and right and right? Why didn't you?"

"I didn't think it necessary, nor do I think so now."

"Well, it was necessary and you know it. God! And speaking of God, why didn't you make it very plain to me that God made the races and put the black folks in Africa with the intention of keeping them there so the missionaries could go tell them that Jesus loved 'em but meant for 'em to stay in Africa? That us bringing 'em over here was all a bad mistake, so they're to blame? That Jesus loved all mankind, but there are different kinds of men with separate fences around 'em, that Jesus meant that any man can go as far as he wants within that fence—"

"Jean Louise, come down to earth."

He said it so easily that she stopped short. Her wave of invective had crashed over him and still he sat there. He had declined to be angry. Somewhere within her she felt that she was no lady but no power on earth would prevent him from being a gentleman, yet the piston inside drove her on:

"All right, I'll come down to earth. I'll land right in the livingroom of our house. I'll come down to you. I believed in you. I looked up to you, Atticus, like I never looked up to anybody in my life and never will again. If you had only given me some hint, if you had only broken your word with me a couple of times, if you had been bad-tempered or impatient with me—if you had been a lesser man, maybe I could have taken what I saw you doing. If once or twice you'd let me catch you doing something vile, then I would have understood yesterday. Then I'd have said that's just His Way, that's My Old Man, because I'd have been prepared for it somewhere along the line—"

Her father's face was compassionate, almost pleading. "You seem to think I'm involved in something positively evil," he said. "The council's our only defense, Jean Louise—"

"Is Mr. O'Hanlon our only defense?"

"Baby, Mr. O'Hanlon's not, I'm happy to say, typical of the Maycomb County council membership. I hope you noticed my brevity in introducing him."

"You were sort of short, but Atticus, that man—"

"Mr. O'Hanlon's not prejudiced, Jean Louise. He's a sadist."

"Then why did you all let him get up there?"

"Because he wanted to."

"Sir?"

"Oh yes," said her father vaguely. "He goes about addressing citizens' councils all over the state. He asked permission to speak to ours and we gave it to him. I rather think he's paid by some organization in Massachusetts—"

Her father swung away from her and looked out the window. "I've been trying to make you see that the Maycomb council, at any rate, is simply a method of defense against—"

"Defense, hell! Atticus, we aren't on the Constitution now. I'm trying to make you see something. You now, you treat all people alike. I've never in my life seen you give that insolent, back-of-the-hand treatment half the white people down here give Negroes just when they're talking to them, just when they ask 'em to do something. There's no get-along-there-nigger in your voice when you talk to 'em.

"Yet you put out your hand in front of them as a people and say, 'Stop here. This is as far as you can go!'"

"I thought we agreed that—"

Her voice was heavy with sarcasm: "We've agreed that they're backward, that they're illiterate, that they're dirty and comical and shiftless and no good, they're infants and they're stupid, some of them, but we haven't agreed on one thing and we never will. You deny that they're human."

"How so?"

"You deny them hope. Any man in this world, Atticus, any man who has a head and arms and legs, was born with hope in his heart. You won't find that in the Constitution, I picked that up in church somewhere. They are simple people, most of them, but that doesn't make them subhuman.

"You are telling them that Jesus loves them, but not much. You are using frightful means to justify ends that you think are for the good of the most people. Your ends may well be right—I think I believe in the same ends— but you cannot use people as your pawns, Atticus. You cannot. Hitler and that crowd in Russia've done some lovely things for their lands, and they slaughtered tens of millions of people doing 'em. . . ."

Atticus smiled. "Hitler, eh?"

"You're no better. You're no damn better. You just try to kill their souls instead of their bodies. You just try to tell 'em, 'Look, be good. Behave yourselves. If you're good and mind us, you can get a lot out of life, but if you don't mind us, we will give you nothing and take away what we've already given you.'

"I know it's got to be slow, Atticus, I know that full well. But I know it's got to be. I wonder what would happen if the South had a 'Be Kind to the Niggers Week'? If just for one week the South would show them some simple, impartial courtesy. I wonder what would happen. Do you think it'd give 'em airs or the beginnings of self-respect? Have you ever been snubbed, Atticus? Do you know how it feels? No, don't tell me they're children and don't feel it: I was a child and felt it, so grown children must feel, too. A real good snub, Atticus, makes you feel like you're too nasty to associate with people. How they're as good as they are now is a mystery to me, after a hundred years of systematic denial that they're human. I wonder what kind of miracle we could work with a week's decency.

"There was no point in saying any of this because I know you won't give an inch and you never will. You've cheated me in a way that's inexpressible, but don't let it worry you, because the joke is entirely on me. You're the only person I think I've ever fully trusted and now I'm done for."

"I've killed you, Scout. I had to."

"Don't you give me any more double-talk! You're a nice, sweet, old gentleman, and I'll never believe a word you say to me again. I despise you and everything you stand for."

"Well, I love you."

"Don't you dare say that to me! Love me, huh! Atticus, I'm getting out of this place fast, I don't know where I'm going but I'm going. I never want to see another Finch or hear of one as long as I live!"

"As you please."

"You double-dealing, ring-tailed old son of a bitch! You just sit there and say 'As you please' when you've knocked me down and stomped on me and spat on me, you just sit there and say 'As you please' when everything I ever loved in this world's—you just sit there and say 'As you please'—you love me! *You son of a bitch!*"

"That'll do, Jean Louise."

That'll do, his general call to order in the days when she believed. So he kills me and gives it a twist . . . how can he taunt me so? How can he treat me so? God in heaven, take me away from here . . . God in heaven, take me away. . . .

VII

PART VII

18

She never knew how she got the car started, how she held it in the road, how she got home without a serious accident.

I love you. As you please. Had he not said that, perhaps she would have survived. If he had fought her fairly, she could have flung his words back at him, but she could not catch mercury and hold it in her hands.

She went to her room and threw her suitcase onto the bed. I was born right where this suitcase is. Why didn't you throttle me then? Why did you let me live this long?

"Jean Louise, what are you doing?"

"Packing, Aunty."

Alexandra came to the side of the bed. "You have ten more days with us. Is something wrong?"

"Aunty, leave me alone for Christ's sake!"

Alexandra bridled. "I'll thank you not to use that Yankee expression in this house! What's wrong?"

Jean Louise went to the closet, snatched her dresses from their hangers, returned to the bed, and crammed them into her suitcase.

"That's no way to pack," said Alexandra.

"It's my way."

She scooped up her shoes from beside the bed and threw them in after her dresses.

"What is it, Jean Louise?"

"Aunty, you may issue a communiqué to the effect that I am going so far away from Maycomb County it'll take me a hundred years to get back! I never want to see it or anybody in it again, and that goes for every one of you, the undertaker, the probate judge, and the chairman of the board of the Methodist Church!"

"You've had a fight with Atticus, haven't you?"

"I have."

Alexandra sat on the bed and clasped her hands. "Jean Louise, I don't know what it was about, and the way you look it must have been bad, but I do know this. No Finch runs."

She turned to her aunt: "Jesus Christ, don't you go telling me what a Finch does and what a Finch doesn't do! I'm up to here with what Finches do, and I can't take it one second longer! You've been ramming that down my throat ever since I was born—your father this, the Finches that! My father's something unspeakable and Uncle Jack's like Alice in Wonderland! And you, you are a pompous, narrow-minded old—"

Jean Louise stopped, fascinated by the tears running down Alexandra's cheeks. She had never seen Alexandra cry; Alexandra looked like other people when she cried.

"Aunty, please forgive me. Please say it—I hit you below the belt."

Alexandra's fingers pulled tufts of tatting from the bedspread. "That's all right. Don't you worry about it."

Jean Louise kissed her aunt's cheek. "I haven't been on the track today. I guess when you're hurt your first instinct's to hurt back. I'm not much of a lady, Aunty, but you are."

"You're mistaken, Jean Louise, if you think you're no lady," said Alexandra. She wiped her eyes. "But you are right peculiar sometimes."

Jean Louise closed her suitcase. "Aunty, you go on thinking I'm a lady, just for a little while, just until five o'clock when Atticus comes home. Then you'll find out different. Well, goodbye."

She was carrying her suitcase to the car when she saw the town's one white taxi drive up and deposit Dr. Finch on the sidewalk.

Come to me. When you can't stand it any longer, come to me. Well, I can't stand you any longer. I just can't take any more of your parables and diddering around. Leave me alone. You are fun and sweet and all that, but please leave me alone.

From the corner of her eye, she watched her uncle tacking peacefully up the driveway. He takes such long steps for a short man, she thought. That is one of the things I will remember about him. She turned and put a key in the lock of the trunk, the wrong key, and she tried another one. It worked, and she raised the lid.

"Going somewhere?"

"Yes sir."

"Where?"

"I'm gonna get in this car and drive it to Maycomb Junction and sit there until the first train comes along and get on it. Tell Atticus if he wants his car back he can send after it."

"Stop feeling sorry for yourself and listen to me."

"Uncle Jack, I am so sick and damn tired of listening to the lot of you I could yell bloody murder! Won't you leave me alone? Can't you get off my back for one minute?"

She slammed down the trunk lid, snatched out the key, and straightened up to catch Dr. Finch's savage backhand swipe full on the mouth.

Her head jerked to the left and met his hand coming viciously back. She stumbled and groped for the car to balance herself. She saw her uncle's face shimmering among the tiny dancing lights.

"I am trying," said Dr. Finch, "to attract your attention."

She pressed her fingers to her eyes, her temples, to the sides of her head. She struggled to keep from fainting, to keep from vomiting, to keep her head from spinning. She felt blood spring to her teeth, and she spat blindly on the ground. Gradually, the gonglike reverberations in her head subsided, and her ears stopped ringing.

"Open your eyes, Jean Louise."

She blinked several times, and her uncle snapped into focus. His walking stick nestled in his left elbow; his vest was immaculate; there was a scarlet rosebud in his lapel.

He was holding out his handkerchief to her. She took it and wiped her mouth. She was exhausted.

"All passion spent?"

She nodded. "I can't fight them any more," she said.

Dr. Finch took her by the arm. "But you can't join 'em, either, can you?" he muttered.

She felt her mouth swelling and she moved her lips with difficulty. "You nearly knocked me cold. I'm so tired."

Silently, he walked her to the house, down the hall, and into the bathroom. He sat her on the edge of the tub, went to the medicine cabinet, and opened it. He put on his glasses, tilted his head back, and took a bottle from the top shelf. He plucked a wad of cotton from a package and turned to her.

"Hold up your mug," he said. He filled the cotton with liquid, turned back to her upper lip, made a hideous face, and dabbed at her cuts. "This'll keep you from giving yourself something. Zandra!" he shouted.

Alexandra appeared from the kitchen. "What is it, Jack? Jean Louise, I thought you—"

"Never mind that. Is there any missionary vanilla in this house?"

"Jack, don't be silly."

"Come on, now. I know you keep it for fruitcakes. Gracious God, Sister, get me some whiskey! Go in the livingroom, Jean Louise."

She walked in her daze to the livingroom and sat down. Her uncle came in carrying in one hand a tumbler three fingersful of whiskey, and in the other a glass of water.

"If you drink all this at once I'll give you a dime," he said.

Jean Louise drank and choked.

"Hold your breath, stupid. Now chase it."

She grabbed for the water and drank rapidly. She kept her eyes closed and let the warm alcohol creep through her. When she opened them she saw her uncle sitting on the sofa contemplating her placidly.

Presently he said, "How do you feel?"

"Hot."

"That's the liquor. Tell me what's in your head now."

She said weakly: "A blank, my lord."

"Fractious girl, don't you quote at me! Tell me, how do you feel?"

She frowned, squeezed her eyelids together, and touched her tender mouth with her tongue. "Different, somehow. I'm sitting right here, and it's just like I'm sitting in my apartment in New York. I don't know—I feel funny."

Dr. Finch rose and thrust his hands into his pockets, drew them out, and cradled his arms behind his back. "We-ll now, I think I'll just go and have myself a drink on that. I never struck a woman before in my life. Think I'll go strike your aunt and see what happens. You just sit there for a while and be quiet."

Jean Louise sat there, and giggled when she heard her uncle fussing at his sister in the kitchen. "Of course I'm going to have a drink, Zandra. I deserve one. I don't go about hittin' women every day, and I tell you if you're not used to it, it takes it out of you . . . oh,

she's all right . . . I fail to detect the difference between drinking it and eatin' it . . . we're all of us going
to hell, it's just a question of time . . . don't be such
an old pot, Sister, I'm not lyin' on the floor yet . . .
why don't you have one?"

She felt that time had stopped and she was inside a
not unpleasant vacuum. There was no land around, and
no beings, but there was an aura of vague friendliness
in this indifferent place. I'm getting high, she thought.

Her uncle bounced back into the livingroom, sip-
ping from a tall glass filled with ice, water, and whiskey. "Look what I got out of Zandra. I've played hell
with her fruitcakes."

Jean Louise attempted to pin him down: "Uncle
Jack," she said. "I have a definite idea that you know
what happened this afternoon."

"I do. I know every word you said to Atticus, and I
almost heard you from my house when you lit into
Henry."

The old bastard, he followed me to town.

"You eavesdropped? Of all the—"

"Of course not. Do you think you can discuss it
now?"

Discuss it? "Yes, I think so. That is, if you'll talk
straight to me. I don't think I can take Bishop Colenso
now."

Dr. Finch arranged himself neatly on the sofa and leaned in toward her. He said, "I will talk straight to you, my darling. Do you know why? Because I can, now."

"Because you can?"

"Yes. Look back, Jean Louise. Look back to yesterday, to the Coffee this morning, to this afternoon—"

"What do you know about this morning?"

"Have you never heard of the telephone? Zandra was glad to answer a few judicious questions. You telegraph your pitches all over the place, Jean Louise. This afternoon I tried to give you some help in a roundabout way to make it easier for you, to give you some insight, to soften it a little—"

"To soften what, Uncle Jack?"

"To soften your coming into this world."

When Dr. Finch pulled at his drink, Jean Louise saw his sharp brown eyes flash above the glass. That's what you tend to forget about him, she thought. He's so busy fidgeting you don't notice how closely he's watching you. He's crazy, all right, like every fox that was ever born. And he knows so much more than foxes. Gracious, I'm drunk.

". . . look back, now," her uncle was saying. "It's still there, isn't it?"

She looked. It was there, all right. Every word of it.

But something was different. She sat in silence, remembering.

"Uncle Jack," she finally said. "Everything's still there. It happened. It was. But you know, it's bearable somehow. It's—it's bearable."

She was speaking the truth. She had not made the journey through time that makes all things bearable. Today was today, and she looked at her uncle in wonder.

"Thank God," said Dr. Finch quietly. "Do you know why it's bearable now, my darling?"

"No sir. I'm content with things as they are. I don't want to question, I just want to stay this way."

She was conscious of her uncle's eyes upon her, and she moved her head to one side. She was far from trusting him: if he starts on Mackworth Praed and tells me I'm just like him I'll be at Maycomb Junction before sundown.

"You'd eventually figure this out for yourself," she heard him say. "But let me speed it up for you. You've had a busy day. It's bearable, Jean Louise, because you are your own person now."

Not Mackworth Praed's, mine. She looked up at her uncle.

Dr. Finch stretched out his legs. "It's rather complicated," he said, "and I don't want you to fall into the tiresome error of being conceited about your complexes—you'd bore us for the rest of our lives with that, so we'll keep away from it. Every man's island, Jean Louise, every man's watchman, is his conscience. There is no such thing as a collective conscious."

This was news, coming from him. But let him talk, he would find his way to the nineteenth century somehow.

". . . now you, Miss, born with your own conscience, somewhere along the line fastened it like a barnacle onto your father's. As you grew up, when you were grown, totally unknown to yourself, you confused your father with God. You never saw him as a man with a man's heart, and a man's failings—I'll grant you it may have been hard to see, he makes so few mistakes, but he makes 'em like all of us. You were an emotional cripple, leaning on him, getting the answers from him, assuming that your answers would always be his answers."

She listened to the figure on the sofa.

"When you happened along and saw him doing something that seemed to you to be the very antithesis of his conscience—your conscience—you literally could not stand it. It made you physically ill. Life became hell on earth for you. You had to kill yourself, or he had to kill you to get you functioning as a separate entity."

Kill myself. Kill him. I had to kill him to live . . . "You talk like you've known this a long time. You—"

"I have. So's your father. We wondered, sometimes, when your conscience and his would part company, and over what." Dr. Finch smiled. "Well, we know now. I'm just thankful I was around when the ructions started. Atticus couldn't talk to you the way I'm talking—"

"Why not, sir?"

"You wouldn't have listened to him. You couldn't have listened. Our gods are remote from us, Jean Louise. They must never descend to human level."

"Is that why he didn't—didn't lam into me? Is that why he didn't even try to defend himself?"

"He was letting you break your icons one by one. He was letting you reduce him to the status of a human being."

I love you. As you please. Where she would have had a spirited argument only, an exchange of ideas, a clash of hard and different points of view with a friend, with him she had tried to destroy. She had tried to tear him to pieces, to wreck him, to obliterate him. Childe Roland to the dark tower came.

"Do you understand me, Jean Louise?"

"Yes, Uncle Jack, I understand you."

Dr. Finch crossed his legs and jammed his hands into his pockets. "When you stopped running, Jean Louise, and turned around, that turn took fantastic courage."

"Sir?"

"Oh, not the kind of courage that makes a soldier go across no-man's-land. That's the kind that he summons up because he has to. This kind is—well, it is part of one's will to live, part of one's instinct for self-preservation. Sometimes, we have to kill a little so we can live, when we don't—when women don't, they cry themselves to sleep and have their mothers wash out their hose every day."

"What do you mean, when I stopped running?"

Dr. Finch chuckled. "You know," he said. "You're very much like your father. I tried to point that out to you today; I regret to say I used tactics the late George Washington Hill would envy—you're very much like him, except you're a bigot and he's not."

"I beg your pardon?"

Dr. Finch bit his under lip and let it go. "Um hum. A bigot. Not a big one, just an ordinary turnip-sized bigot."

Jean Louise rose and went to the bookshelves. She pulled down a dictionary and leafed through it. "'Bigot,'" she read. "'Noun. One obstinately or intolerably devoted to his own church, party, belief, or opinion.' Explain yourself, sir."

"I was just tryin' to answer your running question. Let me elaborate a little on that definition. What does a bigot do when he meets someone who challenges his opinions? He doesn't give. He stays rigid. Doesn't even try to listen, just lashes out. Now you, you were turned inside out by the granddaddy of all father things, so you ran. And how you ran.

"You've no doubt heard some pretty offensive talk since you've been home, but instead of getting on your charger and blindly striking it down, you turned and ran. You said, in effect, 'I don't like the way these people do, so I have no time for them.' You'd better take time for 'em, honey, otherwise you'll never grow. You'll be the same at sixty as you are now—then you'll be a case and not my niece. You have a tendency not to give anybody elbow room in your mind for their ideas, no matter how silly you think they are."

Dr. Finch clasped his hands and rested them on the back of his head. "Good grief, baby, people don't agree with the Klan, but they certainly don't try to prevent them from puttin' on sheets and making fools of themselves in public."

"Why did you let Mr. O'Hanlon get up there?" "Because he wanted to." Oh God, what have I done?

"But they beat people, Uncle Jack—"

"Now, that's another thing, and it's just one more thing you've failed to take into consideration about your father. You've been extravagant with your talk of despots, Hitlers, and ring-tailed sons of bitches—by the way, where did you get that? Reminds me of a cold winter's night, possum hunting—"

Jean Louise winced. "He told you all that?"

"Oh yes, but don't start worrying about what you called him. He's got a lawyer's hide. He's been called worse in his day."

"Not by his daughter, though."

"Well, as I was saying—"

For the first time in her memory, her uncle was bringing her back to the point. For the second time in her memory, her uncle was out of character: the first time was when he sat mutely in their old livingroom, listening to the soft murmurs: the Lord never sends you more than you can bear, and he said, "My shoulders ache. Is there any whiskey in this house?" This is a day of miracles, she thought.

"—the Klan can parade around all it wants, but when it starts bombing and beating people, don't you know who'd be the first to try and stop it?"

"Yes sir."

"The law is what he lives by. He'll do his best to prevent someone from beating up somebody else, then he'll turn around and try to stop no less than the Federal Government—just like you, child. You turned and tackled no less than your own tin god—but remember this, he'll always do it by the letter and by the spirit of the law. That's the way he lives."

"Uncle Jack—"

"Now don't start feeling guilty, Jean Louise. You've done nothing wrong this day. And don't, for the sake of John Henry Newman, start worrying over what a bigot you are. I told you you were only a turnip-sized one."

"But Uncle Jack—"

"Remember this also: it's always easy to look back and see what we were, yesterday, ten years ago. It is hard to see what we are. If you can master that trick, you'll get along."

"Uncle Jack, I thought I'd gone through all that being-disillusioned-about-your-parents stuff when I took my bachelor's degree, but there's something—"

Her uncle began fidgeting with his coat pockets. He found what he was seeking, pulled one from the package, and said, "Have you a match?"

Jean Louise was mesmerized.

"I said, do you have a match?"

"Have you gone nuts? You beat hell out of me when you caught me at it . . . you old bastard!"

He had, unceremoniously, one Christmas when he found her under the house with stolen cigarettes.

"This should prove to you there's no justice in this

world. I smoke sometimes, now. It's my one concession to old age. I find myself becoming anxious sometimes . . . it gives me something to do with my hands."

Jean Louise found a match flip on the table by her
chair. She struck one and held it to her uncle's cigarette. Something to do with his hands, she thought. She
wondered how many times his hands in rubber gloves,
impersonal and omnipotent, had set some child on its
feet. He's crazy, all right.

Dr. Finch held his cigarette with his thumb and two
fingers. He looked at it pensively. "You're color blind,
Jean Louise," he said. "You always have been, you
always will be. The only differences you see between
one human and another are differences in looks and
intelligence and character and the like. You've never
been prodded to look at people as a race, and now that
race is the burning issue of the day, you're still unable
to think racially. You see only people."

"But, Uncle Jack, I don't especially want to run out
and marry a Negro or something."

"You know, I practiced medicine for nearly twenty
years, and I'm afraid I regard human beings mostly on
a basis of relative suffering, but I'll risk a small pro-
nouncement. There's nothing under the sun that says
because you go to school with one Negro, or go to school
with them in droves, you'll want to marry one. That's

one of the tom-toms the white supremacists beat. How many mixed marriages have you seen in New York?"

"Come to think of it, darn few. Relatively, that is."

"There's your answer. The white supremacists are really pretty smart. If they can't scare us with the essential inferiority line, they'll wrap it in a miasma of sex, because that's the one thing they know is feared in our fundamentalist hearts down here. They try to strike terror in Southern mothers, lest their children grow up to fall in love with Negroes. If they didn't make an issue of it, the issue would rarely arise. If the issue arose, it would be met on private ground. The NAACP has a great deal to answer for in that department, too. But the white supremacists fear reason, because they know cold reason beats them. Prejudice, a dirty word, and faith, a clean one, have something in common: they both begin where reason ends."

"That's odd, isn't it?"

"It's one of the oddities of this world." Dr. Finch got up from the sofa and extinguished his cigarette in an ashtray on the table beside her. "Now, young lady, take me home. It's nearly five. It's almost time for you to fetch your father."

Jean Louise surfaced. "Get Atticus? I'll never be able to look him in the eye again!"

"Listen, girl. You've got to shake off a twenty-year-old habit and shake it off fast. You will begin now. Do you think Atticus is going to hurl a thunderbolt at you?"

"After what I said to him? After the—"

Dr. Finch jabbed the floor with his walking stick. "Jean Louise, have you ever met your father?"

No. She had not. She was terrified.

"I think you'll have a surprise coming," said her uncle.

"Uncle Jack, I can't."

"Don't you tell me you can't, girl! Say that again and I'll take this stick to you, I mean that!"

They walked to the car.

"Jean Louise, have you ever thought about coming home?"

"Home?"

"If you will refrain from echoing either the last clause or the last word of everything I say to you, I will be much obliged. Home. Yes, home."

Jean Louise grinned. He was becoming Uncle Jack again. "No sir," she said.

"Well, at the risk of overloading you, could you possibly give an undertaking to think about it? You may not know it, but there's room for you down here."

"You mean Atticus needs me?"

"Not altogether. I was thinking of Maycomb."

"That'd be great, with me on one side and everybody else on the other. If life's an endless flow of the kind of talk I heard this morning, I don't think I'd exactly fit in."

"That's the one thing about here, the South, you've missed. You'd be amazed if you knew how many people are on your side, if *side*'s the right word. You're no special case. The woods are full of people like you, but we need some more of you."

She started the car and backed it down the driveway. She said, "What on earth could I do? I can't fight them. There's no fight in me any more. . . ."

"I don't mean by fighting; I mean by going to work every morning, coming home at night, seeing your friends."

"Uncle Jack, I can't live in a place that I don't agree with and that doesn't agree with me."

Dr. Finch said, "Hmph. Melbourne said—"

"If you tell me what Melbourne said I'll stop this car and put you out, right here! I know how you hate to walk—after your stroll to church and back and pushin' that cat around the yard, you've had it. I'll put you right out, and don't you think I won't!"

Dr. Finch sighed. "You're mighty belligerent toward a feeble old man, but if you wish to continue in darkness that is your privilege. . . ."

"Feeble, hell! You're about as feeble as a crocodile!"
Jean Louise touched her mouth.

"Very well, if you won't let me tell you what Melbourne said I'll put it in my own words: the time your friends need you is when they're wrong, Jean Louise. They don't need you when they're right—"

"What do you mean?"

"I mean it takes a certain kind of maturity to live in the South these days. You don't have it yet, but you have a shadow of the beginnings of it. You haven't the humbleness of mind—"

"I thought fear of the Lord was the beginning of wisdom."

"It's the same thing. Humility."

They had come to his house. She stopped the car.

"Uncle Jack," she said. "What am I going to do about Hank?"

"What you will eventually," he said.

"Let him down easy?"

"Um hum."

"Why?"

"He's not your kind."

Love whom you will, marry your own kind. "Look, I'm not going to argue with you over the relative merits of trash—"

"That has nothing to do with it. I'm tired of you. I want my supper."

Dr. Finch put his hand out and pinched her chin. "Good afternoon, Miss," he said.

"Why did you take so much trouble with me today? I know how you hate to move out of that house."

"Because you're my child. You and Jem were the children I never had. You two gave me something long ago, and I'm trying to pay my debts. You two helped me a—"

"How, sir?"

Dr. Finch's eyebrows went up. "Didn't you know? Hasn't Atticus gotten around to telling you that? Why, I'm amazed at Zandra not . . . good heavens, I thought all of Maycomb knew that."

"Knew what?"

"I was in love with your mother."

"My mother?"

"Oh yes. When Atticus married her, and I'd come home from Nashville for Christmas and things like that, why I fell head over heels in love with her. I still am—didn't you know that?"

Jean Louise put her head on the steering wheel. "Uncle Jack, I'm so ashamed of myself I don't know what to do. Me yelling around like—oh, I could kill myself!"

"I shouldn't do that. There's been enough focal suicide for one day."

"All that time, you—"

"Why sure, honey."

"Did Atticus know it?"

"Certainly."

"Uncle Jack, I feel one inch high."

"Well, I didn't mean to do *that*. You're not by yourself, Jean Louise. You're no special case. Now go get your father."

"You can say all this, just like that?"

"Um hum. Just like that. As I said, you and Jem were very special to me—you were my dream-children, but as Kipling said, that's another story . . . call on me tomorrow, and you'll find me a grave man."

He was the only person she ever knew who could paraphrase three authors into one sentence and have them all make sense.

"Thanks, Uncle Jack."

"Thank *you*, Scout."

Dr. Finch got out of the car and shut the door. He poked his head inside the window, elevated his eyebrows, and said in a decorous voice:

"I was once an exceedingly odd young lady—
Suffering much from spleen and vapors."

Jean Louise was halfway to town when she remembered. She stepped on the brake, leaned out the window, and called to the spare figure in the distance:

"But we only cut respectable capers, don't we, Uncle Jack?"

19

S he walked into the foyer of the office. She saw Henry still at his desk. She went to him.

"Hank?"

"Hello," he said.

"Seven-thirty tonight?" she said.

"Yes."

As they made a date for their leave-taking, a tide was running, returning, and she ran to meet it. He was a part of her, as timeless as Finch's Landing, as the Coninghams and Old Sarum. Maycomb and Maycomb County had taught him things she had never known, could never learn, and Maycomb had rendered her useless to him as anything other than his oldest friend.

"That you, Jean Louise?"

Her father's voice frightened her.

"Yes sir."

Atticus walked from his office to the foyer and took

down his hat and stick from the hat rack. "Ready?" he said.

Ready. You can say ready to me. What are you, that I tried to obliterate and grind into the earth, and you say ready? I can't beat you, I can't join you. Don't you know that?

She went to him. "Atticus," she said. "I'm—"

"You may be sorry, but I'm proud of you."

She looked up and saw her father beaming at her.

"What?"

"I said I'm proud of you."

"I don't understand you. I don't understand men at all and I never will."

"Well, I certainly hoped a daughter of mine'd hold her ground for what she thinks is right—stand up to me first of all."

Jean Louise rubbed her nose. "I called you some pretty grim things," she said.

Atticus said, "I can take anything anybody calls me so long as it's not true. You don't even know how to cuss, Jean Louise. By the way, where did you pick up the ring-tailed variety?"

"Right here in Maycomb."

"Dear goodness, the things you learned."

Dear goodness, the things I learned. I did not want my world disturbed, but I wanted to crush the man who's trying to preserve it for me. I wanted to stamp out all the people like him. I guess it's like an airplane: they're the drag and we're the thrust, together we make the thing fly. Too much of us and we're nose-heavy, too much of them and we're tail-heavy—it's a matter of balance. I can't beat him, and I can't join him—

"Atticus?"

"Ma'am?"

"I think I love you very much."

She saw her old enemy's shoulders relax, and she watched him push his hat to the back of his head. "Let's go home, Scout. It's been a long day. Open the door for me."

She stepped aside to let him pass. She followed him to the car and watched him get laboriously into the front seat. As she welcomed him silently to the human race, the stab of discovery made her tremble a little. Somebody walked over my grave, she thought, probably Jem on some idiotic errand.

She went around the car, and as she slipped under the steering wheel, this time she was careful not to bump her head.

About the Author

H ARPER LEE was born in 1926 in Monroeville, Alabama. She is the author of the acclaimed *To Kill a Mockingbird*, and has been awarded the Pulitzer Prize, the Presidential Medal of Freedom, and numerous other literary awards and honors.

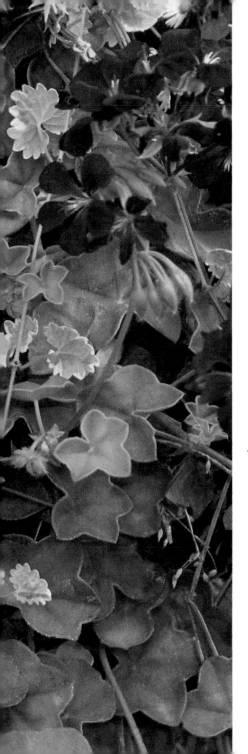

Success with

Hanging Baskets
and
Trailing Plants

MARTIN WEIMAR

Series Editor:
LESLEY YOUNG

LANDOLL'S

Foreword

Contents

Many people love the idea of a hanging garden on their balcony or patio and it is not at all difficult to design and create an overhead display of flowers and scented herbs in a favorite corner or above a garden seat. In this useful guide, Martin Weimar shows you how to transform your balcony or patio with the help of hanging baskets, boxes, and other interesting plant containers.

There are lots of practical tips on securing the containers and on ways of grouping plants in them, as well as advice on the right way to water your plants and on overwintering them. Full-color step-by-step illustrations show the correct way to do all that is necessary to create a lovely, year-round display. The section on design suggests attractive ways of grouping plants and the instructions given are easy for a novice gardener to follow. The book is divided into sections on sun-loving, semi-shade-loving and shade-loving plants to enable you to choose the right plants for each site.

The herbs in this basket smell delicious in the sunshine.

Petunias.

Patience-plants.

The author
Martin Weimar is a gardener and flower artist who has contributed to numerous art exhibitions. For many years he has given courses on designing with plants and has written several successful guides on this subject.

The photographer
Jürgen Stork has worked as a freelance photographer since 1982, mainly in the areas of fashion, advertising and nature. He has contributed photographs to many periodicals and to many of the titles in the "Success with" gardening series.

The illustrator
Renate Holzner lives in Regensburg and works as a freelance illustrator and graphic designer. Her wide range extends from line drawings to photo-realistic computer graphics. Among her regular clients are many well-known publishing companies.

NB: Please read the Author's note on page 60 in order that your enjoyment of hanging baskets and trailing plants may not be spoiled.

Hanging flowers

There is no reason why flowering plants should remain firmly rooted in the ground. With a little help from you your plants can conquer the heights on airy balconies and patios.

Photo above: Patience-plants are decorative in shady places.
Photo left: Rudbeckia, lobelia, ivy, and patience-plant waiting to be planted in baskets.

Hanging flowers

Cascades of flowers on different levels

Many people would love to accommodate more and more plants on a balcony or patio that is already packed with luxuriant greenery but are not sure where to fit them in. Do not despair: there is more room – above your head – and this guide will show you a multitude of possibilities for adding to your plant collection. You can design attractive arrangements in hanging baskets or even plant them in your own individually designed plant containers. If you choose the right plants and care for them properly, your overhead garden will turn into a feast for the eye and can even provide food for the table.

The Hanging Gardens of Babylon

One of the seven wonders of the ancient world was the legendary garden that Semiramis, Queen of Babylon, is supposed to have created some 3,000 years ago. She built the famous Hanging Gardens of Babylon, so the story goes, to remind her of the beautiful mountainous area that she came from. The gardens were built on a slope, in many step-like terraces, one above the other.

You could design a hanging garden of your own on a balcony or patio, for example with a plant stair (photo, right) or by using a table covered in flowering plants (see p. 43).

Beauty for every season

Annual plants are ideal for planting in a hanging garden. During the course of a single year, these plants will grow and flourish and will often bloom continuously throughout a whole season. In addition, with annuals, the trouble of overwintering is avoided. Each season different plant groupings can be put together to take full advantage of their flowering times.

Spring flowers, like pansies, forget-me-nots, primroses, or wallflowers, are ideal for an early, frost-hardy arrangement.

Summer flowers, like petunias, pelargoniums, or lobelias can be planted after the last cold snap of late spring. They make an attractive eye-catching feature during the summer months. When fall arrives, they can be removed or, depending on the type of plant, overwintered in frost-free conditions (for overwintering, see p. 56).

Fall plants like *Erica*, chrysanthemums or asters will cope with a few degrees of frost. Many spring-flowering plants are offered for sale as early as the previous fall. With the correct care during the winter (see p. 56), they will remain hardy and present a continuous display from fall until late spring.

Perennial planting

A hanging garden of perennials can be maintained for many years. This will, of course, require a certain amount of attention to correct care and overwintering (see p. 56). Many hardy perennials (see plant list, p. 40) will flower for only a short while but will continue to look good for the rest of the time because of their attractive green foliage.

Planning ahead

You will be able to enjoy your planting arrangements without any real problems if you consider some important points before you begin.

● Observe the light and climatic conditions at the chosen site and choose plants that will thrive in these conditions.

● Use suitable containers and make sure they are adequately secured (see pp. 10-17).

● When placing containers in certain positions, think of plant care and access etc. (see pp. 44-57). Plants that are difficult to reach generally end up being given less care.

● Make sure nothing is dangling down in your way or hinders access to areas used often, for example a seat. Always hang the

A flowering staircase.

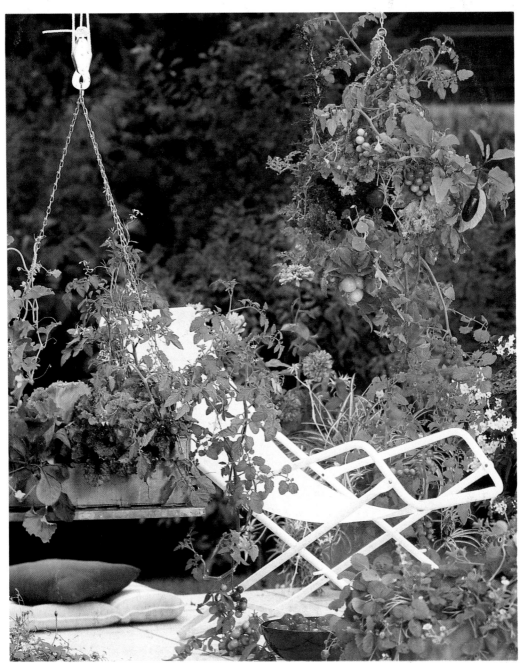

Fruit and vegetables ready to pick.

containers in such a way that you will be unable to injure yourself on them and so that neither the plants nor your furniture can get damaged.
● Choose plants with the most suitable shapes of growth for the intended position.
● When securing heavy containers in their position, think about weight distribution and any legal responsibility you may have (see p. 15).

Designing with plants

You can increase the effect of individual plants if you remember a few rules of good design when combining them (see design ideas, pp. 20-43). A clever selection and the arrangement of plants according to their shapes of growth are particularly important points when planting a hanging garden.

Shapes of growth

You can grow plants so that cascades of flowers and foliage burst out of the containers. Look for plants with very different shapes of growth.
● Creeping or rhizome-forming plants like convolvulus (*Convolvulus sabatius*), *Scaevola*, ground ivy (*Glechoma hederacea*), strawberry plants, *Chlorophytum comosum,* and ivy are ideal for making decorative hanging curtains.
● Plants that grow in the shape of large cushions, like *Portulaca, Dorotheanthus bellidiformis,* and *Gazania* (see p. 23) work best if they are planted close to the edge of the container. Here they will form an attractive link between the plants that grow upward and those that hang downward.
● Plants that are bushy and pendulous, for example hanging fuchsias, hanging pelargoniums, or hanging begonias, will send a wealth of blooms upward as well as downward (see p. 38).
● Some climbing and trailing plants, such as *Rhodochiton atrosanguineus* or nasturtium, will not require climbing aids and will grow easily over the middle and upper sections of an arrangement (see p. 32).
● Plants with upright growth, like kitchen herbs (see p. 24), are ideal for the upper level.

Planting for the best display

The level at which plants are to be grown will also determine your choice of shape and attitude of growth.
Hanging containers *at eye-level* look very effective with a combination of different shapes of growth. The upper, middle and lower parts of the planting will all be easy to see.
Plants placed *below eye-level* look best with upright, cushion-forming and bushy, overhanging plants. However, only the upper parts of the plants and those hanging over the edge of the container will be visible to the onlooker.
Containers placed *above eye-level* do not require any plants that send their flowers upward. Here, all shapes of growth can be used provided they look decorative from below.
Balcony railings, banisters, plant tables, and plant stairs can all be equipped with different shapes of growth depending on the local conditions and climate.

Hanging flowers

Buying plants

Nurseries, garden centers, and markets offer a wide selection of seasonal plants as well as ready-to-plant, flowering young plants. Your decision will depend not only on the price – young plants are cheaper – but also on the way you intend to plant them (see pp. 12-13). Vegetables are obtainable as young plants only. Growing your own plants from seed is recommended if you wish to cultivate rarities (see planting night-scented plants, p. 62) in your hanging garden and they are not available as seedlings. A few seed mail-order firms offer special seed mixtures for hanging gardens.

The right soil

You can use the same pre-fertilized plant compost for hanging containers that you would for balcony boxes and can obtain the various different types of compost in the trade. Garden soil is too heavy for use in containers and has a tendency to become compacted very easily. A good, light soil with a high capacity for storing water can be obtained by mixing 3 parts of garden soil with 3 parts of well-rotted, sifted garden compost and 2 parts each of peat or sand. Alternatively, mix garden soil and purchased flower compost in a ratio of 1:1.

Positioning the plants

Depending on the site and conditions (see p. 36), you can arrange plants to one side to make a splendid display, or in the round. Garden centers offer a wide range of containers for variations on both of these basic concepts.

Hanging baskets

One of the most ideal containers for planting an attractive all-round arrangement is a large-mesh, stable basket made of painted wire, with chains for hanging it up. Such planting containers have been used very successfully for years in many countries. A profusion of flowers pours from every opening, as both the walls and the bottom of the basket are planted through. Nowadays these baskets can be obtained almost anywhere in a range of sizes and colors, semi-spherical or with a flattened bottom. Planting them successfully requires a little skill, however (see pp. 12-13).
Alternative: If you do not own a ready-made basket, you can use a large-mesh bicycle basket made of painted wire or something similar (see photo, p. 42).
Accessories: Wire baskets require strong, ornamental hooks or brackets (see p. 13) for securing them to a house wall.

These baskets can also be obtained in the form of semi-spherical bowls for securing to a wall.

Chains, wires and ropes

Builders' suppliers, hardware stores, rope makers and ship's chandlers can all provide useful supports for securing hanging plants.
Chains can be found in various sizes. They are distinguished by their type and capacity for carrying weight. Circular steel-link chains are very strong and are suitable for securing heavyweight plant containers. Ornamental chains are only suitable for very light containers.

My tip: The best plan is to have chains cut to the right length at the time of purchase. Thick chain links, in particular, cannot be cut or taken apart without using bolt cutters or a hacksaw.

Petunias in brilliant colors. These classic balcony flowers are always charming.

Wire can be obtained on a roll in various thicknesses. Galvanized or green plastic-coated tying wire is particularly suitable. Tying wire of the sort used for making garlands or wreaths is too weak.

Galvanized wire ropes are obtainable in different gauges. They are distinguished by their weight-carrying capacity. They will need to be equipped with rope clamps (see p. 17) for hanging them up. They can be cut with sharp pliers or wire cutters.

Warning: The ends of lengths of cut wire are sharp and can cause injuries.

Plastic-coated ropes and straps are also suitable for hanging up containers. Fixing and securing them is relatively uncomplicated and they are very strong and durable. They are also obtainable in bright colors to give a plant arrangement that extra something, but do consider whether this could clash with the colors of the flowers in the basket.

Planting baskets

If you look around any garden center or residential street you will be amazed by the luxuriantly flowering hanging baskets used for decorating balconies and patios. You can easily make your own beautiful hanging baskets if you follow a few rules.

Equipment

The following accessories are required:
a basket with a chain (see p. 10);
inserts to keep the compost in the basket and cover the lining (see below). Traditionally, sphagnum moss was used but moss from your own lawn or loose coconut fiber matting from a florist or garden center is better for ecological reasons. Cardboard, textile, or foam inserts can be obtained from garden centers. Some of these are biodegradable, recyclable products.

NB: Loose lining material is not a substitute for compost. You should use lining material of the correct thickness for lining the walls of the basket so that your plants have as much compost as possible to hold nutrients and water;
polyethlene to keep moisture in and prevent water from running out unhindered;
plants – for a basket with a diameter of 14 in (35 cm), depending on the size of the plants, about 10-15 plants depending on how large they grow and their habit of growth. Ideas for suitable plants are given throughout this book in the relevant sections.

1 A basket with insert and lining.

3 Carefully thread the plants through the wall.

2 Cover only the bottom with the lining.

4 Wrap moss around the neck of the root.

Using young plants

Advantages: They are less expensive. The small rootstocks are easy to insert through the mesh of the wire.
Disadvantages: It will take longer from planting to flowering. There is a smaller selection of these in garden centers and nurseries than of ready-grown, mature plants.

Using mature plants

Advantages: A large selection of plants is available. The plants flower sooner.
Disadvantages: They are more expensive and have larger rootstocks. A few special tips will help with planting:
● Pull the wire mesh apart a little so that there is more room to insert the plants.
● Cut the wire open using wire cutters.
● Larger plants can be carefully divided if several of them are growing in one pot.

Preparing the basket

(illustrations 1 and 2)
You can prepare the basket in two different ways.

1 First, completely cover the inside of the basket with a prepared insert (see illustration 1), moss or coconut fiber, then lay in the liner. The insert will hide the liner and prevent the compost from falling through the planting holes. Planting will require some deftness as each plant has to be pushed through narrow holes made in the two layers.

2 The neck of the root of each plant is surrounded with moss or coconut fiber after the plant has been inserted. No liner is used to line the inside of the basket before you start, but it is added gradually as you insert the plants. The disadvantage with this method is that the compost may dry out faster.

My tip: Cover the floor of the basket with coconut fiber or moss and liner, covering the

5 *An attractive wall bracket will complement a hanging basket.*

inside to a height of about 2 in (5 cm) (see illustration 2). This "dish" will hold water and also prevent it from running through and dripping away when watering. Do not make any holes in the insert and start planting above it. You can also insert a saucer or something similar in a very flat basket.

Special ways of planting

(illustrations 3 and 4)
There are two possibilities.

1 Carefully wrap the plant quite tightly in foil or cellophane, taking care not to damage any part of the plant, and insert it through the basket mesh shoots-first, from the inside to the outside (see illustration 3).

2 Insert it rootstock-

first from the outside inward.

How to plant

Hang the basket up at chest height, then prepare it as above. Remove the plants from their pots. Water dry plants first.
Planting should always be done from the bottom upward; i.e. plant the floor of the basket first.

● Cut a slit in the insert for each plant.

● Push the plant through the mesh and insert it to the beginning of the stalk. Close the opening around the neck of the root (see illustration 4). Distribute half of the plants in this way at the bottom of the basket.

● Sprinkle compost between the roots and press down. Repeat the procedure at the top and water.

Design tip (see illustration 5): When the basket has been freshly planted, it will look untidy. This will sort itself out after a few days when the shoot tips and leaves begin to turn toward the light.

Containers can be found in many shapes and styles.

Plant containers

You can obtain plant containers in many different materials.

Ceramic containers: Plants look particularly good in earth-colored or terracotta hanging containers. Unglazed containers promote the growth of roots as the walls of the vessel are porous; this also means, however, that water will evaporate more quickly and the compost will dry out faster. As some such containers are not frost-proof, it is best to check this point before purchase. Colorful glazed containers are an additional decoration for your plant collections. Their great weight makes large ceramic containers very stable. Hanging containers should be safely secured because of their weight (see pp. 16-17).

Stoneware containers: Stoneware boxes are available everywhere in garden centers. They are tip-proof, frost-proof, and let the roots breathe.

Plastic containers: They are ideal for hanging plants because of their light weight and because they do not break easily. They retain moisture in the compost as their walls are not porous. They tend to be rather unattractive but the sides are soon covered up by hanging plants.

Wooden boxes, willow baskets: Containers made of natural materials, like wooden boxes (see pp. 27 and 31), fruit crates (see p. 35), or willow baskets, make attractive plant containers which harmonize with the plants. Their durability is, however, rather limited because of constant moisture from watering. The life of wooden containers can be extended by applying a protective coat of paint or plant-friendly wood preserver. Another possibility is to line the inside with polyethylene sheeting (do not forget to make holes to let water run away!). The same goes for baskets made out of any natural materials. The baskets should be checked frequently as both the floor and handles may rot away.

Semi-spherical-shaped containers for planting against a wall: These containers, made of terracotta (see photo, p. 22) or plastic, are very suitable as an ornament on a wall and will not take up much space. Baskets of the same shape can also be obtained.

NB: Every container will require a drainage hole so that rainwater or regular water is not stored inside the containers to waterlog the plants.

Holders for single pots: Potholders made of wire are also obtainable for single pots (see p. 42).

Complying with the law

If you own your house, you should be able to use your balcony or patio in whatever way you wish. If you own or are living in an apartment which has a balcony, you must make sure that nothing you do infringes upon the rights of, nor endangers or inconveniences, your landlord, other tenants, or the general public. As a rule, with the exception of the outside façade, a tenant may secure plant containers to balcony railings or on a patio and install plants in them, provided this is done safely.

NB: Check the weight-carrying capacity of the balcony.

A few important points should be considered if you are a tenant:

● Before securing boxes to the outside of balcony railings, check whether your tenancy agreement expressly permits this, otherwise the landlord may prohibit such use. If you own your apartment, there may also be rules of usage governing the installation of plant containers on the property.

● Make sure you secure the plant containers in such a fashion that even a storm will not tear them from their anchoring. Use balcony box fixtures with a safety lip (see p. 17).

● Only use chains, ropes, hooks, and dowels with sufficient carrying capacity for holding up hanging containers and baskets. The weight will increase

Environmentally friendly containers made of recycled material.

dramatically when the plants are being watered. As a guide, use the weight data in the design section (see pp. 18-43).

● Suspend hanging containers or baskets only from galvanized chains or wires or plastic-coated ropes. Untreated chains or wires may rust under the influence of moisture (watering, rain) and come away. Ropes made of natural fiber may rot and break.

● Check all fixtures at regular intervals.

● Make sure that water dripping down does not damage the façade or run onto a neighboring property or onto the street below. Always stand a bowl under plants you are watering

(see illustration, p. 54).

● Only ever spray plants with protective agents when there is no wind. Always make sure that spray mist cannot drift onto a neighboring balcony.

Making and securing your own containers

You can easily make your own original hanging flower bed or vegetable garden without a great deal of technical expertise.

Hanging plant bed
(illustrations 1 and 2)

A base for a hanging bed that can then be covered, according to your taste, with containers and plants is easily and quickly assembled without a great deal of technical knowledge and using parts obtainable from most builders' merchants. You will only require tools for securing it to the ceiling. When purchasing parts, you should make sure that they all have the correct carrying capacity (after watering, the bed will weigh about 40 pounds/18 kg). Also make sure that the parts fit together before you begin.

Equipment
● 1 metal grid, as used for scraping shoes or for covering cellar window pits. Grids like this can be obtained in various different sizes. If you intend using a fruit crate as a plant container, one measuring 16 by 24 in (40 by 60 cm) will be large enough.

● 4 circular steel-link chains (length 40 in/100 cm each) with a carrying capacity of at least 40 pounds (18 kg). Have the pieces of chain cut to size when you purchase them.
● 4 S-hooks for attaching the chains securely to the metal grid.
● 1 adjustable chain link with thread (see illustration 5) to gather the four chains together at the top.
● 1 block and tackle (see p. 55) for lowering and raising the plants for watering.

My tip:
Galvanized or painted parts will last longer.

Assembling the hanging bed

● Attach a chain to each corner of the metal grid using an S-hook.
● Gather the four chains together at the top by means of an adjustable link.
● Attach the block and tackle to the ceiling and fix the rope.
● Suspend the hanging bed from the block and tackle.

Safe anchorage
(illustrations 3-6)

The anchoring point on a ceiling or wall has to carry a considerable weight. Depending on the materials from which the wall or ceiling is made, the possibilities for securing attachments may vary.

1 A colorfully painted fruit box makes an attractive plant container.

2 An S-hook attaches a chain to the metal grid.

3 Balcony box fixture with safety lip.

4 Rope clamps secure the ends of the rope.

5 Adjustable chain link with screw fixture.

● Always use plastic-coated dowels to install fixtures in brick or rendered walls or ceilings (see illustration 6). They can be obtained in various sizes. Use a drill to bore a hole of the correct thickness and length for the dowel (always use a masonry bit), insert the dowel in the hole (if necessary gently tap it in with a hammer), and screw the hook into the dowel. Before drilling, make sure there are no electric cables underneath. If you are not used to handling a drill, it is better to let a professional do the job as you could be in danger of injuring yourself!

● If you are making a hole in a massive wooden beam, use a screw-in hook. In the case of open balconies (or on an arbor, etc.), wrap a chain or plastic-coated rope around the beam and attach the plant container to this. Take extra care with wooden ceilings or walls as the carrying capacity of panels is very low and a screw-in hook will only be adequate for a very lightweight plant container. It would be better to bore right through the wood and insert a dowel in the concrete or stone behind it.

● Wall fixtures, like ornamental hooks and brackets (see p. 13), should always be supported at the bottom and secured with further screws.

● Fixtures with safety lips can be obtained for balcony boxes (see illustration 3). These will prevent the box from tipping off.

Various other aids will also help to secure hanging containers. **S-shaped hooks** can be used to connect a chain attached to the container and the actual chain used for suspension. They are also useful for other joins. They come in many different sizes.

Rope clamps (see illustration 4) can be used to fix the ends of wires and plastic-coated ropes. They can be obtained for different gauges of rope.

Adjustable chain links (see illustration 5) are single chain links that can be opened on one side and closed again. They are excellent for gathering several chains together.

6 A dowel holds the hook securely in the ceiling.

17

Stylish ideas

With a little basic knowledge about gardening and a lot of imagination, a beautiful display of plants can be created in almost any position. Check through the suggestions in the following pages.

Photo above: Gazania displays its full beauty in sunlight.
Photo left: With the right aids, such as polyethylene, coconut fiber, and the correct tools, it is not difficult to design an attractive hanging basket.

Stylish ideas

The right position is most important

Before buying your plants, you should take a very good look at the position in which you are intending to grow them. Whether they thrive will not depend entirely on water and nutrients but also on the light and the prevailing climatic conditions they will be asked to live in. Different plants have different requirements with respect to light, temperature, wind, and rain. To make the choice of plants for your intended position easier, the following design ideas for groups of plants have been arranged for plants that prefer sunny, semi-shady, and shady positions. The special requirements of free-hanging planting arrangements have also been taken into consideration. The exposed nature of the planting containers means that it is sometimes easier to care for some sun-loving plants in semi-shady conditions and that they will grow even more luxuriantly there. Before deciding, you should make sure that you know which conditions prevail on your balcony, patio, etc.

● Which direction does the position face?

● Is there a roof or awning over the intended position or do trees or a house wall protect the position from direct sunlight?

● What are wind and rain conditions like?

Plants for sunny positions

Spring planting
pansies (*Viola wittrockiana* hybrids)
English daisies (*Bellis perennis*)
bulbous plants such as tulips (*Tulipa*)
narcissi (*Narcissus*)
crocuses (*Crocus*)

Summer planting
Gazania hybrids
Livingstone daisies (*Dorotheanthus bellidiformis*)
portulaca (*Portulaca*)
Swan River daisies (*Brachycome iberidifolia*)
pelargoniums (*Pelargonium*)
petunias (*Petunia* hybrids) ☠
fleabane (*Erigeron karvinskianus*)
Scaevola saligna

Fall planting
violets (*Viola cornuta* hybrids)
heath (*Erica herbacea*)
chrysanthemums (*Dendranthema grandiflorum* hybrids)
ivy (*Hedera helix*) ☠

A sunny position

South-facing balconies, patios, or roof gardens are typically the sunniest positions, which also means that there is a lot of heat during the day in the summer and, depending on the position, the air may not move much. Sensitive plants may burn here. In all cases, you will have to water a great deal. If you are not sure whether you will always be able to water frequently, you should go for a particularly robust selection of plants (see p. 23) or consider the installation of semi-automatic or automatic irrigation.

Positions that face southeast or southwest should be less vulnerable to such extreme conditions. The same goes for a situation where a tree, a house wall opposite, or a roof protects the plants from too much sunlight. The position is classified as shady if the balcony is facing south but has a roof or something similar which keeps the sun off completely. This fact should be reflected in your choice of plants (for plants that like shady positions, see pp. 36-43).

Look at the chosen site at various times during the day as conditions may alter as the sun moves round.

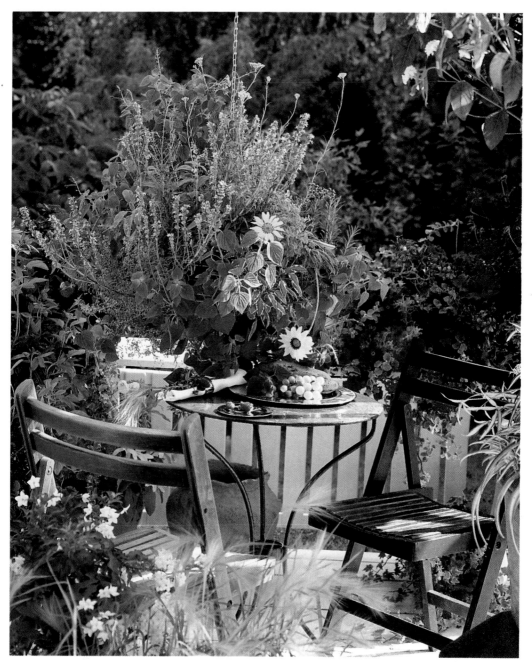

A herb basket above the table releases its spicy scent.

21

Stylish ideas

An exotic blend of colors

This is where plants from hot, dry climatic zones meet up. All the plants in this basket enjoy plenty of heat and lots of sunshine and can also manage on little water – ideal for a sunny position. They will not mind if they do not receive water regularly on schedule as they either have a built-in water reservoir or a special talent for using up the precious liquid frugally. In their countries of origin they have evolved to cope with long periods of drought.

Plants for a wire basket with a diameter of 14 in (35 cm):
5 gazania *(Gazania* hybrids)
3 Livingstone daisies *(Dorotheanthus bellidiformis)*
4 portulaca *(Portulaca)*
2 convolvulus *(Convolvulus sabatius)*
Total weight of the group: 22 pounds (10 kg).

Planting and care
All plants can be bought from the last month of

spring onward. You can increase the number of different colors in your arrangement if you use varieties that come in a range of colors. *Gazania, Dorotheanthus* and *Portulaca* are usually planted several to a pot in nurseries and often produce several different colors in one pot. Prepare the wire basket and insert the plants (see pp. 12-13). Plant a *Convolvulus sabatius* at both the front and the back of the bottom of the basket. Its long, trailing shoots will look best growing freely downward. Toward the top of the basket alternate *Gazania, Dorotheanthus* and *Portulaca*.
Water the basket well (place a bowl underneath!) and keep it as evenly moist as possible. Fertilize weekly. Cut out any dead and faded flowers and foliage as this will encourage the formation of new flowers. These plants react sensitively to continuous rain and waterlogging. During longer periods of wet weather, it is a good

Terracotta wall container.

idea to protect the arrangement from too much moisture by hanging the basket underneath an overhanging roof.

For people who are away from home all day
The glowing, colorful flowers of these plants are open only during the day and when the sun is shining. If you are not at home all day, you should probably choose plants whose flowers are open all the time (see the flower swing, pp. 30-31).

Terracotta hanging container.

Choice of colors
Plants originating from regions with plenty of sunshine are often very brightly colored. If you like strong colors, you can combine them with complementary colors. If you feel this would create too much of a garish splash, you can also use a combination of quieter shades or tones.

Design tip
The plants used here will also suit smaller containers with very little compost in them. They are ideal for summertime plantings in ceramic hanging containers or half-bowl-shaped containers made of terracotta.

Compact and full of color.

An aromatic herb basket

Plants with highly scented flowers or leaves are always a pleasure for the senses. Honey melon sage, lemon thyme, and curry plant provide a real feast of wonderful aromas. As these plants are usually to be found growing on the ground, it is generally necessary to bend down to enjoy the full impact of their scent as you crush their leaves and flower heads in your fingers.
However, if you plant various scented plants in a hanging basket and suspend this at nose level, the plants will release their pleasant perfume at just the right height. If you suspend the basket using a block and tackle, you can even go a step further and vary the level at which the plants hang (see p. 55).
In addition, an airy position like this is the ideal place to grow kitchen herbs with superb flavors. It will make things even easier still if you hang the basket right beside an outdoor table on your

Most herbs have very delicate flowers.

Pocket amphora.

balcony or patio, then you can pick the herbs fresh to eat with your meal. Depending on the plants chosen, such a combination of plants can prove quite robust if subjected to short-term periods of drought (see plant list, p. 25).

24

Plants for a wire basket with a diameter of 14 in (35 cm):
2 honey melon sage (Salvia elegans)
1 sage (Salvia officinalis "Tricolor")
1 golden sage (Salvia officinalis "Aurea")
1 scented-leafed pelargonium with an aroma of nutmeg and white/green variegated leaves (Pelargonium fragrans "Variegata")
1 scented-leafed pelargonium with a fruit scent and red leaves
1 curry plant (Helichrysum italicum)
1 hyssop with pink flowers (Hyssopus officinalis)
2 large quaking grass (Briza maxima)
2 lemon thyme (Thymus x citriodorus)
These plants are not commonly available everywhere but you should be able to purchase them through specialty mail-order nurseries.

An alternative collection

If you want to grow your own herb garden in a hurry, you can fall back on the usual kitchen herbs, for example basil (Ocimum basilicum),
marjoram (Majorana hortensis), dill (Antheum graveolens), or parsley (Petroselinum crispum). These herbs not only smell nice but can also be used to give flavor in cooking.

My tip: Hanging baskets can even be transformed into vegetable gardens (see photo, p. 8) if they are planted all the way around with young vegetable plants. Total weight of the arrangement: 18 pounds (8 kg).

Planting and care

Plant after the last frosts in the last month of spring. Prepare the basket (see pp. 12-13). Honey melon sage needs the most room so plant one of these to the right and left of the bottom of the basket wall. Between these, at the front and back, plant lemon thyme which grows in cushions. Distribute the other herbs all over the basket.
Fill up all the empty spaces between the plants with compost. Press the compost down and water the basket well. Fertilize
regularly (see fertilizing vegetables, p. 46). If you have the space available, you can overwinter this arrangement in a frost-free room during the winter months (see overwintering, pp. 56-57) as all these plants are perennials. Cut the plants back before overwintering them.

My tip: Honey melon sage (Salvia elegans) has a profusion of foliage and requires lots of water. If you are unable to water regularly, it would be better to choose a plant that does not mind a bit of dryness or else hang the basket in a semi-shady position.

The following plants require **less water** than most:
sage (Salvia officinalis), rosemary (Rosmarinus officinalis)
lavender (Lavandula angustifolia)
oregano (Origanum vulgare)
marjoram (Majorana hortensis)
sedum (Sedum reflexum)
various species of
thyme (Thymus)
lavender-cotton (Santolina chamaecyparissus)
winter savory (Satureja montana)

Tip on containers

Ceramic pocket amphorae present an attractive possibility for overhanging plantings. You can plant herbs or even strawberry plants in the pockets. These containers are also sold under the name of strawberry pots in garden centres.

Be aware that the larger strawberry barrels do become very heavy when planted up. They can become impossible to move or lift, so you must decide where you wish to place the pot or barrel before you plant it up.

Stylish ideas

Strawberry fair

By growing the right varieties of strawberries and giving a little extra care, you can be certain of a rich harvest of fruit over several months. The lovely white flowers also make an attractive feature. The strawberry plants ensure their own propagation by producing long runners which form tiny new strawberry plants. These young plants look very pretty when they produce flowers at the ends of the runners, followed by fruit. A rustic tub barrel made of light oak looks superb when full of strawberry plants.

Plants for a container with a diameter of 12 in (30 cm):
1-5 strawberry plants (*Fragaria*)
The best plants for this arrangement are hanging or climbing strawberries which will be available in garden centers from the last month of spring into the first month of summer. These types flower and produce fruit all summer long. They are sold as large container plants or as small young plants. The number of plants you will require for a planting in a wooden container will depend on the size of the individual plants. If you cannot find any plants to buy during these months, you will certainly be able to obtain them during the last month of summer which is the best planting time for garden strawberries.

An alternative suggestion

The small Alpine strawberries make a dainty ornament as well as producing tasty fruit. If you wish to grow the fruit only as a visual delight, you can also use the "fake" strawberry (*Duchesnea indica*). This grows vigorously; its fruits are the same size as wild strawberries but have no flavor. The flowers are yellow.
Total weight of the planting: 37 pounds (17 kg). Make sure the attachment is particularly strong and secure as this container is a considerable weight.

Planting and care

Before planting, check whether the container is equipped with drainage holes.
Place a drainage layer in the bottom of the container, for example clay pellets (Hortag), to a level of about 2 in (5 cm) and then cover this layer with permeable fabric. This drainage layer will not only protect your plants from the effects of waterlogging but will also reduce the overall weight of the planting. If you want to reduce the weight even more, you can double the thickness of the drainage layer.
Fill the remainder of the container with compost and plant the strawberry plants. Press the compost down so that the rootstocks are well covered with compost on all sides and then water well. If the runners of the strawberry plants become too long, they can be trimmed.
Fertilize strawberries in the same way as herbs and vegetables (see p. 46).
Depending on the variety, strawberries are particularly susceptible to mildew if the humidity is high and temperatures are constantly changing (see p. 50). To build up the plants' immunity, and as a preventive, we recommend watering your plants regularly during the growth period with mare's tail brew, nettle brew, comfrey brew, or yarrow brew, all of which contain silicic acid (see p. 52).
You will receive years of pleasure from this arrangement if you position it in a sheltered spot outside or overwinter it indoors at no more than 41°F (5°C) (see p. 56).

Securing containers

If the wooden container has no means of attachment, drill three holes at equal intervals in the top of one of its walls and insert S-hooks.

Make sure the distance between the holes and the top edge of the container is great enough to prevent the wood from giving way. Hang a circular-link steel chain from each hole. Gather the three chains together at the top with an S-hook or an adjustable chain link.

Wooden barrel.

Tip on containers

Do-it-yourself enthusiasts may wish to transform an old wooden barrel into a strawberry barrel. A particularly attractive effect is created if the strawberry plants do not just cascade out of the top of the barrel but also out of additional holes that can be sawn into the walls of the barrel.

Strawberries make an attractive arrangement.

Stylish ideas

A semi-shady position

These sites are characterized by receiving plenty of light but without constant, aggressive, intense rays from the sun. Burning noontime sunlight should generally be avoided. On the other hand, this sort of position does not mean that the plants are sitting in deep shadow. Semi-shady positions are generally east- or west-facing. An east-facing balcony receives softer morning sunlight. A west-facing balcony receives rays from the afternoon and evening sun but, being the side more exposed to weather, it may often be battered by storms and rain. Your hanging containers should, therefore, be very well secured in west-facing positions. In all cases, the prevailing conditions on site should be considered. Even south-facing balconies in full sunlight, or shady north-facing ones, may become semi-shady if, for example, a tree blocks out the sunlight or a neighboring house wall reflects the sun's rays.

Choosing plants

A semi-shady position is ideal for hanging plants as the relatively small amount of compost in the containers will not dry out so fast. On the other hand, sun-loving plants will thrive here just as much as in a sunny position.

Plants for semi-shady positions

Spring planting
forget-me-nots (*Myosotis sylvatica*)
pansies (*Viola wittrockiana* hybrids)
double daisies (*Bellis perennis*)
primulas (*Primula vulgaris* hybrids)

Summer planting
black-eyed Susan (*Thunbergia alata*)
morning glory (*Ipomoea*) ☠
climbing nasturtium (*Tropaeolum peregrinum*)
nasturtium (*Tropaeolum majus*)
Lotus berthelotii
pelargonium (*Pelargonium*)
lobelia (*Lobelia erinus*)
begonia (*Begonia semperflorens* hybrid) ☠
tuber begonia (*Begonia – tuber begonia hybrids*) ☠
Calceolaria integrifolia

Fall planting
heather (*Calluna vulgaris*)
fall asters (*Aster*), various species

As you can see from these lists, with simple care you can take full advantage of a suitable position to grow a wide range of plants. Plants that form lots of leaves in a very short time do particularly well in a semi-shady position. Among these are a wide selection of climbing plants.

Symbols used in the gardening trade

Purchased plants often have labels attached to them. These labels bear symbols giving the requirements of the plant with respect to position and light.

○ **sun:** This plant requires, or can cope with, full sunlight and heat, even at noon. A completely sunny, south-facing position will be necessary for the production of plenty of flowers.

◐ **semi-shade:** This plant requires a bright position without intense midday sunlight. Morning and evening sunlight, i.e. east- and west-facing positions, are ideal for this plant. Even light shade is suitable for growing this sort of plant.

● **shade:** This plant can cope with, or prefers, shade.

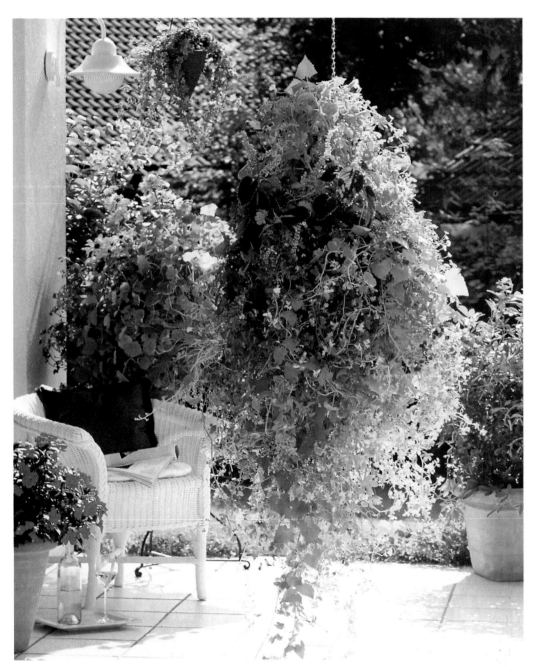

This hanging basket provides an attractive visual screen.

A colorful flower swing

Traditional balcony flowers in glowing colors create a wonderful effect from a distance. The hanging varieties are also excellent for trailing over a balcony railing. Using an interesting or original container, you can place these easily cared-for, continuous-flowering plants in a free-hanging position.

Plants for a box 28 in (70 cm) long:
1 hanging pelargonium (*Pelargonium peltatum* hybrids)
1 *Bidens ferufolia*
5 nasturtiums (*Tropaeolum majus*)
1 *Scaevola saligna*
Total weight of the planting: 44 pounds (20 kg)

Planting and care

Scaevola saligna, *Bidens ferufolia* and hanging perlargoniums can be bought as ready-to-plant plants from the last month of spring onward in nurseries and garden centers. Nasturtiums can be obtained in the form of young plants or you can grow them yourself from seed. Fill a third of the box with compost. Place the pelargonium on the left, the *Bidens* and the *Scaevola* in the center, and the nasturtiums on the right. Fill the box with compost, press down, and water well. Nasturtiums will flower more profusely and produce fewer leaves if you do not fertilize them too often. In order that the other plants will receive an adequate amount of fertilizer, use controlled-release fertilizer or fertilizer sticks in a targeted way around their root systems (see p. 46). In this way you can avoid the use of liquid fertilizer. Regularly remove dead flowers and leaves. If the nasturtiums threaten to

Heath in a pot.

smother the other plants, cut them back a little.

Securing the container

Balcony railings: You can attach the box of plants to the railings with special fixtures (see illustration 3, p. 17).
Free-hanging: If you wish to suspend the balcony box from the ceiling, you will require an overbox (paint it to protect it from rotting) which you can build yourself with a bit of experience or have a carpenter make for you. Make sure it has an attachment which you can easily make yourself.
● Stand the balcony box in a rather wider box made of heavy wood. Allow a gap of 1¼ in (3 cm) between the inner and outer boxes so that the inner one can be removed easily.
● Make sure that both the inner and outer boxes are equipped with drainage holes.
● Stand the box on narrow wooden battens so that excess water can run away unhindered.

● Take two narrow-gauge iron pipes, which correspond in length to the width of the overbox, and pass them underneath each end of the overbox; insert chains through these pipes and suspend the box from the chains (see photo below).
My tip: If you wish to grow perennial plants, insert a layer of polystyrene between the two boxes as protection against the cold.

Color tip

If you enjoy the pink shades of pelargoniums during the summer, you can have the same colors again in the fall by planting winter heath.

Flower box attachment.

A free-hanging balcony box on chains.

Stylish ideas

This cascade of flowers forms an attractive visual screen.

Visual screens

This basket is enveloped in luxuriantly growing plants that will produce long shoots and dense foliage in the shortest period of time. It is simply overflowing with eye-catching nasturtiums and various varieties of *Asarina barclaiana*. The latter are distant relatives of the snapdragon and are generally grown as climbing plants.

Nasturtiums.

If no climbing aids are present, the long, trailing shoots will hang down over the edge of the container. This basket provides a dense visual screen and an eye-catching decoration all in one (see photo, p. 29).

32

Plants for a wire basket with a diameter of 16 in (40 cm):
3 climbing nasturtiums (*Tropaeolum peregrinum*)
2 nasturtiums (*Tropaeolum majus*)
2 hanging pelargoniums (*Pelargonium peltatum* hybrids)
1 ground ivy with white and green variegated leaves (*Glechoma hederacea* "Variegata")
2 *Asarina barclaiana*
2 *Asarina scandens*
1 *Rhodochiton atrosanguineus*
1 convolvulus (*Convolvulus sabatius*)
3 coleus (*Coleus blumei* hybrids)
Total weight of the planting: 40 pounds (18 kg).

Planting and care
The right time to plant is after the last frosts, about the middle of the last month of spring. You can purchase the plants in nurseries and garden centers or grow them yourself from seed during the middle of the second month of spring. Prepare the basket and plant it (see pp. 12-13). All the plants, with the exception of pelargoniums and coleus, can be distributed evenly on the base and walls of the basket. Only the colorful coleus and pelargoniums should be placed in the upper portion and on the surface of the basket. When planting, make sure that the spaces between the rootstocks are completely filled with compost.
Water the basket well; after three weeks use a liquid flower fertilizer once weekly.
If one of the plants begins to dominate the arrangement, cut back its shoots. You can break up this arrangement before the first frosts in the fall. Plant the pelargoniums, convolvulus, and coleus in individual pots and overwinter them in a frost-free position.

My tip: To help the climbing plants to produce a more bushy appearance after planting them in the basket, pinch out the tips of the first shoots. This will encourage the formation of plenty of lateral shoots.

Morning glory sown from seed.

Design tip
If you want to cover a wall or the railing of a balcony or patio with greenery but do not have enough room on the ground or floor for a large plant container, you can hang a basket of climbing plants near a trellis or balcony railing. Carefully tie the long shoots from the basket to the railing. The plants in the basket will then climb all over the trellis or railing throughout the summer. When positioning the basket, remember that after its climbing shoots are entwined around a support, you will no longer be able move the basket about. This means hanging it up in such a way that it is easy to reach for watering.

An alternative planting
To obtain a cheap planting for your hanging basket, after the last frosts in late spring, sow morning glory (*Ipomoea*) seed or scarlet runner beans (*Phaseolus coccineus*) directly into a basket filled with compost or into a ceramic hanging container. Keep the compost evenly moist during germination. After about ten days, the plants will begin to germinate and, throughout the entire summer, will grow all over the container. The *Ipomoea* has brilliant blue flowers and the bean flowers are an intense scarlet as their name suggests.

A hanging vegetable garden

You can plant a vegetable garden in a very small space in this way. The basic construction is simple and you can put it together from parts that can be found in any builder's merchant. The actual plant container is made from a painted fruit box that can easily be purchased at a weekly market or in a greengrocery. Naturally, if you do not wish to grow vegetables, this hanging garden can be filled with flowering plants instead.

Plants for an orange box of the dimensions 24 by 16 in (60 by 40 cm):
1 cherry tomato plant
1 red cabbage
3 lettuce plants (choose varieties with different leaf colors and shapes)
1 gourd
red basil plants
Total weight of the planting (inc. the metal grid): 35 pounds (16 kg).

Securing the container

This hanging bed

requires a basic construction comprising four chains and an attached metal grid (see p. 16). It will be easier to care for the plants if it can be lowered for watering. A block and tackle arrangement should be installed for this purpose (see p. 55).

Planting and care

You can start to plant after the last frost at the end of spring. You will find a large selection of young vegetable plants in garden centers at this time. Use a fruit box, preferably with high sides, as this will ensure a large volume of compost for the plants. Give the box a coat of paint before planting as this will make your arrangement more attractive. Let the paint dry properly and then

Water melon.

line the inside of the box with polythene sheeting. Cut several holes in the bottom of the sheet so that excess water can run out. Before planting, fill the box with compost and insert the plants. Place the red cabbage at the front so that it inclines forward, plant the tomato on the left, and then place the other young plants between them.
You can sow lettuce seeds in the gaps and harvest them before the other vegetables have grown very big. The lettuces will germinate quickly and produce salad leaves. In addition, they will later produce pretty, creamy-white, star-shaped flowers that look enchanting among the other plants. After three weeks, fertilize the

Eggplant.

vegetable garden weekly (see p. 46). Check for pests regularly.

My tip: Cherry tomatoes do not have to be tied to sticks. They produce very attractive yellow flowers and their miniature, brilliant red fruits are quite eye-catching as well as delicious.

Positioning

If you place this arrangement beside an outside table, you can pick fresh tomatoes straight from the plant to eat with your meal. Cress is also ideal for this method of growing or you could even sow a whole boxful of lettuces. Naturally, this kind of hanging bed can also be filled with herbs (see p. 24).

Design tip
Vegetables can produce
a very attractive effect.
The creamy-colored
flowers of lettuce can be
very ornamental.
These flowers are formed
when the lettuce "bolts"
and the flower head
shoots up.
Water melons and
eggplants also make
interesting and delicious
additions to your hanging
vegetable garden.

*Line the inside of the
box with polyethylene.*

A painted fruit box makes a good container.

Stylish ideas

A shady position

A shady site requires just as careful a choice of plants as a sunny one. North-facing positions are perpetually in the shade as direct sunlight will never reach them. However, even a square courtyard or a planting position directly under a tree with dense foliage will create very shady spots. Because there is less sunlight in shady positions, the plants placed there and the surface of the compost in the container tend to lose less water through evaporation. This means that moisture is retained for longer in the compost. One advantage of this is that the plants do not need to be watered so often. On the other hand, there is a disadvantage if the plants become waterlogged as this may cause damage to the roots (see p. 53). Although there is a smaller selection of plants that feel at home in a shady position, with a little careful thought you can still have a profusion of summery flowers on your north-facing balcony. You can also resort to short-term decoration by using plants that can be replaced with others when they have finished flowering. This sort of short-term use is best achieved by standing the plant in its pot inside the hanging container. This will enable you to exchange it for another easily and quickly.

Plants for shady positions

Spring planting
forget-me-nots (*Myosotis sylvatica*)
primulas (*Primula vulgaris* hybrids)
spring anemones
(*Anemone blanda*)

Summer planting
tuber begonias *(Begonia –* tuber begonia hybrids)
ivy (*Hedera helix*)
Tradescantia
Chlorophytum comosum
Mimulus luteus
fuchsias (*Fuchsia* hybrids)
patience-plants (*Impatiens walleriana*)

Fall planting
heather (*Erica heracea*)
heather (*Calluna vulgaris*)
fall asters (*Aster*), various species
forget-me-nots (*Myosotis sylvatica*)
Gaultheria procumbens
chrysanthemums
(*Dendranthema grandiflorum* hybrids)

My tip: Have fun experimenting with a selection of plants as many plants are very adaptable. Some sun-loving plants will still produce flowers in the shade although they do not develop quite so profusely.

Reaching for the light

Sunlight is vital for plants so they tend always to grow toward the source of light and will produce most flowers in sunny conditions. The part of the plant that is farthest from light tends to become bare and often becomes unsightly. Positions that are not built up and obtain light from all sides are, therefore, ideal for the creation of attractive, all-round plantings. In order to encourage this ideal all-round growth in unfavorable conditions, for example on a cramped balcony that is roofed over, one method is to paint the walls etc. white. You should not continually turn an arrangement to expose all sides of it to the light. This creates great stress for the plant and hinders its growth.

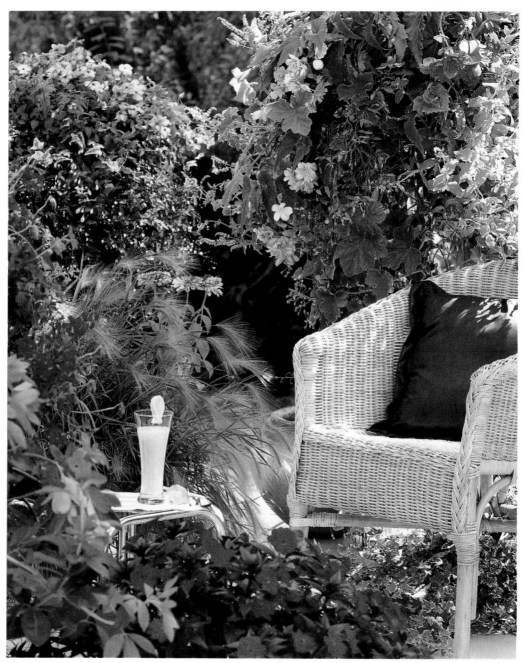

A profusion of plants can be grown even in a shady position.

Stylish ideas

Baskets of begonias and fuchsias

This elegant basket arrangement, containing hanging begonias in shades of pink and apricot amid variegated green and white foliage, will bring clusters of flowering color to even the shadiest nook (see photo, p. 37).
The small-flowering fuchsias are ideal for shady positions. Although they are true children of the sun, mint, scented-leafed pelargoniums, and ground ivy with its aromatic foliage will quickly become accustomed to a shady position.

Plants for a wire basket with a diameter of 14 in (35 cm):
2 hanging begonias (*Begonia* – tuber begonia hybrids)
3 hanging fuchsias (*Fuchsia magellanica*)
1 *Rhodochiton atrosanguineus*
3 ground ivy (*Glechoma hederacea* "Variegata")
2 pineapple mint (*Mentha suaveolens* "Variegata")
2 *Chlorophytum*

comosum
2 scented-leafed pelargoniums with a scent of peppermint (*Pelargonium tomentosum*)
Total weight of the planting: 26 pounds (12 kg).

Planting and care
Plant after the last frosts at the end of spring. The plants for this pretty combination can be bought at garden centers and nurseries or from mail-order firms. This arrangement will take its overall balance from a subtle combination of different shapes of growth (see p. 9). The graceful curtain of foliage (see photo, p. 57) and downward-trailing shoots have their stable base in the compact, bushy plants at the top of the basket. Prepare the wire basket and install the plants (see pp. 12-13).
In the lower and middle levels of the basket, plant ground ivy and *Rhodochiton atrosanguineus* alternated with scented-leafed pelargoniums and hanging fuchsias. Distribute the remaining

plants at the top near the sides of the basket and over the surface. Water the plants well and begin fertilizing three weeks later. Pick out dead flower heads and leaves. The more vigorously growing plants, like mint and pelargonium, should be lightly cut back from time to time if they start crowding the other plants.

My tip: Mint can be obtained in many different varieties. Not only do the many types of mint have differently scented leaves but they also grow vigorously and have interesting, attractive foliage. You can also use them as herbs in cooking.
If you cannot find any pineapple mint in garden centers but still wish to have variegated green and white decorative foliage, try planting *Plectranthus*, which is easier to obtain, or simply use an ivy (*Hedera*) with variegated leaves.

Color
Hanging begonias come in many different colors, from deep red and

glowing yellow to delicate pink and white, and with double and single blooms. All pastel shades go well with the variegated green and white leaves of ground ivy and pineapple mint. A particularly enchanting effect can be obtained with a combination of apricot and pink or by mixing different shades of pink. You could design your basket entirely in shades of one color if you add white tuber begonias and fuchsias to the white and green foliage. If in doubt, you should go for fewer colors in a combination and plant flowers of each color in one or two larger groups.

A profusion of fuchsias

Fuchsias are wonderfully adaptable plants to use in designing baskets and hanging containers. The hanging fuchsias are best for this mode of

Pineapple mint.

planting. The colors, sizes, and shapes of the flowers of the hanging varieties are just as varied as those of the upright-growing varieties, for example "La Campanella" (white/violet), "Elfriede Ott" (salmon/pink), or "Annabel" (white).

The scented-leafed pelargoniums spread an aroma of peppermint.

Bellflowers and grasses

Experiment by planting unusual plants in an unusual container. For example, here a small selection of woodland plants have been grown in a section of guttering as an interesting and novel hanging box that is perfect for a shady patio or balcony. All the plants shown here are perennials and the arrangement can be kept outside during the winter.

Plants for a section of guttering with a length of 28 in (70 cm):
2 large selfheal (*Prunella grandiflora*)
3 yellow corydalis (*Corydalis lutea*)
1 giant bellflower (*Campanula latifolia*)
1 barrenwort or bishop's hat (*Epimedium x rubrum*)
2 tufted hairgrass (*Deschampsia cespitosa*)
1 periwinkle with green/white leaves (*Vinca major* "Variegata")
Total weight of the planting: 18 pounds (8 kg).

This guttering container can be filled with woodland plants.

Making the plant container

The container consists of one section of roof guttering, with two end pieces to close both ends of the gutter and chains for suspending it. The best solution is to let a plumber or expert handy person put it together for you.

Guttering comes in several different widths and the measurements do not refer to the diameter of the gutter itself but to the width of the metal/plastic/PVC etc. before it is bent into a gutter shape.

Wall attachment.

The best gutters for this purpose are those made of metal or stout PVC that are about 13¼ in (33 cm) wide before shaping. They will hold more compost and the plants will do better. Avoid waterlogging by drilling several holes in the bottom of the gutter. The finished bed will be suspended on chains, so holes for these have to be made at both ends, front and back, about ¾ in (2 cm) below the upper edge, using a drill. Insert an S-hook in each hole to which you can attach the chains.

An alternative method

Wire ropes can be used instead of chains. Push a piece of wire through a hole drilled in the guttering from the outside, draw it along the inside wall of the guttering, and push it out through another hole drilled at the other end. Repeat this along the other side of the guttering.

My tip: The most attractive gutters are those made of galvanized metal that will not rust. Copper gutters are only suitable for planting if they have been coated with bitumen on the inside. Plastic and PVC gutters are also obtainable in the construction trade. They are not as attractive as the metal ones but can be painted any color you like. They have the advantage of being less heavy when planted up but do remember to use a robust plastic gutter.

Planting and care

Hardy perennials can be bought all year round in garden centers and nurseries. The best time to plant is during the first two months of spring, which gives the plants time to acclimatize well before the fall so that they can face the winter months with a well-developed root system.
A particularly interesting effect is obtained with this kind of arrangement if you distribute tall and low-growing plants unevenly along the gutter, for example by creating a focal point at the right end with taller plants. Place a few low-growing plants between the tall ones. They will form a link to the left end of the arrangement and the low-growing species of plants. From the middle of spring until the end of summer, use liquid fertilizer every two weeks. Make sure the arrangement is kept moist during the winter (see pp. 56-57). Do not cut the plants back until the following spring. The seed heads of the grasses and the trailing shoots of periwinkle will look most decorative throughout the winter. If one of the plants should die during the winter, you may wish to plant pansies or forget-me-nots in the gaps.

Fixing a wall attachment

The usual roof gutter fixtures (obtainable in the construction trade) can be used to transform a gutter into a wall garden (see small photo, p. 40). This attachment can be fixed to the wall with dowels and screws.

Containers

Galvanized metal buckets look good next to a plant container made out of a gutter. The handle of the bucket can be used for suspending it. The best idea is to plant the entire arrangement of plants in a plastic bucket with holes in its base and then insert this into the metal bucket. This will enable excess water to run out of the compost and into the metal bucket which should be emptied daily, if possible, to prevent waterlogging.

Bucket with insert.

Stylish ideas

A romantic flower table

This decorative plant arrangement is perfect for the summer. It has uncomplicated, continuously flowering hanging plants.

Plants for a bowl with a diameter of 24 in (60 cm):
6 patience-plants (*Impatiens walleriana*)
4 hanging fuchsias (*Fuchsia* hybrids)
1 large ivy for a hanging container and 3 small ivies with different colored foliage (*Hedera helix*)
2 *Tradescantia* of different species or varieties

Planting and care

Tradescantia and ivy are available in garden centers all year round and at reasonable prices. Patience-plants and fuchsias can be bought from the last month of spring onward. Before planting, make sure that the plant container has drainage holes at the bottom. Cover the bottom of the bowl with a thin layer of compost. Place the green/white *Tradescantia* and the large ivy to the left, hanging over the edge of the bowl and, on the right, plant the other *Tradescantia*. Place the fuchsias and the smaller ivy plants at the front and back between the first two groups of plants. The center of the bowl should be filled with compost to form a small mound where the patience-plants should be planted.
Regularly remove dead flower heads and leaves. Cut the ivy and *Tradescantia* back if they start to grow all over the flowering plants.
Do not place the bowl directly on the surface of the table. Slip short battens of wood under the bowl so that the drainage holes do not become blocked. *Tradescantia* and ivy can be planted individually in containers in the fall and then used as robust indoor plants even in dark positions within a room.

My tip: Ivy plants are often placed several to a pot by gardeners. You can carefully divide their rootstocks and plant them separately.

Design tip

A certain degree of artistic flair can be achieved with this arrangement if the edge of the bowl is left visible in several places. When the arrangement is established, the edge of the bowl should be clipped free to expose it in certain places every so often.

Containers

You can create an elegant effect with this kind of arrangement if you use containers with flat edges. You will also achieve a luxuriant overall effect if you choose a terracotta urn as a container.

Securing pots

There are various ways of securing pots to a balcony railing. (see illustration 3, p. 17, for an example)
Decorative baskets and ordinary pots obtained from garden centers are ideal for holding replaceable plants or for short-term decoration.
● Bicycle baskets are also suitable for this purpose.

Two decorative wire pot holders.

This cascade of flowers covers everything except the legs of the table.

Successful care

What could be finer than to sit on your
balcony or patio contemplating a firework
display of colorful flowers high above
your head? It can all be achieved by
using plants in baskets and hanging
containers. To ensure that your efforts
are well rewarded and will give pleasure
for as long as possible, however, it is
worth establishing a regular program of
good care. The advice given in the
following pages will help you to do this.

*Photo above: Petunias are popular balcony
plants.*
*Photo left: Spray bottle, ceramic cones, and
watering can are important aids for watering.
Liquid fertilizer, fertilizer sticks, and granules
supply the plants with nutrients.*

45

Successful care

Fertilizing

Plants in containers have to make do with a minimum of compost and are still expected to provide a long-lasting profusion of flowers and vigorous growth. As the nutrients contained in the compost are generally used up after a very short time, you should definitely start fertilizing two to three weeks after planting.

Types of fertilizer

Fertilizer is obtainable in solid and liquid forms, for watering or sprinkling on. It is easy to measure doses of liquid fertilizer into water. Controlled-release fertilizers are also practical. They are offered in granule form to be mixed into the compost or sprinkled onto it later. They will then release nutrients at an even rate over a period of 10-12 weeks. Overfertilizing and the resultant damage to the plants is impossible if controlled-release fertilizer is used properly as, by its very nature, it releases nutrients slowly. The same goes for fertilizer sticks. These should be completely inserted into the compost around the rootstock. The number of sticks to use will depend on the diameter of the container and the number of plants. Fertilizer sticks and controlled-release fertilizer are also ideal if you are combining plants which have varying requirements for nutrients (see p. 30). Use a compound fertilizer for flowering plants. Fertilizer intended for leafy plants, on the other hand, will only encourage the formation of foliage.

Fertilizer for edible plants

If herbs and vegetables are intended only as ornaments, they can be fertilized in the same way as other plants. If, however, they are intended for consumption, the plants should be supplied with nutrients in a different fashion. Growth-promoting fermented herbal brews can be used all summer long. With this form of mild, organic fertilizing, the nitrate content of vegetables and lettuce is much lower than if you use mineral fertilizers. You can also mix a small handful of hoof/horn chips into the compost. Biological fertilizers based on molasses are also obtainable from garden centers.

Tips on fertilizing

Please note the following points.
● Continuous rain will wash nutrients out of the compost. This is why plants often look yellowish and unhealthy after sustained periods of rainy weather. Giving them additional doses of fertilizer will usually help them to recover rapidly. Use liquid fertilizer twice weekly, diluted in water and according to the manufacturer's recommended dosage. You can also give the additional benefit of leaf fertilizer. Spray the plants with water containing this fertilizer. The nutrients are then absorbed through the surfaces of the leaves.

NB: Never fertilize plants in full sunlight as this will cause burns on the leaves. The best time is in the evening as the plants will then have time to absorb the fertilizer during the night.
● Dry planting arrangements should be watered with fresh water first and then fertilized, otherwise the roots may suffer burns.
● Granules or water containing fertilizer should not be allowed to come into contact with the leaves (if they do, rinse them off immediately).
● It is better to fertilize plants more often and less plentifully than seldom but in huge doses!
● Plants that are to be overwintered should not be fertilized from the first fall month to let their shoots ripen before they are moved into their winter quarters.
● You can place liquid fertilizer in a reservoir if the plants are being semi-automatically irrigated (see p. 48).

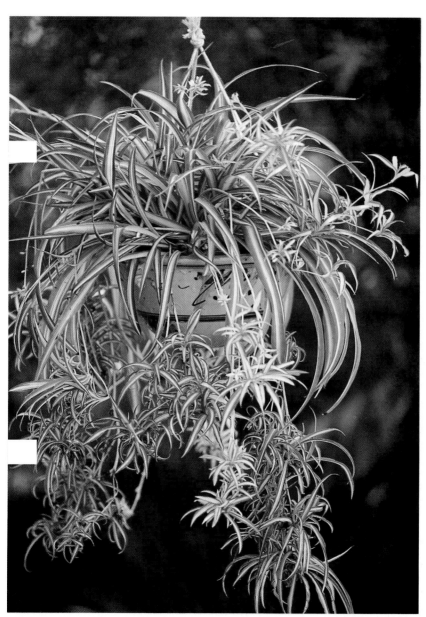

Spider plants (Chlorophytum comosum) produce long, decorative plantlets. These plants are undemanding but will develop particularly well if they are fertilized regularly during their growth phase.

Watering systems

1 A spray attachment on a pole will help you to water high containers.

To ensure that your hanging garden will thrive and grow vigorously, it will be necessary to water regularly. Both the plants and the hanging containers will lose water through evaporation all the way round and they will require regular and plentiful watering. There are several very different systems of watering that will ensure an adequate and manageable system. You should always make a point of avoiding damage caused by water dripping from hanging containers (see p. 54).

of these materials do not draw water away from plants so the total amount of water given remains available to sustain the plants in their growth.

Watering by hand
(illustrations 1 and 3)

Watering cans: The simplest method is watering with a can with a spray attachment. If the plant containers are hanging up high, you should have taken this into consideration when planning beforehand and have a set of steps handy. These, in turn,

will require additional space for storage.

A spray stick attachment (see illustration 1): This spray-head attachment on a long stiff pipe can be attached to a garden hose. Even containers that have been secured way above your head can be watered comfortably from ground level using this method.

A pump can (see illustration 3): Special watering vessels with a pump attachment for watering hanging containers are now available in many garden centers. A hand pump conducts water via a pipe up to the hanging container.

Watering plant containers

You can prevent excessive water evaporation through the walls of the containers if you use plastic, stoneware, or glazed ceramic containers. Unlike unglazed, porous clay pots, vessels made

2 Ceramic cones and a container of water will replace daily watering for several days.

Semi-automatic watering
(illustration 2)

Irrigation systems that are reasonably priced and easy to install are able to supply water automatically to plants for several days at a time.

Various different types are available in the specialist trade.

Ceramic cones (see illustration 2): Watering is carried out by means of a cone with a thin hose attached to it, the end of which is completely immersed in a container full of water. The cone should be inserted into the compost right to its top. Use two cones for large containers. For boxes of plants, use one at intervals of every 6-8 in (15-20 cm). The surface of the water in the feeder vessel must be lower than the top of the cone. Positioning the reservoir higher or lower will affect the amount of water conducted to the plant container. Light-impermeable material for the reservoir will discourage the formation of algae.

Water reservoirs: Flower boxes can be obtained with built-in water reservoirs. The compost sucks water up through a wick leading to a tank in the double floor of the container. The reservoir is replenished via a refill pipe.

3 A pump can for very high containers.

Fully automatic irrigation
(illustration 4)

You will hardly need to bother with hand-watering at all any more if you install a fully automatic irrigation system. Even long absences will present no problems. The installation is quite involved but the cost and the effort will be rewarded with considerable easing of regular work and an even, superb growth of plants. In these systems water conduction comes from the main

supply through a valve and an in-built pressure control. The water is distributed through thin plastic hoses. The amount of water and the rhythm of watering is controlled by varying mechanisms. Some systems are even computer-controlled.

Water supply: There are two systems for regulating this.

1 A ceramic "feeler" is inserted into the compost for each irrigation circuit. If the compost begins to lack moisture, the "feeler" emits an electronic impulse that opens a valve to provide more water. When the compost is moist enough, the "feeler" activates the closing of the valve.

2 Regulation via a time clock ensures that water is supplied at regular intervals.

Disadvantage: The supply of water is not controlled by the requirements of the plants and changes in the weather as is the case with a ceramic "feeler."

NB: Check the function of semi-automatic or fully automatic irrigation systems regularly to avoid unpleasant surprises. Occasionally, problems may occur. In all cases, a newly installed system should be closely observed over a certain period of time, just as a trial run.

4 Automatic irrigation will care for the plants while you are away from home.

Pests, diseases, and mistakes in care

While watering, you should regularly take time to do a thorough check of your plants, especially the leaves and shoot tips, in order to spot trouble as soon as possible. Only quick action can prevent pests and diseases from spreading and endangering neighboring plants. Mistakes in care can also be the cause of an occurrence of disease and pests. For example, plants that are placed in a position that is not suitable for their requirements, are watered the wrong way, or are not receiving sufficient nutrients will all be weakened and this will make them particularly susceptible to disease or attack by pests.

Aphids

Symptoms: Aphids (greenish or brownish-black) suck the sap out of buds, young leaves, and shoots, causing sticky, rolled up or crinkled leaves. Ants often follow as they utilize the sticky honeydew produced by the aphids for feeding their young.
Cause: Moist, warm weather and/or weakened plants. If humidity drops again, the aphid attack often subsides. Severe infestation can also occur if plants are overfertilized.
Remedy: Prevention through species-targeted care. Use plant protection agents when plants are infested (see p. 52).

Spider mites

Symptoms: The undersides of leaves are coated in fine web-like structures; light-colored dots on leaves.

Spider mites.

Cause: Dry, warm, stagnant air and/or weakening of the plant through mistakes in care.
Remedy: Plant protection agents. Prevent with good circulation of air. In advanced stages, web-like structures appear in the leaf axils.

Powdery mildew

Symptoms: A flour-like film on the top and undersides of leaves as well as on stalks and flower buds. Withering of leaves in advanced stages.
Cause: Temperature fluctuations as well as constantly wet leaves during cool, wet weather.
Remedy: Do not wet the leaves when watering. Protect the planting arrangement from rain. Prevent by using plant-fortifying agents (see p. 52). Affected parts can be carefully cut off and destroyed. Subsequently, thoroughly clean tools and your hands to avoid spreading the fungus.

Sunburn

Overfertilizing

Dryness

Nutrient deficiency

Symptoms: Reddish-brown or grayish-silver discoloration of the leaves which does not always appear on the whole plant but usually only on the parts of the plant that face the sun. It is easy to confuse the symptoms with those of spider mite infestation.
Cause: Exposure to intense sunlight, ozone burns (particularly on medium-warm days), or frost damage during light night frosts.
Remedy: Prevent through the choice of a position suitable for the species. Newly purchased plants or overwintered plants have to be acclimatized gradually. Protect plants from night frost (see p. 57). There is no protection against ozone damage.

Symptoms: Individual parts of shoot tips, buds, flowers, or leaves turn brown and start to develop mold. They do not dry up and do not drop off either. The greater part of the plant is not affected by the problem.
Cause: Overfertilizing. In particular, sensitive plants are most affected, for example those with variegated green and white foliage or soft leaves or herbs. Regular doses of fertilizer that are exactly right for nutrient-hungry plants will cause this reaction in more sensitive plants.
Remedy: Immediately cease regular fertilizing. Cut off affected parts.

Symptoms: Clearly discernible parts of individual leaves become discolored yellowish-brown and dry up.

Nutrient deficiency.

Cause: Lack of water in plants that can normally cope with little water (e.g. pelargoniums).
Remedy: Water more frequently. Cut back parts that have become unattractive. Water and fertilize regularly.

Symptoms: Yellow discoloration of older leaves. The plant becomes bare lower down and looks unhealthy and yellowish. Particularly noticeable after drenching rain showers and in summer plants that grow very fast, like petunias.
Cause: Nutrient deficiency through lack of proper fertilizing, particularly in plants that require lots of food. Heavy rain that washes nutrients out of the soil will also cause symptoms of deficiency.
Remedy: Spray the plant with leaf fertilizer in the evenings or in dull weather (see fertilizing, p. 46). Then fertilize once weekly.

Successful care

Plant protection

Prevention is the best form of plant protection. Avoiding mistakes in care (see pp. 50-51) means that you can eliminate most types of disease. If pests or diseases do appear, check first of all whether the affected plants are provided with the best conditions of growth for their species.

Note the following points.

● Choose the right position.

● Use the right kind of fertilizer and apply the correct dosage. Too much fertilizer can make a plant just as susceptible to disease as nutrient deficiency.

● On hot summer days, water your hanging plants, for example those in baskets, at least twice and do it plentifully, the best times being mornings and evenings. Remember that groups of plants will also dry out on cloudy days with strong winds. Plants placed right up against a house wall or under balconies and overhanging roofs will often not receive any rainwater.

● Water the plants very thoroughly. If the arrangement has dried out, water it several times in succession.

Mechanical methods

The simplest method of preventing infestation by pests is to collect the pests by hand, spray the leaves with a strong stream of water, or cut off affected parts of the plant.

Biological measures

A number of biological methods can be used for pests.

● If the infestation is not severe, or even as a preventive, you can use brews, fermented brews, or plant extracts. If an infestation has become severe, however, such remedies may not prove satisfactory. Furthermore, they should not be used too often as the plant may become damaged through a reaction to the brews. Plant extracts can be bought in garden centers.

● A well-tried home remedy that you can easily prepare yourself is a soap solution mixed with mineral spirits. Insects that eat the leaves or suck the sap of plants, like aphids and spider mites, can often be successfully controlled with this. Dissolve 1 tablespoon of soft soap in 4 cups (1 liter) of tepid water and add 1 tablespoon of mineral spirits. Spray the colonies of pests with the solution several times at intervals of a few days.

● Garlic brew works well against fungal infections. Crush 1 clove of garlic and pour 4 cups (1 liter) of boiling water over it. Let it cool, strain, and then spray undiluted.

● Preparations that are made out of paraffin or oil. They are non-toxic and do not, therefore, act as a nerve toxin on pests but, instead, clog up their breathing ducts with a film of oil. These preparations should not be used too often or they will also clog up the minute transpiration slits of the plants being treated.

● Pyrethrum extracts are derived from the flowers of an African chrysanthemum. They act as a nerve toxin on pests.

Warning: Although preparations containing pyrethrum are made from plant extracts, they are toxic to humans and animals as well if they enter the bloodstream. Do not use these agents if you have an open wound. Always wear gloves when handling these preparations and never inhale the spray mist. Do not use them in the close vicinity of aviaries, beehives, ponds, rivers, or aquariums and keep them away from children and pets.

Chemical agents

These really should be your very last resort when all other methods have failed or an infestation occurs in epidemic proportions. In fact it is often better to replace the affected plants instead of using chemical agents which require so many accompanying precautions.

● Never use highly toxic agents.
● Follow the rules for dosage and use stated on the packaging and also observe the suggested spraying intervals.
● Wear rubber gloves and do not eat, drink, or smoke while spraying. Do not inhale the spray mist.
● Only spray on windless days so that the agent cannot drift on to a neighbor's property.
● Never spray in sunlight as this may cause the plants to burn. It is better to spray in the mornings, evenings or when the sky is overcast.
● Always keep plant protection agents in the original packaging. Never, ever store them together with foodstuffs or within reach of children or domestic pets.
● Remains of spray solutions should not be kept as they quickly become ineffective. They should be put into sensitive waste disposal, not poured down the drains (check with your local council).

Healthy Gazania plant.

Healthy rootstock.

Sick rootstock.

Roots

All plants will develop well if they are watered and fertilized properly according to the requirements of their species. Disturbances in their growth pattern may occur if they receive too much or too little water. In both cases, the plant will wilt and become limp. A quick glance at the root system may help you to determine the cause.

Correct watering: With regular amounts of the right quantity of water for the particular species, a light-colored, felty root system (see central photo) is a recognizable sign of a healthy plant. The roots are intact and the transportation of water and nutrients from the bottom upward takes place without any problems.

Incorrect watering: The roots of the plant will become damaged if there is waterlogging or water is provided irregularly. They will first turn brown, then black and begin to rot (see bottom photo). The parts of the plant above the soil will begin to wilt and die because they cannot obtain water. The symptoms are very similar in plants that have suffered either drying out or waterlogging.

Watering and care

A beautifully proportioned hanging garden can transform any area. Throughout the year you can change the look and atmosphere simply through your choice of planting arrangements. However, an arangement that starts off looking beautiful can become a nightmare if the care you give is inadequate or inappropriate. Plants that are difficult or uncomfortable to reach often end up being neglected so that they are not watered or looked after properly. The result is infestation with pests, disease, or, at the very least, lack of proper growth.

The importance of planning

When planning and designing you should ensure that there will be easy access to your hanging garden. This does not mean that you must always keep a tall ladder standing beside a hanging container that is out of easy reach. With the help of easily installed block and tackle equipment or pulleys that can be purchased from a builder's merchant, this kind of arrangement can be raised and then lowered to the right height for you to care for the plants easily.

Water damage
(illustration 1)

Excess water will simply drip downward, particularly from hanging baskets.
● Place the arrangement in a position where the water can run away properly and will not damage anything underneath it. The ideal place is above a stone-flagged area with cracks between the individual slabs. On no account should excess water be allowed to run onto a neighboring balcony or patio.
● When watering, stand a bowl underneath to catch the water running through (see illustration 1). Placing an old cloth inside the bowl will prevent the running water from splashing over the edges.
● Water that runs through should not be allowed to drip onto plants underneath. Such constant showers from above would soon damage them.

2 *Complete immersion is a relief for dry plants.*

Emergency watering
(illustration 2)

Another way of watering hanging plants is to immerse them. This is recommended if the compost in the pot has dried out to the point where it will no longer absorb water during ordinary watering. To do this, lower the hanging container or remove it from its hook and immerse it in a bath of water until no more air bubbles are seen to rise to the surface of the water. You may have to hold the pot down at first.

1 *Always place a bowl underneath when watering.*

When carrying out this procedure, make sure that the shoots do not end up lying in the water or are damaged, or made dirty. The best way to avoid this is to hang the shoots carefully over the edge of the bath of water.

Rope and pulley
(illustration 3)

Pulleys are practical aids for lowering large, heavy plant containers. They can be purchased in the construction trade, from builders' merchants or in ship's chandlers specializing in sailing accessories. They are distinguished by the thickness of the rope and their carrying capacity. Simple or double rope pulleys are ideal for hanging containers or baskets that are not very heavy. Some pulleys are fixed with a screw at the top which means that the entire device can be screwed quite easily into a wooden beam. Others are made for attaching sideways, for example to a house wall. If you use a number of pulleys, you

3 The pulley guides the rope.

can run the rope over quite a distance and in different directions. This makes sense if fixing the rope close to the container is impossible, for example if your garden seat is right beside it. Even if it is conducted across several pulleys, the rope should still move evenly, without sagging. Use a hook firmly fixed in a handy position for tying up the end of the rope. It is possible to buy a kit that comes complete with all essential parts for a practical installation of ropes and pulleys.

Block and tackle
(illustration 4)

In the case of heavy hanging containers, free-hanging balcony boxes (see p. 30) or baskets, you may wish to install a block and tackle between the ceiling and the container (see pp. 16-17). With the help of this device you can lift and lower heavy weights very easily. A reasonably priced block and tackle from a builder's merchant, with a lifting capacity of 440 pounds (200 kg) will be quite sufficient for your purposes. Some means

of securing it, in the form of a hook, for example, should be installed in order to fix the rope at the desired height.

Do make sure the apparatus is securely fixed and can lift the weight you propose to hang from it. If you are not a good handy-person, it might be a good idea to have the pulley or block and tackle installed by a professional.

4 A block and tackle make it easy to lower the plants into a comfortable position for you to reach.

Successful care

Caring for your plants

The correct care depends on the requirements of the species of plant. Always check your plants when carrying out daily watering in order to spot pests or diseases in their early stages so that you can immediately take measures against them. Less-involved measures of care, such as removing dead flower heads, tying up, or cutting back, will increase growth and willingness to flower among your plants. Plants are living organisms with a strong urge to survive. With the right care and in the optimal position, they will flower endlessly except during natural, seasonal rest periods or if there has been some kind of growth disturbance.

Removing dead flower heads

It is the natural function of plants to produce flowers and, later on, seeds. The formation of seed, however, also brings about the fading and withering of the flower as its natural purpose has now been fulfilled. By regularly removing dead flower heads, you will prevent the formation of seeds and encourage the production of more flowers. Also, no dead petals will be left to drop down onto other parts of the plant where they will start to decay, thus providing a fertile bed for diseases. If the flower

has a long stalk, remove the stalk along with the dead flower head. The trigger for seed formation in many balcony plants often comes in the form of great heat and long periods of drought. In their countries of origin, these plants would only flower during a wet period. When the dry period begins, flowering ceases.

Cutting back

Dead parts of the plant should be cut off with scissors and destroyed as they can become veritable "nurseries" for diseases of all kinds. Cut back shoots that are too long and also plants that threaten to smother their neighbors or rampage all over the container. Many plants become bushier when they are cut back in a systematic fashion. This is a useful exercise if only one meager shoot is present. After carrying out plant protection measures, cutting back can encourage plants, that have become weakened through attack by disease or pests, to produce new shoots. A rejuvenating cut encourages flower formation after the first crop of flowers.

Replacing plants

Plants are easy to replace, for example as the flowering season changes, if they are placed in

individual pots. Individual plants that have become unsightly amid a group of hanging plants can be carefully dug out with a trowel. Fresh compost and a new plant can be inserted in the hole. Follow the same procedure for dying plants in baskets. Cut off dead plants in the sides and base of the basket at the neck of the root. These bare patches will soon be covered over by neighboring plants. You can freshen up the used compost in long-term plant groups if you loosen the surface around the rootstocks and sprinkle fresh compost here.

Overwintering

Outside: Hardy groups of plants can be overwintered outside with a few careful precautions. Remember that, whether full or empty, containers that remain outside must be frost-proof. Ceramic containers will often crack in winter, particularly if the compost in them is moist and begins to expand during freezing weather. Plastic containers should not crack when frozen. They should be kept either in a frost-free room or, if you do not have such a space, under a roofed-over area outside. Cover containers with plants in them with brushwood or something similar and water them on frost-free days. Remove hanging containers and place them in

Begonias and fuchsias will flourish if they are given good care.

suitable winter quarters. Hardy plants removed from baskets should be planted in pots in the fall.

Overwintering in frost-free conditions: Groups of plants that are expected to be sensitive to cold should be cut back before taking them inside to be overwintered in a position that is as bright and cool (but frost-free)

as possible. A cool conservatory is ideal. Many plants will even flower here during the winter. During the coldest time of year, water them sparingly but do not let them dry out.

Protection against early or late frosts

A hanging planting arrangement with plants that are sensitive to frost is easy to protect from light frosts in the spring or fall if it is moved to a frost-free position overnight or covered over and wrapped up all around in polyethylene or something similar.

Index

Index

Index

Author's note

This volume gives advice on growing and caring for hanging plants on balconies and patios. Some of the plants described here are toxic, can cause skin irritation, or may trigger allergies. Very toxic plants, and even less toxic ones that might still cause considerable damage to health in susceptible adults or children, have been marked with a warning symbol in the lists of plants (see pp. 20, 28 and 36). Please make absolutely sure that children and domestic pets do not eat any parts of these plants. Also make sure that plant containers are firmly secured to avoid accidents and in accordance with your legal responsibilities. Further advice on this matter can be found on pages 15, 16, 17 and 54. Follow the manufacturer's directions meticulously when using plant protection agents and also note my recommendations on pages 52-53. Store plant protection agents and fertilizers (even organic ones) in a safe place where they will be inaccessible to children and pets. Their consumption can lead to damage to health.

If you receive any wounds while handling soil or compost, it is advisable to consult a doctor to discuss the possibility of having a tetanus injection.

Acknowledgments

The author Martin Weimar and the publishers wish to thank Claudia Worner, florist and gardener, for her help in the taking of these photographs. Thanks also go to Angelika Sage, who offered the use of her balcony and patio for photography.

Cover photographs

Front cover: *Gazania hybrids, Dorotheanthus bellidiformis, Portulaca and Convolvulus sabatius.*

Photographic acknowledgements

The photographs in this volume were all taken by Jürgen Stork, except for:
Henseler: p. 50 top right, bottom;
Schaefer: p. 51 top left;
Weimar: p. 51 top center left, top center right, top right, bottom;
Zunke: p. 50 top left, top center

This edition published 1996
by Landoll, Inc.
By arrangement with
Merehurst Limited
Ferry House, 51-57 Lacy Road,
Putney, London SW15 1PR

© 1992 Gräfe und Unzer GmbH, Munich

ISBN 1-56987-694-0

Text copyright ©
Merehurst Limited 1996
Translated by Astrid Mick
Edited by Lesley Young
Design and typesetting by
Paul Cooper Design

A candlelit dinner on the patio

What could be nicer on a summer's evening than to dine outdoors on a patio where the warm evening air is filled with the enchanting scent of star balm (*Zaluzianskya capensis*) and tobacco flowering (*Nicotiana suaveolens*). In this hanging garden these two have been combined with ivy. The best way to grow these plants is from seed during the second month of spring and then to plant them in hanging containers after the late frosts in the last month of spring. If you wish, you can add *Nicotiana sylvestris* (left in the photo) which also has a lovely evening fragrance.

An enchanted evening setting with candles and scented plants.